Revenge on the Ca

Anthony Coles

A Smith Story

Chapter	Title	Page

Preamble

'I want you to do a job for me. I'll pay you a million dollars.'

The young man looked across the café table at the elegantly suited man who had sat down uninvited.

'What's the job?'

'I want you to help me kill someone.'

'Who?'

'My brother.'

The young man just looked on calmly as his guest got up and put a business card flat on the table.

'Call me,' he said and walked out of the café.

Chapter 1: Opening Events

The beach at La Plagette was typical of many, if not most, of the beaches on that stretch of coast. It was a narrow strip of clean sand that filled a curved inlet rather like a thin membrane of skin between one's fingers where they join the hand. The sand had simply filled in the curve encouraged by years of gentle urging waves that were driven by the tiny rises and falls in the Mediterranean tide. Had the beach been on the Atlantic coast some four hundred miles to the west, the whole thing would have been different. The violence of the Atlantic storms would have thrown that thin smattering of sand to the four winds and created an inlet that was deeper and harder with the coast driven back into the rock shore. Here in Provence the little bay had been almost caressed into shape; gently shelving down into the sea and rising less than a couple of metres to the rough grass and scrubby dunes. The nearest villages of Leucate and Quartier de la Falaise were well to the south and the larger town of Perpignan was some thirty miles even further away. The dunes extended well inland and that, more than anything, was the reason for choosing the place. At this time of night, it was almost completely deserted. That was another reason.

It looked a long way from being the ideal place. Once Moroni had decided to add people trafficking to his already extensive portfolio of criminal activities, the search had been on for a landing site. Getting the refugees away from North Africa was easy enough. There were many people willing to do that for him and, with a certain amount of coercion, they would act as his agents in collecting the money from desperate families willing to pay almost anything in the hope of a new life somewhere in Europe. If the business grew, it might merit sending his own people over there to supervise and collect the money. He was pretty sure that the price he was quoted as a good deal short of what was actually being paid by the refugees. Moroni didn't often pay middlemen when he didn't have to. He would see. But for the moment the job was in its infancy.

The only real problem wasn't getting the refugees across from Africa. It was a long journey, sure enough; particularly all crammed together in small fishing boats that regularly plied the waters between North Africa and Spain. They could then be transferred to military-style RIBs for the final few miles for the run to the shore. The problem was where to land. Moroni's territory was extensive. He was based in Toulouse and oversaw virtually all crime, major and petty, in the south-west of France. While that took in a lot of country, the coast only stretched between the Spanish border at Cerbère and Montpellier to the east for a distance of about one hundred and twenty miles. A great deal of that coastline was built over and given to tourism. There were very few places that were isolated enough for his purposes. So, to some extent, they would have to risk it. After much discussion the little beach at La Plagette was chosen. It was one of the less popular beaches for tourists and, at least to the north, shielded from view by a substantial cliff up to a small military lookout post that was only occasionally manned during the day and never at night. Unlike many of the neighbouring beaches, there were no houses or any buildings at all anywhere near so that at night the small strip of sand was normally deserted. In any case speed was the essence and there was a narrow road that ran along the coast very near the beach from which it was only a few moments' drive onto a fast road away from the landing site.

The night was warm and overcast and from the beach there were no visible lights. A slight breeze was blowing from the south east over the sea. Two large container trucks had been painted grey and were parked on the road above the beach. A large number of Moroni's men were on the beach, forming a corridor up to the road, wearing black-clothes and balaclavas; conspicuously armed with automatic weapons. The plan was to land the refugees and get them into the trucks as quickly as possible for a fast trip into the hinterland where they could be thrown out in small groups in a sufficiently remote location not to raise any great interest.

The group waited and before long three large converted RIB appeared over the horizon. Moroni had stripped all the seats out and installed electric motors in each so that the approach could be made as silently as possible. The original petrol outboards had been retained in for emergencies and longer journeys.

The three boats were beached, and their occupants started a rush to disembark. Their joy at reaching what they thought to be their destination was short-lived as they were roughly formed into a line and made to file towards the waiting trucks. The boats left as soon as they could. Occasionally one or two tried to break away but were brutally beaten back into line. Many had to be forced with clubs and gun butts up the ramps into the trucks. The trucks had just begun to leave on the relatively short journey across to the main E15 motorway and beyond into the hills to the south of Carcassonne when a police helicopter, searchlight blazing, sprang over the cliff to the north and bathed the whole scene in light. At the same time two columns of flashing blue lights approached from north and south as a well organised trap was sprung. The loud megaphone shouted instructions from the helicopter telling everyone to stop, get out of the trucks, put down their arms and lay face down on the roadway. The refugees were to be left imprisoned on the transports for the time being.

It was only Moroni's instructions that, if anything went wrong, there was to be no gunfire. He wanted to prevent a bloodbath. It was one thing having one particular operation screwed up for some reason. He had had many such setbacks in the past and presumably would again. It was however entirely different to face a full-blown gun battle with the French police with the inevitable casualties and then to suffer the investigation that would follow. So, when the CRS arrived, they found the whole scene surprisingly quiet apart from the cries from inside the trucks.

Now, a few days later, Moroni presided over a meeting of his senior lieutenants in the private room of the Restaurant Michel Sarran on the Boulevard Armand Duportal in Toulouse. Moroni was well known for his temper and these men who between them ran most of the organised crime between the Rhône and the Spanish border were nervous. The refugee operation had gone wrong and that would normally have occasioned fireworks from the boss. But all they saw was their host, immaculately dressed as usual, sitting at the head of an equally immaculately dressed table, smiling benignly at them all. Those who really knew the man feared the worst.

'Gentlemen, let me set your minds at rest. You will all survive this lunch, unless you eat yourselves to death, of course. That is perfectly possible in this restaurant. I want to talk business and inevitably the events of last Monday must be discussed. We have to know why the refugee operation went wrong. We need to plan whether this experiment is one that we will continue or just pass on to other activities. Today also happens to be my birthday and I make it a point never to kill anyone on my birthday.'

A series of very uncertain smiles crossed the faces of the hard men around the table. They could handle the boss when he was angry or fierce. They had practice at that. But a sweet and cheerful Moroni was a different and very rare animal and a much more dangerous one. One by one they congratulated their host on his birthday; not sure whether that was another piece of some great and complicated conspiracy that would suddenly go very wrong indeed. Moroni himself was enjoying himself greatly. These were not men you could usually impress. They had all come up the hard way to earn their place at his table. They had become very rich by stealing, killing, running all the rackets it was possible to devise; dealing in everything that could be dealt in. All had started when they were kids in the slums; doing it themselves. From there they graduated to having others to do it for them until one day Moroni had got them together and stopped them fighting amongst each other for territory and power and taught them to combine their talents and their armies. Now they were all seated in the best restaurant in Toulouse, clothed in Armani and Hugo Boss, in thrall to the only man around the table who was not carrying a gun.

'Come, Gentlemen. Trust me. We are here to talk, certainly, but let us also enjoy the talents of Maître Sarran who will produce something that I guarantee you will remember for ever.'

A first course of *vol-au-vent de huitres et coquillages* was put in front of them and Moroni gave the waiters time to pour glasses of Saint Aubin and then leave before carrying on.

'I feel I should explain why I'm not incandescent with rage over the events of last week as some of you probably expected. We were grassed on by someone and we need to find out who and why of course and do something terrible to the people involved. But the reality is that this refugee business is unusual. Last week we imported close to a hundred people into France at a rate of five thousand dollars each. They probably actually paid more but the locals in Africa who organised it all need their cut. Equally importantly, we got the money up front. All we did was to put three cheap rubber boats together and have them at the right place in the Mediterranean at the right time. Ignoring the end result that, incidentally, doesn't concern me in the least, we earned half a million dollars for doing fuck all. Forgive me if I profess rather to like that.'

The first course was finished and cleared away to be replaced by Cabillaud. Glasses of a white Saint Josef from Bernard Gripa decorated the starched white cloth. Moroni went on.

'This is clearly a good business, irrespective of what happened the other day. There seems to be an inexhaustible supply of these refugees with the means to pay these sorts of fees without any guarantee of a successful outcome to the venture. The words 'money', 'old', and 'rope' come to mind.'

There was a general nodding of heads around the table. They all tucked into the fish and finished it in short order. It was absolutely delicious. Again, the waiter appeared as if by magic and the course was exchanged for a pigeon dish accompanied with a glass of Languedoc from Montcalmes. So the meeting went on.

'I want to hear your opinions on how to proceed with this project. The post mortem on what happened the other day can wait. You all know what has to be done to find these people so I suggest you get on with it. A one hundred thousand Euro bonus to whoever eliminates the bastards who grassed us up in the nastiest and most public way possible. What is more important now is how we change things so that it doesn't go wrong again.'

There followed a general discussion that Moroni let run. He knew that it was important that he took them along with his ideas whether or not they agreed. After a lot of wandering around the subject, much of which, to be honest, Moroni ignored, one man, Pierre Chirosi, started with some remarks that began to make sense.

'As far as I can see the only thing in the way of this being a success is the problem of somewhere safely to land these people. Our coastline is entirely too crowded with tourist developments and holiday homes. We need somewhere to be left in peace. The only place I can see that fits the bill between the Spanish and Italian borders is the Camargue. Miles of unattended isolated beaches. There are no holiday villages or police patrols, no night time tourists; precious few in daytime either. Just the occasional nature-lover wandering about on a bicycle. Perfect, I would have thought.'

There was a silence around the table while they all digested the thought. It sounded pretty easy. Nothing wrong they all thought until someone piped up.

'Bulls.'

There was a slightly stunned silence until someone else asked: 'what'?

'Bulls', the answer came again.

Again, a silence. Moroni knew exactly what was going on but he was happy to let the joke run a little. Before long, the author felt compelled to explain.

'Two weeks ago, two wonderfully green German nature tourists on bicycles stopped alongside a field containing a herd of Camargue bulls which, as we all know, are the main crop and pride of many Camargue farmers. Reports vary as to whether the young bulls had been fighting amongst each other or not. But they were thoroughly worked up and on seeing said pair of Germans in their shorts, anoraks and water bottles, broke through the wire fence and killed one and injured the other.'

'And your point is?' someone asked in an exasperated voice.

The man smiled.

'Nothing that lives on the Camargue should be underestimated, my friend. The farmers over there are a race apart.'

There was clearly little sympathy for this idea. These were men who were accustomed to being on top, taken seriously and yielding to no-one. The idea that a bunch of farmers could stand in their way was preposterous. Perhaps that was the main reason they would always be subservient to the man at the head of the table who also added his voice of caution.

'Pierre is right and you might do well to take note. These farmers are unlike any people you have dealt with before. They don't scare easily, if at all. They are secretive. They're both clever and cunning - a combination that some of you, my friends, might do worse that to cultivate yourselves. They also stick together. They have family loyalties that go back hundreds of years; loyalties that form the strongest bonds of the sort that many of you will never understand. Just bear in mind that during the war, even the Germans with all their troops left these farmers alone. Sure, they occupied the whole Camargue as they did everywhere else but the let these farmers just get on with the business of farming. If we intend to try to use their undeniably deserted coastline for our little project, we are going to have to be very clever about approaching them. We will have to choose our allies very carefully. We will have to find the ones who are unhappy or resentful in their lives. We have to find some of these farmers who will be prepared to break some of their own rules.'

There was a silence around the table while they tried to understand what the boss was saying. Usually it was easy enough to get what they wanted. Enough force, enough violence, real or imaginary, and enough money was all it took to get their way. Moroni noted that again it was Pierre Chirosi, the man who ran the eastern part of their territory and who was based in Montpellier who wanted to know more.

'What do you mean by rules, Sebastien? Rules can be broken by us as well as by them and, anyway, who makes these rules? Who enforces them?'

There was another pause while the main course made way for a selection of exotic-looking puddings. Moroni, who never touched sweet foods, waited until they had all made their choices. He knew that he would handle this project himself. He certainly didn't think that too many of the men round the table had the necessary skills to handle these farmers. However, he knew that he must try at least to make them understand how different this place was to where they normally operated. Their territory extended through many country areas and there were thousands of farmers throughout their normal bases of operation. Normally there was little profit to be had from them and they were, by and large, left alone.

'What you must try to understand,' Moroni explained, 'is that unlike us, these people have been farming this part of the world for hundreds of years and it has never been easy. But they have survived by working hard at difficult work. They are a strange combination of self-reliance and inter-dependence, but it is this reliance on each other that makes them strong. They help each other, especially at harvest or if things have to happen that require more than just one or two. But above all there is a man called Emile Aubanet.'

There was a general increase in attention. Most of the assembled company were a bit at a loss so far, but now the boss had mentioned one individual the whole picture got simpler - or so they thought.

'For centuries the farmers of the Camargue have essentially formed a single group; a club if you like. This club formed their government. It represented them all because it was them all. However, this club was run by one man. The position has been handed down from generation to generation, certainly for the last two or three hundred years. It is rather like a royal family. But this is not a dictatorship. It is entirely advisory and only exists as long as all the farmers want it to. The present holder of the office could be deposed simply by being asked to stand down. This family must have been doing something right because that has not happened in three hundred years. Aubanet's father got them all through the war and now the son has run things with much general satisfaction ever since the old man died fifty years ago. Very little happens on the Camargue without Emile Aubanet's knowledge and approval.'

'So why can't we get to the man Aubanet?'

'The man is rich, powerful, completely independent and a Camargue farmer. He is also politically better connected both locally and nationally than almost anyone you've ever met. He has friends in both the gendarmerie and police. Note I said friends but not of the paid-for type we have. He is ridiculously well informed, surrounded by friends who rely on him. He is very well guarded and stays pretty close to the middle of his farm. Although no-one is completely safe, of course, he is as bulletproof as is possible to imagine.'

Again, there was a pause but Moroni hadn't finished.

'Before we talk about how to approach our problem of getting some access to the Camargue which inevitably means finding some way of getting past Emile Aubanet, there is another issue that relates to all this. For some reason our friend Alexei Girondou seems to have got a foot in the door already.'

As he anticipated there was a loud murmuring around the table. Girondou was the great bête noire. They had been trying for years to take over the territory to the east of the river Rhône and had failed. The frowns were still on their wearer's faces as Moroni continued.

'We seem to have a situation now where not only have the farmers of the Camargue seemingly forgotten their traditional hatred of the men from Marseille but Girondou and Aubanet seem to have become family friends. Now that makes life a lot more difficult for us.'

'How has this happened? Why that swine from Marseille rather than us? I feel positively insulted.'

A small and slightly pensive smile crossed Moroni's face.

'Well as far I as can figure some sort of a mystery man seems to have come on the scene and has not only made some sort of connection between Girondou and Aubanet but has also shacked up with Aubanet's daughter.'

'So what do we know about this man, then?'

'Very little indeed. He is English apparently and lives in Arles. If even a few of the stories that circulate about him are true, he's a pretty formidable unit. Not a man to be crossed, I gather.'

He broke off as a member of his audience sniggered. It was a mistake and the perpetrator felt the weight of a very fierce stare.

'Unless I am not making myself clear, I am saying that until we know a lot more about this man and what he is capable of we leave him severely alone. If even twenty percent of the stories I have heard about him are true, you will probably come off second best in any case. So, leave him alone for now.'

Coffee and glasses of cognac were served for those who wanted them before he continued his briefing.

'So, considering that if we are to try to take advantage of the Camargue and the relative isolation of its beaches for our operations, I'd like to hear suggestions on how we might consider cracking this particular nut; given ...' he spread a particularly sharp glance around the table. '... it might involve slightly more than the subtlety we usually use.'

There was something of an embarrassed silence. Subtlety was a good distance from an everyday life skill for most of these men, as, in fact, was planning of any sort. The problem Moroni had set them was simply too hard. In the end and of no surprise to Moroni it was Chirosi again who spoke up.

'Well, Boss, I haven't thought it through of course but there may be one approach that could work.'

He immediately had their attention; from Moroni as he had expected Chirosi to be the one to come up with something and from the others who were relieved that Moroni had not started to single individuals out for suggestions.

'For some time, I have heard rumours that Emile Aubanet is considering standing down from the position as head of the family. He is in his mid-seventies and his predecessors have all at some stage given the thing over to a succeeding son before they got too old to be of use. He has been a popular leader with very few enemies and there is no reason why a hand-over shouldn't happen successfully. However, on this particular occasion there might be something of a wrinkle.'

This was news to everyone around the table. A significant number might not have been entirely sure where the Camargue actually was. But Moroni certainly found his interest piqued. Anything

15

from the east interested him. His great rival and enemy was Alexei Girondou and he had always seen the Camargue as a barrier to his own ambitions further east. He nodded at the man to encourage him to continue.

'Well, the wrinkle is that Aubanet only has a daughter. For the first time in the family's history there is no male heir to pass the job on to. Now this may not be a problem of any sort. The woman is highly competent. She has been running the family businesses for a long time very successfully. These are businesses, by the way, that extend way beyond farming and turnover more than fifty million Euros a year. She has also been involved with farming and the rest of the Camargue all her life and if anything if not more widely liked than her father then certainly equally as well. Now this may be nothing but, as we know, the Camargue is a deeply conservative place and I was wondering if there might be some opposition to a woman taking over what has traditionally been a man's job - irrespective of how well she is regarded. If this is the case there might be a few discontented souls who would be more susceptible to any approach we might make than usual.'

Chirosi stopped and looked up the table. He wanted to get some impression of what the boss was thinking. He didn't care what the others felt but he didn't want to risk Moroni dismissing his suggestion. He was pleased to see that he had the man's complete attention.

'Go on, Pierre. This is interesting.'

So, basking in the unusual use of his Christian name, he did.

'Well, I do happen to know a few farmers down there who for various reasons are less than happy with the status quo. Obviously this may not be for any reason directly to do with the Aubanet family or, for that matter, be anything to do with an imminent promotion of a woman to the top job. Out of any group of people there are always some who are worse off than others and feel unhappy, and farmers are usually better at complaining than most. I already know of a few of them who, shall we say, divert somewhat from the traditional image of the happy family of Camargue farmers. These are men who have their resentments and may not be quite as locked in to the Aubanet family myth as most. One or two of them farm in a small way quite close to the coast and may be of interest for that reason. One in particular I know hates the Aubanets.'

Now Moroni really was interested. Hard facts were what he was after not just idle speculation.

'Who?'

'Well there is a small farmer who has a hundred or so acres on the south west corner of the Étang de Vaccares called Cordiez who seems to be unhappy'

'Why?'

'Well to be frank I think the man is just generally pissed off. He's that sort of bloke. Never a good word to say about anyone. But he certainly isn't making a fortune doing what he does. He might well be someone who would be open to an approach and a large wedge of cash. I know his son is a junior bullfighter and that is a trade where you need a good deal of money. Certainly, more than the old man has got. Might be worth a try. I also think that if we looked, we could find a few more like him.'

There was another silence while Moroni thought all this through and the others just waited.

'OK. Thank you, Peter, for the idea. At least you had one.'

The rest of the assembled company shifted uncomfortably.

'We might as well start with this Cordiez person and see if there is any chance of getting a few disgruntled farmers on our side. If they're not making too much money, there must be a chance that they can be bought, Peter?'

'Well I don't see any harm in going to have a word with him, certainly. Perhaps I can get him to a meeting of some sort preferably away from home.'

'Why?'

Well there is always a chance that we might be spotted.'

'Spotted? By whom?'

Even Moroni was contemptuous.

'Well, by anyone really. It can be quite difficult to get that deep into their territory without being spotted especially in that damn great Merc of yours. It's not a common vehicle in that part of the world.'

Moroni was flabbergasted.

'You mean that these stone age farmers have enough electronic surveillance to notice an AMG Mercedes nosing around? I don't believe it.'

'No electronics. Just a lot of very sharp eyes and bucketloads of curiosity. They'll spot you mark my words. At this stage, best leave it to me to organise this first meeting at least.'

Moroni shrugged.

'OK. This was your idea so run with it. Let me know what you can organise. Just bear in mind that I want to get something moving quickly.

He cast a baleful eye along the two sides of his dinner companions.

'And I still want some input from you lot. This is the best idea we've had for a long time to make a lot of relatively risk-free money and I want to own it. If you can't think of anything clever then at least find out what went wrong last week. I want some heads on platters.'

Chapter 2: Chess and a Conversation

There is a story, possibly apocryphal, that one day in the late nineteenth century during the June Royal Ascot horse race meeting, George, 4th Baron Harris, broke the strict dress code required of guests in the Royal Enclosure. Instead of wearing the ubiquitous full morning dress he attended in a suit made of his eponymous tweed. His host, King Edward VII, was heard to ask, 'Goin' ratting, Harris?' It was a story that often make Smith smile inwardly when he met his friend David Gentry for Gentry was an exceedingly tweedy sort of a person. These days as the average temperature in Arles in Provence was considerably higher that it had been during their previous lives together in London, Gentry was less often to be found dressed in full tweeds. It was originally clothing designed to keep a person alive while striding over a Scottish hillside in the teeth of a full winter blizzard, gun in hand, in pursuit of grouse or pheasant or even capercaillie. These days, Gentry limited himself to a waistcoat or even a light jacket. Harris Tweed is by no means either heavy or rough. It can be a soft as cashmere.

But for all his current rather splendid accommodation in a vast and impenetrable old house in the very centre of the town, Smith always associated his friend with their place of work for many years before their mutual retirement. Gentry's natural habitat was a windowless room buried a couple of floors below the street under one of those huge, grey, stone buildings that line many of the streets around London's Whitehall; each distinguished only with a small, well-shone brass plaque bearing an uninformative legend like "Department of Overseas Trade (Annex C)" or "Ministry of Supply" or "Commonwealth Institutions Regulatory Committee". The heating in these old building never worked and Gentry had settled on tweed as a means of staying alive while seated at his desk.

So as the two sat at Gentry's elegant chess table, Smith was again reminded of the Lord Harris story. This time it was indeed just a waistcoat, and an unusually restrained one at that, but it was enough to trigger the memory. The game had started in silence; each man being accompanied by glasses their own preferences in whisky; Banff malt for Gentry, well-iced and watered supermarket blend for Smith. They knew each other's games well having been friends for more than forty years and for most of that time they had worked for what is euphemistically known as Her Majesties Government, or HMG for short, in the murky world known as intelligence. Smith's involvement had only been sporadic. He had only been involved when the powers that were – whoever they actually were – thought that they needed his particular combination of skills. The rest of the time he happily plied his trade teaching art history to American university students. Their little bit of HMG's service was not one of the well-known groups known publicly by their acronyms in the alphabet soup customarily used to identify such things: MI5, MI6 also known as SIS. Neither was it one of the lesser known ones like Defence Intelligence that did the military bits of the foreign remit or the newly-formed Office for

Security and Counter-Terrorism – OSCT inevitably. Their little group had no name, no official identity. It appeared in no reports nor was ever the subject of cabinet briefings or oversight. It had no official budget. Smith didn't know anyone else in the department. Other than Gentry he never met anyone. The people he worked with in the field usually came from a bewildering variety of places. Like him, he supposed. His contact was Gentry and he alone. One evening after a particularly difficult operation in the then communist Albania he had actually asked his friend what their department actually did. The man looked highly embarrassed at the question and answered only reluctantly:

'Well, er. Um. What can I say? We sort of do the little things that need tidying up around the place; things that others might find it difficult, being in the public gaze and things all the time.'

That was all he got. Smith was fully aware that "tidying up" usually meant killing people for that was something he was good at and "the place" around which they did their "tidying" was the entire world. Gentry planned the jobs and Smith carried them out. It was as simple as that.

The chess progressed, in silence and seriously. They were both excellent players with Gentry being rigorous and disciplined to Smith's somewhat more unorthodox approach. Considering their very different skills they were surprisingly evenly matched. This occasion saw one of their more traditional encounters. Smith played white and opened with King's Gambit and the game progressed along traditional

22

lines. Gentry countered with Falkbeer. It was only after the game progressed into its middle phase that Smith noticed something was amiss. Gentry made a mistake. It was highly unusual especially in a game where they were both keeping to the accepted rules. Almost unheard of. Smith decided to ignore it and carry on and it was only a few moves later that it happened again. This time Smith pushed his chair back and addressed his partner.

'OK Gentry. Something on your mind?'

Gentry tried to look innocent.

'Whatever makes you think that, Peter?'

'Two mistakes in seven moves in the Falkbeer Countergambit that you could normally follow faultlessly in your sleep. That's what.'

Gentry nodded.

'Yes. Perhaps I am not concentrating as much as I should. Maybe I'm getting old, I suppose.'

They both moved from the chess table and dumped themselves in the two armchairs either side of the fire place. Smith waited.

'You may have heard about a people trafficking operation that went wrong, over near Narbonne a week or so ago.'

Smith nodded.

'Well, this morning I got a call from an old chum in the UK.'

This didn't narrow the field much. Gentry was one of the best-connected people in HMG past or present. His network also extended over most of Europe. Retirement hadn't altered that.

'Chum?' Smith wanted some detail because he recognised where Gentry was headed. A little job was on the horizon.

'Er, well, a chum in Hereford,' came the reluctant answer.

Smith was instantly all attention. Although they had moved from that rather pretty little English market town buried in the Welsh marches some years ago to the even sleepier village of Credenhill some ten kilometres to the north west of the town, Hereford was still the much-used euphemism for home of the 22nd Special Air Service Regiment, know to all and sundry as the SAS or, more colloquially, as "The Regiment".

Gentry took a deep breath and started in.

'I don't know the details, of course, but they have a sort of exchange programme with the French 4th Special Forces Helicopter Regiment who are based in Pau. The French want to develop their aerial soldiering skills, I hear. There are usually some exchanges with French troops coming to Hereford for training and some of our lot acting as instructors down here. Well, it seems that the intel that led to the immigrant smuggling episode being intercepted by the Gendarmerie came from one of our people who was doing some sort of surveillance on some local mobster who was behind that attempt. I have no idea if the man was acting on his own initiative or whether this was some sort of French op and he was just lending a hand. Anyway, to cut a long story short, the soldier was found two days after the op in a ditch beside the road with a 9mm round through his mouth.'

24

Gentry seemed visibly upset which struck Smith as being a little strange. In the past Gentry had approached all aspects of their work together with a particular *sang froid*, irrespective of how nasty were the things they were contemplating. He also couldn't work out why this was any of Gentry's business.

'This chum from Hereford. Why was he calling you?'

Now Gentry was looking more than uncomfortable, and he just sat there uncomfortably saying nothing. Suddenly Smith realised what was going on.

'Good God, Gentry. You were Regiment yourself, weren't you? I never guessed.'

Now the discomfort was mixed with a slight pride.

'Well, Peter. There was never any reason for you to know, I suppose.'

To say that Smith was impressed was an understatement. Any image of a tweedy academic living far away from the front line just planning the life and death of others from a safe distance was banished for ever from his mind. This little force was currently by far the best five hundred soldiers in the world. None of the many troops of elite forces around the world came near. Very quickly Smith cottoned on. The Regiment, rather like some of its equivalent groups around the world, took care of their own.

'Right, old chum. I would guess you have it in your mind to find out who killed this man. Given that some SAS people are in Pau officially on training duties and their hosts know all about them, I can't see any reason why they can't find it out for themselves. The fly boys are part of the French Special Forces Command and whoever carried out the successful Narbonne operation it must have been one of the myriad of French police forces. Gendarmerie or Police National, they are all actually parts of the army here in France. If that lot can't find the culprit, then no one can, I would have thought.'

A secondary though struck him.

'Who did the Narbonne op, by the way?'

'Mostly armed gendarmerie with some GIGN men. Air support came, of course, from Pau.'

'And where was the all-important intel fed in to the system?'

'Local Gendarmerie, I believe,' replied Gentry shifting uncomfortably. He knew where Smith was going with this.

Smith realised why Gentry had brought this up with him.

'I'm guessing that Messailles was in charge of the operation. They wouldn't have let this rest in the hand of the local plod. It was much too important. So, the intel came in from the British grunt on the ground and was quickly fired up to Paris where it landed on our friendly Colonel Messailles' desk. Yet another step to the greasy pole to stardom for our pet Gendarme. The operation was successful, but someone, probably from the Paris end of course, leaked back to the local gangster who had planned his latest get-rich-quick scheme and the grunt was executed in the traditional gangland method for informers.'

Gentry nodded silently.

'All that is pretty clear and straightforward. No obvious reason for clandestine phone calls from Hereford down the old-boy network, I would have thought. Except for the fact that that if the French have clammed up about the leak then official channels of enquiry would be very tight shut. Hereford thought you might help as you're on the spot, as it were.'

Gentry continued to look a little uncomfortable.

'Well, as usual, Peter, I think you've got most of it right. Hereford was just wondering if I could do a little local digging. That's all. Part of that is to ask you, of course. See if you knew anything.'

'Well, to be frank, old friend, I don't and to be brutally honest, I don't really care very much. This was no simple civilian who died. It was a fully trained – some might say over-trained – regular soldier killed in the line of what he or one of his bosses thought of, as duty. That's what regular soldiers get paid for. The fact that it was a gangster who pulled the trigger makes no difference. Dead is dead. You may feel some old-boy sense of indignation and get all sentimental for The Regiment and its loss. But I don't. So no, I don't know anything and furthermore I don't feel any need to try to find out. I'm not prepared to risk my arse finding out want happened to a soldier who was doing his job. Sorry.'

Gentry just sat there looking a little miserable. It was rather the reaction he had anticipated. Now if he could just get out of the conversation without further difficulty. But he saw Smith frowning

27

and knew he couldn't. Smith fixed his friend with a slightly more than unfriendly look.

'Peter. Messailles and his peccadillos are known only to you and me and Girondou. No-one else. I would be ..er.. distressed if that rather specific knowledge was spread any more widely than that.'

Sometime before Smith had discovered that the then local regional Commander of Gendarmerie, Claude Messailles was taking handouts from the local Marseille crime boss Alexei Girondou. Nothing that got in the way of his being a good policeman but enough to keep him from taking too close an interest in the gangster's business. Messailles was destined for the top and had been helped occasionally by information that Smith and Gentry had furnished. Messailles was Smith's asset and he wasn't happy at the thought that someone else knew about him.

'No Peter. I've told no-one.' Gentry was adamant.

'Good,' replied Smith. 'Then do dig away in this little mystery if you want. But if you want any advice, then I would be very careful. You seem to have a local French gangster who can get close enough to an experienced and highly trained member of the most elite group of combat soldiers on earth actually to shoot him in the mouth. That, as you should well know, isn't easy. If I were you, I'd stay as far away from that little problem as I could.'

The conversation carried on in a desultory sort of way for a while with Gentry continuing to look miserable before Smith made his excuses and went home. He had a dog to feed.

Chapter 3: New Allies

It was only a day or so before Chirosi phoned his boss.

'Cordiez will be coming south to Céret near the Spanish border for their Feria on 14th July in two weeks. His son is fighting there. It's a long way from the Camargue and right in our territory. I would have thought it is an ideal opportunity to sound him out. It's a long trip from Arles, so they will probably arrive on the previous night and stay until Sunday at the least.'

Moroni was pleased that the man had got into the problem so quickly and the 14th was only a week or so away.

'OK. That's fine. Please make the arrangements and get somewhere civilised for us to stay.

'Us, boss?'

'Yes Pierre. I want you there please. You are the only one who seems to have the remotest idea what's going on. You also live closest to the Camargue and know a bloody sight more than anyone else about these people and what is required to deal with them. I want you to be the main contact with these people. In any case, I have some idea about how we might take the opportunity to have another look at

Girondou's territory and I want you involved in that too. I've just transferred a million Euro advance on the increase in your salary to your Nevis account to compensate for the additional work. Perhaps you might like to think of buying that helicopter you have always lusted over. Play your cards right you could even run it as a business expense if and when you ever decide to start paying taxes.'

Chirosi was thoroughly taken aback. Moroni was not someone he usually associated with making generous gestures.

'Jesus, boss. Thanks.'

Moroni laughed.

'Don't worry. You'll earn every centime twice over. Between now and the 14th I want you to plan this meeting and give me a serious briefing on how we handle this man Cordiez and others like him. I also want a full briefing on the whole Aubanet family thing - solid facts not just some mythological mumbo jumbo. I want to know their strengths and weaknesses better that they do themselves. I also want to know about the mysterious Englishman. The guy is a wildcard and an unknown. Both are dangerous when they are separate but together, they can be lethal. Find out about him and how we take him out of the picture if it becomes necessary.'

'What about Girondou?'

'Don't worry about him for the moment. I have a plan for him and I've been waiting for a long time. Perhaps this might be the opportunity I've been looking for. Leave that one to me, at least for now. Set up the meeting. Find a hotel good enough to impress this man Cordiez and a restaurant good enough to impress me.'

Chirosi rang off and set to work looking for a hotel for the meeting. It was not long before he called again.

'Well, the whole area is not best served with nice hotels, but I thought the Hotel Windsor in Perpignan might be OK for Cordiez and it is with easy distance of the restaurant La Galinette which is probably to your taste and will certainly impress our guest. I assume you'll be driving back after the meeting.'

Moroni noted the date and time and rang off.

Pierre Chirosi wasn't completely relaxed as he drove through the gates of Moroni's estate. He had been working for the man for a number of years now, but this was the first time he had been invited to his house. To many, Moroni was a bit of a mystery. He seemed to have appeared one day out of the blue with a handful of men and before anyone really noticed he had taken over most of the major criminal activities in the south of France to the west of the River Rhône. Anyone who tried to challenge him had just vanished, even when it was just a matter of a small territory or a local protection ring. Other groups, Arabs, Chinese had all tried from time to time and failed. Even the Mafia had agreed to share the business, having to be content with whatever Moroni decided to offer them. Chirosi had been given the east of the region to manage a year or so before and had been left reasonably alone to get on with it. Now, he realised, Moroni wanted something different and the fact that he was based in Montpellier and did at least know some of the basics of what was happening on the other side of the Petit Rhône made him valuable, for the moment. He was, however, apprehensive as at least some of his briefing to his boss was incomplete and one never knew what the reception would be.

His host opened the door to a startlingly modern house that seemed to be located in the middle of a wood some miles to the north west of Toulouse and he was shown into an equally modern rather minimalist office.

Moroni was in a good humour, enough for a modicum of small talk.

'Come in Pierre. Sit down. Can I offer you some coffee? Have a good trip? I hope the traffic wasn't too bad on the AutoRoute. The sooner you get that helicopter of yours the better, I think.'

It was all slightly too much. Moroni was not usually a man for this sort of badinage and Chirosi couldn't really work out what was going on. However, there was nothing for it but to go along and enjoy it while he could. He knew full well that Moroni's mood could change in a flash. Before long coffee had arrived and the briefing started.

'Firstly, Pierre, I would like to thank you for the notes you emailed. It was a bit like going back to school for a history lesson but actually I learned a lot.'

Chirosi had decided that rather than stand there giving his boss a lecture about the history and traditions of the Camargue, he would write it all up in a series of detailed notes. That way Moroni could choose how much he was interested in knowing and Chirosi could avoid going on too long and annoying him.

'I think I understand the basics and the historical position that the Aubanet family have occupied especially during the last war which I found interesting; one brother killing the other. I know that war time collaborators weren't treated very nicely immediately after the war, but for that to happen must have been difficult for a young man. It says a lot about him, I think. However, I now want to know about the present day, especially this business of a changeover of control and whether that might be an opportunity for us.'

'Well, Emile Aubanet is in his mid-seventies and, I believe, wants to spend his time with his herd of bulls and the rest of his farm. Apart from the fact that she is a woman, in all other respects Martine Aubanet is eminently qualified to take over as the de-facto leader of the Camargue farmers. She not only knows everything there is to know about life and work on the Camargue, she is also a highly experienced and successful CEO of a wide range of family businesses that she, almost alone, has built up over the last twenty years.'

Moroni was immediately interested.

'Tell me about the businesses. Maybe I'll have more of a chance to understand this damn family that way than by trying to get inside a farmer's mind.'

'Well the group as a whole is very widely diversified. Apart from their own farm which is one of the larger ones on the marsh, they also have several large commercial fruit and vegetable farms in the Plan de Crau. They also own and operate a number of small vineyards on the banks of the Rhône although none of the wine ever seems to be released onto the market. They have interests in most of the farming-based business in the area, the rice storage and distribution, the remains of the salt industry which now is reduced almost to a tourist product; a couple of large transport and haulage businesses with at least four large storage and distribution depots in Martigues and St Remy de Provence. Then they own several small restaurants in Arles and various surrounding towns and villages, to say nothing of a number of small and medium-sized hotels and pensions. They also have large shareholdings in many local businesses who have bases in Arles or the surrounding area. The whole group has a declared turnover now of more than sixty million euros. If you add it all together, they are also one of the area's biggest employers too.'

Moroni whistled softly.

'Not too shabby for a farmer operating in a very small area of the country.'

Chirosi went on.

'Now if you really want to get in under the skin of this family, there is one very unusual and possible significant point about all this. Many of these businesses are not exactly run on conventional lines. While the Aubanet family always owns a majority in the business, a large proportion of the remainder is always held by the employees. Most of the hotels and restaurants have been bought when they have got into difficulty for one reason or another and then the owners have usually been kept on and they have retained a substantial shareholding. So, they have been got out of whatever trouble they may have been in, given some investment and, presumably management advice, then very much left alone to keep running their businesses themselves.'

Moroni frowned.

'Sounds a bit patriarchal to me.'

Chirosi nodded.

'Yes, and I think that's a significant point. These businesses are not just owned for profit. They are owned as a sort of social investment too. Make no mistake, these businesses make profits and Martine Aubanet has the reputation of being a hard taskmaster on the previous owners who don't do what she wants. This is no charity. But it seems that the people are the most important and I think that is why she is so popular. They understand what she is doing and why.'

'Well if father and daughter are so adored, why do you think there might be any difficulties when the old man hands over control.'

Now Chirosi had to choose his words carefully. He had a lot to lose by giving the wrong advice.

'Well if you remember I only said that this might be a chance and I feel this for two reasons. The first is that with any situation like this, there will always be some people who are unhappy or jealous. People who think of themselves as hard done by or mistreated or ignored or who think they are missing out on something. There will certainly be some historical enmities too. Just because the Aubanets are liked and powerful, doesn't mean they don't have enemies. The second reason is, as I said before, this is a very old-fashioned community and they have some pretty old-fashioned values. Martine Aubanet will be the first woman in their history to be in the driving seat and some will oppose that just on its own merits.'

'And you think that this man Cordiez might be one of these?'

'Well Cordiez is a possibility for someone who might be useful to us for two reasons. Firstly, he is one of the malcontents and secondly because of where he farms. He's basically a complete pain in the arse. For no reason that anyone can guess he is just one of those people who hasn't got a good word to say about anyone and anything. He's always rude, doesn't seem to like anyone and keeps to himself. So, to that extent, at least, he is a suitable candidate. Then he needs money. Fortunately for everyone concerned, his son, Robert, is a thoroughly nice sort of bloke and is well on the way to becoming a fully-fledged bullfighter. This is an expensive business and likely to get more so. The boy is coming up to his *alternativa* and after that he is playing with the big boys. Until he gets his reputation established enough to demand top wages, it is likely to require funding from either sponsors or his old man who certainly doesn't have enough to do that.'

Again, Moroni nodded slowly. This was more that sort of thing he understood. He was used to making money do things.

'OK. I understand that. Now you mentioned where he farmed.'

Chirosi got out a map.

'Let me explain, boss.'

They got out of their armchairs, went over to the desk and bent over the large-scale map of the Camargue that Chirosi had brought with him.

'You see there are about thirty kilometres of beach between Piemanson and Stes. Maries de la Mer, almost none of which is overlooked. There are virtually no houses and precious few roads. The main road to access the beach runs down the east side of the main Étang de Vaccarès and that road happens to run right through Cordiez's farm. Now it is a public road but narrow. The final kilometre or so to the beach is down some very rough tracks indeed. The only metalled road that goes to the whole beach is at the east end but that is very near Port St. Louis which has a full complement of police. Now the logistics of all this is not my field but I would imagine that given the lack of roads leading to and from the beach, we might take advantage of the huge number of little pathways and embankments that criss-cross the hundreds of different waterways, lakes and pools to move the people inshore. It would be very secure, but you would be completely lost without someone to guide you through it all. Given that he farms much of this area, I would imagine that Cordiez would be your man. He would certainly know if there were any police around on any particular night. Now there may be a number of candidates for your ally in the area but given where he farms, I suggest that he is a good place to start.'

Moroni stayed motionless over the map. After a while he muttered almost to himself. 'Now that's interesting.'

'What?'

He jabbed his finger down over the map on a bit that covered to north shore of the Étang de Vaccarès just near the Domaine de Méjanes.

'That canal.' He leant closer. 'The Canal de Pont de Rousty and whatever. It goes directly inland and joins up with a myriad of others. Goes a long way inland, too. Not too difficult to find somewhere to off load groups of people without being seen, I would have thought. We'd need some sort of marsh boat, though.'

He got lost in thought for a moment. Then he straightened up.

'Thank you, Pierre. I think that your initial thoughts are good. At some stage we need to take a really close look at this whole area on the ground but on first glance you seem to have picked a winner. Well done and thank you. You're the only one to offer anything remotely useful. I won't forget it. We'll have a meeting with this Cordiez man and see where we get. Now for the third part of your briefing. This man Smith. What have you found out?'

This was the part Chirosi had been dreading. But nevertheless, he did what he had decided to do.

'To be honest, boss. I haven't discovered very much. He's Welsh, rather than English, in his mid-sixties, retired here with his dog a few years ago leaving two ex-wives and two children back in England. He seems not to have much money and very few close friends locally but seems happy with that. He is a university level art history teacher with an interest in Roman sarcophagi. He spends his time apparently reading, writing and walking his dog.'

'And?'

Moroni, as Chirosi anticipated, was getting impatient.

'Well, he seems to have got involved by accident when Martine Aubanet's husband was killed a year or two ago. He was murdered although no-one knew by whom. The man was a paedophile. I have no idea how it happened but Smith who seems to have come across the body by accident got involved in investigating unofficially for the Aubanets. I also have no idea how or why but your friend Girondou also got involved. I have been told it was something to do with the dead husband stealing EU funds for the preservation of ancient buildings. Presumably Girondou was taking a cut. Whatever. In any case Smith and Girondou have become friends while Smith has become heavily involved with Martine Aubanet.'

'Jesus,' Moroni cried. 'It all sounds like a bad novel. What else'

'Well the odd thing is that a number of people who got involved in this saga, some thugs that tried to kidnap Martine Aubanet as well as some others, all ended up dead. There is another story about Smith getting involved in the investigation of the death of a local policeman who was said to have been killed on a training exercise but was actually caught up in the cross fire of a French scheme to steal and export plutonium from the same beach that now you are thinking of using to import refugees. This also involved various people dying including Girondou's younger brother but that seems not to have

39

harmed their relationship. You may also like to know that one of the people who died was a full-blown colonel in the GIGN and that sort doesn't usually die easily.'

Moroni was all ears.

'And you are suggesting that this man Smith was responsible for all this?'

Chirosi shrugged.

'That's the word. No proof obviously.'

'Jesus Christ! Now you tell me that this is the man who when he's not reading or writing or walking his fucking dog, is in bed with Martine Aubanet?'

Chirosi nodded unhappily.

'Honest, boss. I've tried everything I know. I looked all over the internet. I've checked with our friends in the police, local and national, local politicians. Anyone. I got in touch with our Italian friends in London and they haven't heard of him or they weren't talking. In the end I telephoned our contact in the Élysée. He told me to call back in ten minutes and when I did, he told me in no uncertain terms to forget about the man.'

'Anything else?' glowered Moroni.

Now Chirosi was very nervous.

'Well the man in the Élysée told me that the "hands off" message should be passed to you as well.'

There was an instant when Chirosi thought that he was in for one of Moroni's legendary explosions. But to his surprise and relief, the man became thoughtful.

'Now that's interesting. It takes a lot of help to drop completely off the grid while remaining visible. Friends in very high places indeed.'

He then lapsed into another silence that Chirosi was happy to let run. In fact, he had very little more to say. Basically, the conversation had come to a point where he became an employee again and took some orders rather than making suggestions. He was pleased with that. He reckoned that so far he had come through without too much damage. The next few moments would tell. Finally, Moroni made up his mind.

'Firstly, Pierre. Thanks for all this. You've done a lot of work on this and I appreciate it. I'm going to go forward with this project and I want you with me. I want you to be my eyes and ears on what is happening in the Camargue. Report to me if anything odd goes on or if you think I should know something. Even if it turns out to be nothing.'

Chirosi just nodded, knowing full well he was being handed what could easily turn out to be a poisoned chalice. Moroni went on.

'Now, on a slightly different matter, I just want to have a word about getting in touch with a certain Dutchman. I want you to find out about Girondou's body guard, a man called Henk van der Togt. I want to know all about him, his strengths and weaknesses and how we get to him. After that I will want you to set up a meeting with him. I've got a job for him.'

Chirosi just nodded. He had a feeling that his boss was up to something; something that would happen while people were diverted with this Camargue thing. Interesting times ahead, he felt. Interesting times.

Chapter 4: Gimeaux

The preparations for the Corrida in Arles had been underway for over a year. The committee had obviously finished its deliberation and the news was out. The cartels for the Feria de Riz were known. Arles had two Ferias each year; the first over Easter weekend while the second was held over the second weekend of September and held to celebrate the autumn rice harvest. In many ways the second was sometimes more popular as often the weather was more reliable. The date of the first obviously had to follow the changing Easter date. Periodically it fell early, and the end of winter could catch it. Smith had often sat on the cold stone Amphitheatre steps, well rugged up against the temperature, crushed hard against his neighbours on the already narrow seat allocation by the required thicknesses of coats. September tended to be hotter. Essentially the format of the festival remained pretty constant. Six fights over three days. The most popular was always the Corrida Goyesque where the bullfighters wore suites much more restrained than the traditional multi-coloured suits of lights; suits styled after that originally painted by the great Spanish artist, Francesco Goya. At the same time the sand of the arena proper is painted by a famous artist of the day and there are parades and song and dance before of bullfight itself. Of course, the town around is filled with many bullfight-related shows and activities and numerous temporary bodegas open for the weekend in addition to the many permanent cafés and restaurants offering food, wine and music into the early hours.

This time it was different for something of rare importance was also being offered. It is not generally known that the otherwise insignificant village of Gimeaux outside Arles very close to the road that leads from the town towards Stes. Maries de la Mer contains a much-respected school of bullfighting. Students come from a wide range of towns and villages, some even from foreign countries to practice and train. Occasionally one of these students graduates to the junior ranks of competitive fighters to start his or her career. He then has to improve much further and put in performances of ever-increasing quality against bulls of ever-increasing difficulty until he is judged to be a sufficient quality to take his place amongst the highest ranks of his peers and become a fully-fledged matador. It is a long, difficult and inevitably dangerous business until the successful candidate is offered his *alternativa*; a graduating fight amidst and against his senior colleagues at which he will win his place at bullfighting's top table. It is the climax of the bullfighter's early career and a fight at which someone is taking his *alternativa* is much anticipated. It is an occasion not dissimilar to a christening or a confirmation; a rite of passage for a young person graduating truly into the world of bullfighting.

This year's autumn Feria was one such but even more than usual the weekend was to be savoured for the man in question was from a local family; born and brought up in the farming world of the

Camargue itself. Those who followed bullfighting in the area - and that meant virtually everyone - were simply bursting with pride. The announcement of the Cartels was therefore followed more than usually closely. The announcement was made a goodly number of weeks before the Feria. This was effectively the public announcement of the three matadors who were to share the six bulls and were to comprise each of the Corridas. They are discussed and argued about long before being booked and arranged. It is not just a matter for hiring the matador and his *cuadrilla* - usually comprising two *picadores* and three *banderilleros* and their horses - it is also to arrange his own helpers and assistants, the identities and origins of the bulls themselves as well as the date and timetables of the corridas. Emile Aubanet had been one of the first to be informed and the topic had come up in conversation with Smith a month or two before the event.

'The young Cordiez boy has been granted his *alternativa* next month and although we would have gone to watch anyway, of course, the family has invited us to join them in their box. Martine and I would be honoured if you would join us as well.'

'Emile, I'd be delighted.'

He was being less than honest in giving a reply that obviously pleased the old man for he smiled broadly. In reality, Smith was far from happy. Smith's usual seat was about a third the way up from the ring and half way around its length on the west side. It was an area called the *secondes*. It was shaded during the afternoon and represented the best compromise between levels of view, price and

45

position. His usual neighbours were a very mixed bunch; mostly locals, always knowledgeable and frequently boisterous. No snobs and very few tourists. The former were in the lowest levels nearest the ring itself, the Tribunes, while the tourists usually went to the eastern seats in the mistaken belief that the bullfight was a good place to get a sun tan. Poached alive would be a more accurate description. The occasions when he and Martine went to the fights alone, they sat up there together and had always enjoyed it. To be imprisoned amongst the great and the good was not Smith's cup of tea at all. It was, he thought a little grimly, another example of the walls closing in on him in his retirement. However, he acknowledged that it was a chance to watch the fight from a good deal closer than usual. He also realised that it was another acknowledgement for the acceptance of Martine's much anticipated new position. He also noted Martine's quick smile of gratitude.

'We're also asked to a party at Gimeaux today to celebrate young Cordiez's being awarded his *alternativa*. He'll also possibly give us an exhibition. It should be a good afternoon.'

Smith nodded. This was actually something he would relish. Bullfighters parties were often robust affairs.

The Arles suburb of Gimeaux lies east of the river, to the west of the town, along the road that leads down to the Camargue, and it was along that road that leads to Arles from the Mas des Saintes that Smith, Martine and Emile were travelling, driven, as ever, by Jean Marie. The bullfighting school at Gimeaux is the one of the few such schools in France. While Smith had followed the sport for most of his life, he had never really penetrated this far back into the business of how bullfighters learned their trade.

'So, when do children start their education with the bulls?' Smith asked Emile with whom he was sitting in the back of the armoured Ranger Rover.

Obviously delighted to talk about a subject very near to his heart, Emile warmed to the task of explaining to a novice.

'Well it rather depends on how involved parents wish to get. Some form of education can be introduced into children's education at an early stage. This isn't because they all want their children to become bullfighters, of course. But many families here know how important it is for children to understand the tradition they will be brought up with. If they don't nobody will, I suppose. But those who are serious can start their education very early.'

'How many are serious?'

'Well, if you include those who train for the *courses camarguaise* or to be *razateurs*, then quite a lot. It is a popular training, rather like your British Pony Club. It has an important social function too that goes beyond bulls. It is a way that young people learn a discipline and how to get on with each other; how to depend on each other in a dangerous situation. Many parents think that time spent with training bulls and instructors is better spent than standing around on street corners in Arles waiting for the nearest drug pusher. Children who join the school are highly respected in the community.'

Smith became more and more interested as the old man warmed to his theme. He was clearly a passionate supporter of the whole tradition and was delighted to find such a willing and interested pupil as Smith continued his questioning.

'And the ones who want to become bullfighters. How long do they train?'

'Ah, that is more complicated as the school will weed out the ones who aren't suitable very early. Even for those who wish to follow the path to become a participant in the *Courses Camargaise* the school is a hard place to progress. The standards are high, and the tests are very hard. You must remember that this is a profession where the penalty for getting it wrong is death or great injury. For a prospective professional bull fighter, it is even harder. Much harder. Perhaps each year one or two only finish the course well enough qualified to start as a *novillero* on the long road to become a professional bullfighter.'

'How long will a *novillero* work before he can become a fully-fledged bull fighter?'

'Well, that rather depends on how good he is. It tends to become self-determining. The ones who aren't so good tend not to get contracts to fight or, perhaps, get contracts in smaller or less well-known places. Many just fade away if they think that they won't make it to their *alternativa*.'

'And how many make it?'

'Very, very few. Perhaps one or two in a hundred; if that.'

'Ah,' It was all Smith could think of to say.

At that point Martine got fed up about being left out of the conversation and turned around in her chair.

'That is why we're going to the *école* at Gimeaux. Something rather special is happening. For many years since he was a young child, Roger Cordiez, the son of our farming neighbour, had been in school training to become a bull fighter. He has spent two very successful years as a *novillero* in Spain and in France and now has been granted his *alternativa* and today will be the official announcement of that. We hope that it will take place of the Feria de Riz in September in Arles. So, you are in for a good old Provençale bullfighting party.'

Smith smiled back at her enthusiasm.

'And that entails...?'

'Basically, lots of speeches, some exhibitions put on in the school training ring and a lot to drink. It's a great occasion and we are all very proud indeed. It is a long time since one of our own graduated to the top rank.'

Emile harrumphed.

'Perhaps we might even get a smile out of that miserable old git of a father of his.'

Martine refused to take any notice.

'Oh, come on Papa. He's not that bad.'

'Yes, he is and well you know it, my girl.'

Smith sat back and enjoyed the badinage between father and daughter. For himself, he was certainly looking forward to the afternoon and, not for the first time, felt lucky to be included in something that was so obviously a local tradition. They arrived at the series of low buildings and stables that surrounded a series of concrete corrals that were used to house bulls, most notably the Feria bulls as they were rested at the end of their journey from Spain or Portugal for the two Ferias to which the arena at Arles played host each year. At the centre was the ring, much smaller, of course, than a standard bull ring but a bull ring nevertheless; a place where many young people entered their hopes of future glory high, many destined not to be fulfilled. But for the young Roger Cordiez this was his day of glory.

As soon as the Rover came to a halt, Marine's door was opened by a slim, bronzed young man dressed in a smart version of a working bullfighter's everyday uniform. White shirt and a string tie and dark brown leather trousers, dark leather pumps. It was a very long way from the elaborate suit of lights that would soon be his new working costume. He had obviously been waiting for them to arrive. A broad brimmed hat was held in one hand while the other was extended in offer of assistance. Martine smiled broadly and placed her hand lightly symbolically on his forearm. Once she had alighted, she kissed him enthusiastically on both cheeks.

'Roger, this is a great day. I congratulate you and,' looking over the young man's shoulder,' your parents as well.'

She quickly went past him and greeted his parents who were standing proudly to one side. They both looked a little uncomfortable at standing together but, Martine thought, at least this occasion brought the family together for a short while.

'Monsieur and Madame Cordiez. You have my congratulations and my thanks. Your son brings great honour both to his family and to all of us here in the Camargue.'

Both looked proud and slightly embarrassed at the same time.

'Thank you, Madame Aubanet,' muttered Cordiez.

In the meantime, Jean Marie had seen his master out of the car and Smith was left to his own devices. He was content to hang back a little and observe. Roger Cordiez came around the car and shook Emile Aubanet's hand. Smith was interested to see that the handshake was accompanied by a slight dip of the head.

'Congratulations, young man.' said Emile. 'We are all very proud of you. I wish you well.'

'Thank you, Sir.'

Finally, he shook Smith's hand too.

'Well done, Monsieur Cordiez. A fine achievement.'

The man beamed.

'Thank you. I am absolutely delighted that you and the Aubanet family could join us for our little celebration. It means a lot to me.'

The whole crowd slowly assembled in the ring. The entire *barrestre* was lined two or three deep and the stands were also full. Most of the crowd was clutching glasses of wine or pastis. Smith had managed to pick up one of the latter before the three of them were ushered into the better seats on the grandstand. It was hot, but the section of the grandstand was equipped with a somewhat rickety roof that nevertheless did what it was supposed to do. The Cordiez family were seated at the front of the grandstand from where the lad could be extracted at the appropriate time to receive his plaudits.

As anticipated, there were speeches; numbers of them. Essentially, they all said the same thing and Smith found his attention wandering. The school ring and its surroundings were rather scruffy in a workmanlike sort of way. Rather in the same way as many farmers keep their farms in a semi-permanent state of dilapidation. The whole place needed a lick of paint, but Smith suspected that there probably wasn't a lot of money about for that sort of thing. The large crowd was benign and somewhat respectful; listening to the speeches intently and applauding from time to time. All were well-dressed with most in suits or local costume.

Finally, the announcement they had come to witness was made. It was no surprise, of course. The event would indeed take place at the forthcoming Feria de Riz in September. The special news was that his veteran, the senior bullfighter, the young man's bullfighting Godfather, who oversees this particular rite of passage by symbolically handing over to the young man his cape and sword would be no less a man than Juan Bautista. Bautista was at the very top of his profession, an international superstar, but of even greater significance was that he was also born in Arles and received his own *alternativa* in the Arles arena back in 1999. It could not have been a more popular announcement as Bautista whose presence at the school had been briefly hidden from the public, came into the ring to join the young protégé.

Finally, the official party broke up and everyone headed for the bar. After a while, Smith took himself off for a wander around. Apart from the admin buildings and the practice ring itself the main feature was an extensive layout of large concrete pens with high walls. These were the pens that housed the bulls for the fights. They usually came from breeders in Spain and Portugal some days in advance by truck and were held there to recover from the journey. He became conscious of someone beside him and, on turning around, saw Emile also looking out over the empty corrals. He stood close and linked his arm through Smith's.

'There is a lot of history in this place Peter; our history. The history that matters to us here in the Camargue. If you are interested, I'd like to show you something.'

He led Smith back towards the range of single-story buildings that housed offices, class rooms, tack rooms and storage for all the various bits of equipment necessary to run the school. There were still a lot of people standing around with glasses in their hands chatting to each other; showing no inclination to leave. Emile led Smith down a couple of corridors and then unlocked a door.

'You might say this is our museum or perhaps our archive.'

He led him into a large room that was completely full of bullfighting memorabilia. The walls were covered with a chaotic collection of posters, bull fight flyers and photographs and book shelves filled with everything from card index boxes to groups of figurines. Tottering heaps of programmes were tied together with string. The walls also had some other bullfighting miscellanea pinned up. There were at least six filing cabinets arranged rather randomly around the room as well as a small table and two upright chairs. The floor had a faded carpet of sorts, but this was covered with a myriad of cardboard piled in unsteady - looking towers two, three or four high. Emile came to the rescue with an explanation.

'If you forgive the mess for a moment, this room contains most of the records of our bullfights for the last fifty years.'

He looked around fondly as he waved generally towards the far wall.

'Behind that wall there is an even larger collection that covers the last hundred years or more. You could say that in these two rooms is the true beating heart of the Carmargue. We have our own traditions here. We are farmers after all. But almost everything goes back to the raising of bulls on the marsh which, as you know, started in earnest when the Romans came. It is the bull that is the cement that has kept us together over the centuries. The town of Arles, of course, has its own history but that is separate and different. Arles is not the Camargue and to confuse the two is to make a mistake; one that is made by almost every visitor that comes here. Anyone who doesn't wish to understand that and who takes instant views about the farming of bulls or the fighting of them will never understand what these two thousand years of history mean to us. All that is represented by the contents of these two small rooms.'

They both stood in respectful silence considering the maelstrom of information and memories that surrounded them.

'I believe, Peter, that more than most newcomers to our world here you can understand all this very well; perhaps better than most. It is not just to do with your relationship with Martine. You came here to live of your own free will. You chose to be here. You will therefore understand what today's celebrations here mean, not just to Roger Cordiez and his family, but to all of us who still live and work here. We have many opponents, I know, but today might show you that we will not be defeated. We have survived the last two thousand years and with luck we might make the next few. I just wanted you to see this.'

Smith looked around him unable to say much. It was as if he had been let into a great secret. The old man continued with a gentle smile on his lips.

'I come here from time to time to remind myself of these values that we hold so dear. I also come to wonder whether I should invest some time and not a little money in sorting this out and make a proper archive of all this. But every time I come part of me likes it in the mess it is.'

They left, and Emile Aubanet turned the door key gently. As they walked back to join the party, Smith repeated the earlier gesture and slipped his arm though Emile's.

'Thank you for showing me that, Emile.'

He was answered by just the lightest of squeeze of his arm. He felt that the old man was imagining that he had a son himself, if even for a few brief moments.

Chapter 5: A Meeting in Lyon.

It was a meeting that neither of them thought would ever happen. Both the men who sat facing each other over a generously sized restaurant table were in their mid-forties, each fit and healthy with just the right amount of tan; good complexions and immaculately suited. Moroni used Cifonelli in Paris while Girondou used Anderson and Sheppard of Saville Row. Girondou was a Gucci shoe man while Moroni wore Lobbs. They both, somewhat coincidentally, used Turnbull and Asser for their shirts. The pair oozed an elegant sophistication that few could emulate. Their surroundings were equally sophisticated. The old L'Auberge du Pont had sat next to the Rhône on the Quai de la Plage in Collonges au Mont d'Ory some twenty kilometres up the river from central Lyons for years until a young man called Paul Bocuse arrived in the family and bought it from his parents-in-law to set about creating one of the greatest restaurants in France and, then as now, that means in the world too.

The two men were similar in appearance; so much so that they could be almost brothers. Same height and build; same dark hair greying slightly at the temples. To all intents and purposes, they looked like a pair of highly successful business men meeting for lunch to discuss yet another successful venture that would enrich them even further. To some extent that was exactly what they were. A less casual observer would notice that the atmosphere at the table, half way down the dining room, was not at all the urbane relaxed one might expect.

Both men sat upright as straight backed as the chairs they occupied. Both sipped at chilled coupes of Clos de Mesnil while they examined the menus.

It was Moroni who started the conversation.

'You know I have never been terribly impressed with you, Alexei, but I must admit I am now.'

Girondou looked across the table at his companion with all the suspicion of coming face to face with a slumbering snake.

'Oh?' was the only reply he thought necessary. Ignoring the man's reticence, Moroni went on in a sarcastically amused tone.

'Yes. I always thought that getting a table here at short notice was impossible. I understood that you had to savour the prospect of eating in this temple of French gastronomy for months before you were actually allowed to sample it. Yet here we are, and you got two tables to boot. Incredible.'

He glanced at an adjoining table where two other men sat in silence looking somewhat balefully at each other. These two were also very well dressed although not to precisely the same standard as their masters. They also looked like a pair of businessmen discussing a deal of some sort, but it was clear from their demeanour that neither was very happy in each other's company. They, in contrast, were drinking water. They also had been given menus.

'I hope yours can read,' grunted Girondou.

'Not as well as he can shoot, in all probability, my friend but perhaps well enough to ensure he doesn't starve to death. I just hope you can afford to pay for four rather than just two.'

'Oh,' replied Girondou. 'I don't think that'll be a problem. I made the reservation in your name.'

For a second, Moroni stiffened then, perhaps thinking of the discussion to come, gave a hearty guffaw.'

'Touché, mon ami. Touché. Now what shall we eat?'

'I will stay with the set menu. It should be good enough here. Pike quenelle and Beef Rossini would be my choices.' Girondou replied.

Moroni nodded.

'I agree. I will join you with the beef but start with the foie gras. Perhaps a bottle of Margaux with the meat. One can hardly eat in the best restaurant in the world without drinking the best wine ever created?'

Moroni signalled the waiter. Now it was Girondou's turn to be impressed.

'They don't generally like to be summoned, these waiters. They usually get a bit sniffy.'

Moroni smiled grimly.

'Not with me they don't.'

The waiter listened to their order.

'We'll continue with the champagne with the first course and have a bottle of Margaux '82 with the meat.'

The waiter departed. It was Moroni who continued the conversation.

'And how are the beautiful Angèle and the children?'

Girondou gritted his teeth. He knew that this was a very long way from a polite social enquiry. However, until he found out what this meeting was all about, he could do nothing other than to play along.

'There are all fine, thank you. Very well.'

'Good to hear. I hope the girls are doing well at school. They are just at the age when they become more interested in boys that in their studies; especially two such beautiful ladies as they.'

'Thank you for asking. They're doing fine.' Girondou replied as he remembered that his lunch companion was unmarried and had been so since the events of sixteen years ago.

The waiter re-appeared with the amuse-bouche. This consisted of tiny dish of avocado mousse, half a small cup of cold fresh pea soup and a few shrimps in a lemon yoghurt sauce. Normally neither man had much time for this sort of rather inconsequential approach to eating good food, but both were forced to admit that the three tastes were delicious. Conversation paused while the little dishes were sampled. When they had finished, Girondou offered a suggestion.

'You asked for this meeting, Sebastien and now you have it. Perhaps you might like to say what you want after all these years. It's a long way to come for lunch; even one as good as this.'

Moroni nodded thoughtfully.

'Yes, Alexei we have both come a long way to eat here today just as we have both travelled a long way since we last met. As I recall vividly even now, it was not a pleasant parting.'

Girondou frowned at the memory.

'As I recall too there was good reason for that.'

'Yes, I do believe there was.

A waiter re-filled their glasses with more of one of the rarest and most expensive champagnes on the market while their first little course was cleared away and, on Moroni's instructions, was replaced in short order by the second.

The quenelle came in a single piece surrounded by a classic Normandy sauce that was just fishy enough not to disguise the taste of the pike. A few tiny vegetables and piece of scallop were added to the sauce. Girondou had heard that this dish was more often served with a Nantua sauce, but he usually found that with its bechamel base and crayfish flavour it was too strong to taste the fish. Moroni's fois gras was in a traditional slab of generous proportions and served with a fruit chutney. He called for and got some melba toast.

Moroni finally got to the nub of the meeting.

'Alexei, I want to find a way to work together again. It seems stupid for us to dance around each other as if we both had some dreadful communicable disease. We could do much more if we worked together. We were partners once. When we parted sixteen years ago, we basically divided up the south of France between us. You took the east and I the west. We have managed keep out of each

61

other's hair but now things are changing. The world is getting smaller and God is on the side of bigger battalions these days. We could do much more together than by continuing separately.'

Girondou snorted.

'I doubt that any God that either of us would recognise would wish to take sides with us, Sebastien. For all our fine suits and our fine food and wine, we fall completely into the ungodly category.'

'Yes, you are right, perhaps,' the gangster from Toulouse replied. 'But the fact remains we could be stronger together.'

'And this is what this meeting is all about? You want to join forces after all these years.'

'So, how is business?'

'Oh fine. Nothing to complain about. We have problems from time to time with the odd over-zealous gendarme or some of these new immigrant groups who think that they are harder than us effete French. But they learn to truth pretty quickly. You?'

'About the same, I think. The Mafia stays away but we are getting some trouble from these new Russians but for the moment they seem to be more interested in buying property to use for R&R than getting into any of the rackets. They look to us for holidays rather than business; somewhere to park their enormous yachts and equally enormous backsides. They may become a problem in future but not yet. Nothing yet also from the Orientals. For some reason I don't understand they seem to be steering clear. No, business is OK.'

Moroni switched the topic again.

'Tell me about your guard. Is he any good?

Girondou glanced across at the neighbouring table where both men, faced with a meal the like of which neither had ever encountered before, seemed to have lost a lot of their mutual antipathy.

'He's a Dutchman. Ex DKDB, Dutch diplomatic close protection. Seems efficient enough. Fortunately, he isn't kept too busy. He's a little sweet on Solange, Angèle tells me. Yours?'

'Or he's just a gorilla in a suit. Good with a gun though.'

'Well, that's what you want, after all.'

They had finished their second course and the waiters descended again. The Tournedos Rossini came in the now traditional tower sitting in a lake of thick brown truffle sauce from Périgueux and surmounted by a slab of lightly grilled fois gras and some other inconsequential bits and pieces held onto the top of the pile by a wooden cocktail stick. Both men instantly disassembled the dish and spread it out on their plates so they could actually see what they were eating. Moroni waved away the offer to taste the Margaux much to the annoyance of the sommelier who wanted to make a fuss and just told him to pour the damn thing. If there was anything wrong with it, he'd know soon enough. They resumed eating.

'Let us toast to a spirit of cooperation.'

Girondou thought they were a very long way from that but raised his glass to his nose nevertheless. He didn't need to taste it. What reached his nose was the aroma of the best wine he had ever come across. Both men sat silently while they appreciated what they had in their glasses. It was obviously a great wine. In a subjective world it was probably the greatest they would find in a restaurant and whatever their differences and whatever the tensions between them, this was something special. One this point, at least, Girondou was generous.

'Sebastien. I congratulate you on your choice. This is a wonderful wine. The best wine I have ever tasted.'

Moroni just nodded.

They both attacked their beef with gusto. It was, of course, delicious. The conversation meandered a little; lighting briefly from time to time on aspects of their shared past without doing so in sufficient detail as to become difficult. It was, Girondou thought, the nicest five or fifteen minutes that he had ever spent in his brother's company. It was almost nice enough to make him forget the storm clouds that would obviously roll in before coffee and what the great restaurant Paul Bocuse liked to call Delicacies & Temptations or Fantasies & Chocolates which came at the end of their meal, depending on how each man intended to ignore his current regime.

'What I want to suggest is that in a France that is becoming smaller and more paranoid, we bring our businesses closer. We look for shared opportunities where together we can be greater than we can on our own.'

This was, of course, the nub of the argument. The fact was that in terms of its ability to provide sources of income, Girondou's patch was much better than Moroni's. He had the entire French Riviera with its tourist riches, as well as its restaurants and hotels; thousands of them. It had its reclusive money too. It had casinos and it had Monte Carlo. It had industry along the coast, most especially, around Marseille. It had the port of Toulon. Millions of men employed in a myriad of jobs all of whom presented opportunities for Girondou to make money. Moroni was on shorter commons and that had always irked him. His bit of France ran from Montpellier to the Spanish border. It had Toulouse, of course, a major city but with half the population of Marseilles and it is people that allow crime to make money. Toulouse was a technology city and the more technology there was, the fewer people one found. Much of the rest of the territory was also less fruitful. The coast was populated by people who couldn't afford to live on the Côte d'Azur. Inland it was mostly farming. Toulouse may have been the old man's home base, but his eldest son got the thin edge of the wedge. Moroni had always coveted his brother's territory and this lunch was obviously yet another attempt to steal it without being obvious. Girondou was contemptuous but took care not to show it. There was still half a bottle of the Margaux to go.

The beef was gone, and two very clean plates had to please the chef in spite of a very politically incorrect call for bread with which to mop up the sauce. No matter how snooty the waiter had become when he received the request, Girondou suspected that the late lamented Maître Bocuse would have approved. It takes a hard heart for a chef not to see a customer scraping up the last remnants of his sauce with pleasure. Both decided to give the enormous selection of desserts a

65

miss and have some cheese instead and there was still half a glass of wine each. It was Girondou who took the conversation forward.

'This recent operation at La Plagette didn't go so well, Sebastian. What was that all about?'

The man glowered as the memory of that recent debacle was still very fresh in his mind.

'We were betrayed, of course. The flics knew everything about it.'

'By whom?'

'Believe it or not, some bloody Englishman.'

Girondou was immediately uncomfortable. It was precisely the sort of this that his friend Smith might get up to although this was well out of his usual territory.

'Englishman?' he asked.

'Some fucking soldier who was doing some training with the flyboys in Pau; on loan for some outfit called the SAS. Got involved with the daughter of one of our people. The information got out that way. In any case our man, his daughter and the interfering soldier are all dead. The soldier's going home in a box. End of problem. Teach me to be more careful, I suppose,'

Girondou did wonder where the matter of the British soldier was quite as dead as Moroni imagined but he let that pass. He was more interested in raising a different matter.

'I really don't like this people trafficking business. It is much too political a thing. I know the money's good. I've looked at it too, but it is a bit too political. It strikes me as a good way to get the direct attentions of the bigwigs in Paris. It isn't just a police matter anymore. The politicians will get involved and we both rely on the good offices of people up there. They're perfectly happy to take our money and help to keep the flics off our backs but once we start doing something that affects them politically, I have a feeling that things might change.'

Moroni was dismissive.

'Pah! That's bollocks. Those politicians will do what I tell them. They take enough money from me. They can bloody well keep their consciences in the same pockets as their wallets.'

There was a silence after which Moroni spoke again.

'Well, what do you think?'

Girondou sighed. He wondered if there was any point in delaying the inevitable, especially as the last of the Margaux had been poured.

'Sebastian. You and I have been enemies for long time. We both know why, and I really don't care anymore. It's a fact and that's that. There's no way we can collaborate, and you know that perfectly well. There is absolutely nothing for me in this; nothing I can profit by. I also know it's impossible for us to have any sort of relationship together let alone a working one. As I recall you were the one who wanted to stay in Toulouse. It was your choice. I just got what you thought were the leftovers. It's just tough luck that history has moved on and now you think I have the better territory. Well it's better because I have done a better job of developing it. I suggest we just enjoy the rest of our meal and agree to leave thing exactly as they are, for you'll never get an agreement from me.'

Moroni's colour deepened as his temper rose quickly. This was not a man who was used to people saying no to him.

'You always a sanctimonious prick, Alexei. Well, fuck you. You'll regret this. Mark my words. Your time is limited and when you do fall, I'll be the reason.'

With that he got up suddenly. He reached into his pocket, pulled out a roll of notes. He peeled off six five hundred euro notes and threw them contemptuously across the table at his brother.

'I won't bother killing you, my brother. I'll just kill your family instead.'

With that he swept out of the restaurant followed by a somewhat flustered bodyguard, leaving a stunned Girondou still in his seat.

After a while Henk moved silently into the vacant seat across from his boss.

'You all right, Sir?' he asked quietly.

Girondou just nodded slowly.

'Take me home, please, Henk.' was all he said as he too got up and walked slowly towards the door of the ornate dining room oblivious to the stares of his fellow diners. Henk gathered up the bank notes and added one of Girondou's business cards. He summoned the Head Waiter and pressed the payment into the man's hand.

'If that isn't enough, contact me for the rest.'

It had taken Moroni some time to calm down as the Mercedes sped along the Transeuropéenne towards Clermont- Ferrand on the first leg of their journey home to Toulouse. After some considerably time in thought he called Chirosi on his mobile.

'I want you to find out about Girondou's bodyguard. Henk something. He's a Dutchman. Find out his movements. I want to speak to him.'

He sat back deep into the back seat of the Mercedes and spent the rest of the journey staring sightlessly out of the window as a plan, long formed in his mind began to gain focus.

Chapter 6: New Allies Cemented

Cordiez was still dressed in a suit. It was a pretty shabby one but at least he made the gesture. It was still usual for the families and connections of those most closely involved, the fighters and their teams and the bull breeders, to dress up even if many of the audience no longer did. He usually tried to go to his son's fights when they were within distance. It wasn't always easy financially, but he tried. The boy and his achievements were the only thing he really valued these days. His wife had left him ten years ago, unable to cope with his almost permanent bad moods. She had taken their daughter with her. He had no idea where they lived. He had heard once that they were still in the south of France but her family who came from Avignon had cut him off almost as soon as she left, and no news came from them. The recent brief meeting at Gimeaux was the first since she left him. More or less, the boy had been in full-time schooling all his life and as the amount of training at Gimeaux increased, Cordiez had felt the double hit of the boy being in training and thus being un-available to work on the farm and the expense paying for that training. Usually some of the cost was paid by private sponsorship but in the early days there was very little of that about given that the father was not the most popular of men. So, he sat somewhat uncomfortably in the hotel where he had arranged to meet these two men, taking small sips of a cold beer. He had heard of them both, of course. Most people in the area had. But he had never met them. However, the man he met had hinted that it might be worth meeting his boss and he was offered a stay at the hotel.

'Why not?', he had thought.

Moroni arrived in the hotel car park, driven in his trademark Mercedes S600 as usual, directly from Toulouse. He had little or no interest in bullfighting. He had looked at it some time ago but decided that there was very little money to be made there except by betting and he had many of the bookmakers in his pocket anyway. Chirosi, however, had gone to the fight. Apart from the fact that he was interested in the sport, he had also wanted to keep an eye on Cordiez. The small bull ring at Rue du Cami Ral in Céret in was in the centre of town, surrounded by low cost blocks of flats and a few supermarkets. It was one of the many small rings that were scattered across the south of France and this one held about three thousand people. But since the ban on bullfighting just over the border in Catalonia it had become much more popular and the monied spectators visited now in numbers. Chirosi also drove a Mercedes but a slightly more modest GLS. He timed his arrival at the hotel to be just ahead of his boss and immediately got into the rear of the limousine.

'He's arrived and is waiting in the hotel. His son had a good day at the fight. He was awarded two ears.'

Moroni just nodded. He had only a vague idea of what this meant but he assumed it was good.

'All right. I'll meet you in the restaurant.'

71

It took Chirosi about ten minutes to collect his guest and escort him to the restaurant. Moroni was at his social best.

'Monsieur Cordiez. Thank you for agreeing to this meeting. I appreciate your taking the time to stop on your way home.'

Even Cordiez who was a little overwhelmed both by the hotel and the restaurant was persuaded to leave his usually grumpy personality aside for a while. He was also impressed that this important criminal was interested in talking to him. He was, of course, no fool and understood that there would be a bill to pay for all this flattery and hospitality.

'Congratulations also to your son,' Moroni continued. 'A great success. Two ears.'

It was skilfully done. The flattery was always welcome, and Moroni managed to give the impression that he was both interested in the bull fights and had been there earlier in the day to watch. In turn Cordiez acknowledged the praise with as much grace as he could. The meal began with Moroni ordering for all of them. He assumed that his guest would be thoroughly intimidated by the prices if not by the somewhat overblown descriptions of the courses in that way slightly less than great chefs describe their work.

'Monsieur Cordiez. I assume that you know who I am and what I do for a living.'

The man just nodded, unsure of the extent that this was a topic that could be discussed out loud in a public restaurant. He didn't realise that any table that was remotely within eaves-dropping distance was occupied by Moroni's people.

'I have a business proposition to put to you. But before I offer it, I do feel that I should emphasise that this is all highly confidential. You mustn't discuss this with anyone other than me or Mr. Chirosi here. You know my reputation so you know that I have a certain policy towards people who don't follow my instructions. If you're not willing to accept these conditions, then I suggest we talk no longer and just have a pleasant meal together.'

Cordiez thought for a moment then just nodded. What had he to lose? In any case, this was a powerful friend in a life where he had precious few of them of any sort.

'Monsieur Cordiez. I'll be very frank and honest with you. I am talking to you because I am told you can help me in a new scheme. I intend to help immigrants from North Africa to find new homes in France and the rest of Europe.'

He smiled slightly.

'Now while this might sound a philanthropic activity, I can assure from the start that it is not. It is highly illegal but equally, it is highly remunerative. Personally, I couldn't care less about giving refugees new homes but the possibility of their finding one is one for which many of them are prepared to pay a lot of money. You've undoubtedly read newspaper accounts of this sort of thing in Italy and elsewhere usually when something goes wrong but policing the whole northern coast of the Mediterranean is impossible and there are many more successful importations than there are unsuccessful ones that grab headlines. We have decided after a somewhat unfortunate experiment recently that our particular stretch of the south coast of France is too full of French policemen and German tourists to operate without great risk. The coast of the Camargue, however, is a different story as, although it is well-stocked with tourists during the day, the fact that most of it is almost completely undeveloped and unbuilt on means that they tend to disappear during the night. Also, there are very few roads to carry regular police patrols, and the Coast Guard is busier looking after the interests of rich boat owners at more populated parts of the coast.'

Cordiez finished his latest mouthful before asking the obvious question.

'All that makes sense to me and you can rest assured that I have no interest one way or another in immigration, legal or illegal. As long as they keep the hell off my farm, I don't care. But what do you actually want from me? What can I offer you in exchange for the sort of money that was mentioned by Mr. Chirosi, here? I'm not the only farmer on the Camargue.'

'Indeed, you're not, Monsieur Cordiez. But you farm in precisely the right place to offer us assistance. You live on the only road south to the beach at Beauduc and thus you know most of what happens along it. You also know the inland waterways from the beach if we decide to run our operation from the landing beach inland a little before transhipping the immigrants to other transport for further travel.

We thus need your eyes and your local knowledge. Nothing more. For this we're prepared to pay you a lot of money.'

'And how much is that?' asked Cordiez. They were finally getting to the bit that interested him most.

Moroni smiled. This was a man of similar caste to him.

'Ten thousand Euros each time we plan to land a consignment with a bonus of ten thousand if the whole thing goes off successfully.'

Cordiez looked interested.

'And how many of these consignments, as you put it, do you intend to bring in?'

'At least one a month.'

They all paused while Cordiez did the mental arithmetic. It was clearly more money that Cordiez had seen in many a long year; if ever. It was also a good deal less than what Chirosi knew his boss was prepared to pay. It had also been news to him. It didn't take long for the answer to appear.

'Well. I'd say you've got yourself a partner.'

Moroni disguised that fact that he was a very long way from wanting a partner. A disposable asset would have been nearer the mark, but he let it pass.

'Splendid. Let's drink to our, er, partnership, then.'

Once glasses had been raised, the meal progressed. Moroni returned to the subject.

'Pierre here will be your main contact for all this. He is the man who will pay you and he will organise things when we are arranging a shipment. He will give you a phone number and you will only talk to him. We may wish to find one or two more like-minded people in the area to help with the project, but you must talk with them as little as possible, preferably not at all. You report directly to us. I would prefer it if you only did what we pay you for and that alone. Pierre is also the man to come to if you have any difficulties.'

That was it. The meal proceeded with small talk although Moroni was actually more on a fact-finding mission. After generalities about the man's son and some on the rest of the Camargue, he finally got onto the subject that interested him most.

'Now, this Emile Aubanet. He seems something of a bigwig in the area. How come?'

Cordiez's face darkened to a scowl. His contempt was obvious.

'Oh, he's just someone who has grown too big for his boots. Like a lot of them. They seem to think that because they have big bits of the better farming land, they're somehow better than the rest of us. They should try farming the land I have. Then they would learn what kind of work farming is.'

'But I was told that he's somehow in charge,' Moroni persisted. 'A sort of boss of bosses.'

'Pah!' the man spat. 'Rubbish. He's just a jumped-up old man who happens to come from a family that thinks it owns the place. Well he doesn't own my bit. That's for sure.'

'What do you believe Monsieur Aubanet would think of our little plan. Would he approve?'

Cordiez laughed.

'I very much doubt it. He's much too high and mighty and moralistic. Easy to say when you've got more money than Croesus.'

'What do you think other farmers would think of it; the plan, that is.'

Cordiez shrugged.

'Most wouldn't care one way or the other I suppose. I don't really know. Most people around me don't think of immigrants very much. They usually think of anyone who wasn't actually born here as an immigrant of some sort. There are a few, I know, men like me, who would jump at the chance of making a bit of money. We can't afford to have principles like Monsieur Aubanet.

A look passed between the two gangsters. He seemed to be the right choice, this man. The meal led to conclusion and Moroni took his leave. He shook hands with his guest.

'It's been a pleasure to meet you, Monsieur Cordiez. I look forward to a long and mutually prosperous relationship. I must leave you now as I have another appointment but Monsieur Chirosi has a little something for you. We will be in touch soon.'

And with that he left the restaurant and was spirited away in his Mercedes that had magically appeared at the front door just as he got there. Chirosi had also decided that he didn't relish this man's company for too much longer, so he walked his guest back to the hotel and took his leave of him the foyer.

'I too must leave you now, Monsieur Cordiez. You are our guest here, of course. The hotel bill will be paid by us so don't bother with that and use the bar as you wish. It is all covered. In the meantime, please accept this as a contribution to your expenses.'

He took a well-filled envelope from his inside jacket pocket and handed it over to the man. It contained five thousand euros.

Chapter 7: Transfer of Power

There had been the slightest of breezes overhead as the grand lunch party assembled and the temperature beneath the trees in the walled garden wasn't too high. It was early August so that any respite from the piercing heat that often enveloped life in the Camargue for the last few weeks was welcome even by those who, like many there, had been born to it. Smith stood to one side, glass of a highly iced, weak whisky and water in hand looking on, smiling and nodding to many he recognised and to those who he didn't. It wasn't his party, of course. Indeed, it was only Martine's insistence that got him there at all. He had never been a party animal and had become less so with age. However, it had been made very clear to him that he had to be there, so he just agreed without argument. In fact, it was Émile who had first asked him even before Martine and it was also Émile who had hinted that he was to be slightly more than just a spectator.

'Just keep an eye out, if you would, Peter,' he had said.

'Anything in particular?'

The old man shrugged in a way that meant little.

'Nothing in particular. Just watch. Nothing too obvious.'

Smith shot him a bit of a look. Émile raised a hand in apology.

'Sorry, Peter. Of course, you know more about this sort of thing than I do.'

So he stood by as people came into the garden, each stopping as they arrived to be greeted by Émile and his daughter. The old man was casually dressed in a white shirt and dark trousers with a brightly decorated Camargue waistcoat. Martine was in full Camargue costume, full lightly flower printed skirt with a white apron, a crisp white blouse under an embroidered waistcoat, low heeled shoes. Her dark hair was piled high on her head, decorated with black silk ribbons and she wore a thin string of pearls tightly around her neck and a small jewelled Camargue cross on her lapel. Not for the first time Smith looked on in wonder at this ravishing beauty. From time to time she glanced in his directions and smiled. She knew how much he hated this sort of social event. She also knew how much he enjoyed her dressing up like this.

Once the guests had been greeted and had a cold glass of Crémant in hand they gravitated towards the long table set out under the shade of the many trees that grew in the garden and stood chatting in small groups. Smith also looked across at another small group near the garden door through which, he noticed, all the guests had arrived. The normal entrance to the garden was through the house. It was a group of six, all younger than he. He didn't recognise four of them but one couple he knew. His friend Deveraux had, like him, found that Provence was a good place to lose his past and, also like him, he had found himself a girlfriend who was also in Provençale dress and, as a consequence, looked beautiful. Deveraux was also dressed up somewhat and like most of the male guests was wearing a light jacket. For many it was a courtesy. For Smith and Deveraux, it was also security. It is hard to hide a Glock in the back of your trousers if you weren't wearing a jacket. Ever since his brief conversation with Émile he had decided that the old man needed a bodyguard beyond Jean Marie. Deveraux also was covering his own boss.

After a succession of anodyne exchanges with guests who seemed to know him better than he knew them, Smith was delighted to see a friendly face approaching. Four, in fact. He was hard put to rescue his drink as two extremely beautiful teenage girls flung their arms around his neck, smothering him with kisses. The glass was mysteriously taken from his hand and he could respond in proper manner. At last the two disengaged themselves, to be replaced by a slightly older but equally beautiful lady and receive again another triple kiss on the cheeks; rather more dignified this time. Finally, an extremely elegant man approached, right hand extended while the other held the whisky glass. The Girondou family had arrived.

In the year or two since he had met them and shared some adventures, he had become extremely fond of the family of the man who controlled most of the organised crime in the south east of France from the coast as far north as Lyon. He looked like the archetypal successful French business man. That was hardly surprising as that was precisely what he was. But it was just that his business was slightly less orthodox than most.

'Peter, nice to see you.'

'And you, Alexei, and you. Your family grows more beautiful every time I see them.'

The man smiled with genuine pleasure.

'As does your Martine, I think,' he replied glancing across the garden. 'How an old man like you can catch the eye of such a beauty, I have no idea. Something to do with being Welsh, I suppose.'

Smith just smiled and stood with his friends enjoying the moment. His friend continued.

'So, what's this all about, Peter? I am honoured to be asked, of course, but what is the occasion? Not a birthday, I hope. If so, we would be embarrassed to arrive without a present.'

Smith shook his head and decided that a little lie was in order.

'No, nothing like that, I think. To be frank, I have no idea. We'll just have to wait and see.'

It was a while before everyone was assembled and Martine clapped her hands and asked everyone to sit at the long table. In a gesture that was unusual in its precision, unusual for Provence, that is, each guest had a place name. The table was long and narrow. Émile took his place at the head, of course, while Martine was opposite at the far away other end. Number two, as it were. Each side was lined with some twenty or so guests with men and women generally mixed. As is usually the case on these occasions there was a certain amount of precedence as one got nearer the ends of the table. However, on this occasion, the precedence was an odd one.

The place of honour on Émile's right was given most peculiarly to Smith himself while Alexei Girondou sat opposite Smith on the old man's left. At the opposite end of the table, Martine had her old nurse Madame Durand and retired family housekeeper on her right with

Angèle Girondou on her left. If there was a precedence behind the rest of the seating it escaped Smith, but he was pleased to see that Deveraux and his girlfriend were seated opposite each other in the middle of the table. It was the best place from which to observe their fellow guests. He recognised most of them but not all. There was a small sprinkling of people from the various Aubanet business and a significant number of fellow Camargue farmers.

The table was covered with a wide variety of plates bearing almost everything you could think of that was local to the area. Charcuterie including selections of the many bull meat sausages that were a local speciality, salads of all sorts, plates of baked aubergines, and peppers, seafood and meats of all sorts including the little paupiettes of veal and fish, rice from the Camargue. Almost everything came from the Aubanet farms as did the wine with large jugs of red and rosé spaced regularly along the table. Everyone helped themselves and there was a generally festive atmosphere with loud conversations ebbing and flowing across and along the length of the table.

Arthur, of course, was in heaven. Smith's faithful greyhound had fallen in love with the Aubanet farm a good deal quicker than Smith and was a regular and much - loved guest. The dog did regular circuits around the table receiving titbits as he went. He was also probably the happiest with the seating arrangement as it placed his two favourite people, Smith and Émile Aubanet, together and he regularly returned to that end of the table. Smith was also interested to note that these foraging trips avoided certain people. The dog had always been a good judge of character and more than once in the past had Smith trusted that view.

The main course had been finished and replaced with plates of fruit and cheese. Everyone was replete and deep in conversation with neighbours. Smith had been able to mix his conversations with, as requested, an unobtrusive surveillance of the guests on the opposite side of the table. He noted that Deveraux, being seated on the other side, was doing the same of the people he couldn't see himself. A quick eye contact between the two confirmed that nothing out of the ordinary had been spotted.

So, it was somewhat to everyone's surprise when Émile Aubanet got to his feet. There was no aggressive clinking of a wine glass with a knife to obtain silence. Aubanet had been the leader of their Camargue community for almost fifty years. He had led and advised them, helped them where necessary and defended them too. With absolutely no authority other than tradition and his own personality he had been in charge for as long as most people could remember. He needed no-one to stop the traffic for him. The main point of the lunch had obviously been reached and the table fell silent while everyone turned to face their host.

'Friends. Firstly, I would like to thank you all for coming here today. It is a great pleasure to see you all at the Mas des Saintes as our guests; guests of Martine and myself. In particular, I would like to welcome Alexei Girondou and his family. It was two thousand years ago when Julius Caesar and Pompey were picking sides in their fight, rather as children do in a playground, that Arles and Marseilles found themselves on opposite sides creating a falling out that stupidly still exists today. I think that perhaps it is time for all that to stop and I am delighted to welcome Alexei and Angèle, Solange and Amy to our table here as friends.'

He looked down to his left and then across the length of the table.

'It is a place at which you are always welcome.'

There was a ripple of applause at this and Smith took a silent note of where the greeting was less that enthusiastically received. He knew that Deveraux would as well. The old man continued with a slight gesture down to his right.

'I would also say that this historical reconciliation, if that's what it is, could not have taken place without Peter Smith here. All of you know Peter and many of you have reason to be grateful for that acquaintance. I certainly have. I won't embarrass him by going into details but he the only man alive to whom I owe anything at all. Both debts are ones that I can never repay. Firstly, I owe him my life and secondly, and to me more importantly, is that his friendship with my daughter seems to make her happier than I have seen her since the death of her mother ten years ago.'

There was a respectful murmur from the assembled company. Most of them were old enough to remember the lady. Smith looked down at the table more than a little unhappy about being in this sort of spotlight even for a moment. Somewhat to his displeasure he saw

85

Deveraux grinning widely him. Deveraux alone knew how excruciating Smith felt this unwelcome limelight. Aubanet continued.

'As you all know I have a daughter. You will therefore forgive an old man his indulgence but I look on him almost as a son.'

'A son-in-law would be better,' came a cry.

Everything stopped, and everyone turned towards the bottom end of the table where Madame Durand was to be seen completely unrepentant wagging her ninety-year-old finger at her host with a broad grin on her face. She had been nurse to Martine, and housekeeper to the family all her life and throughout that time had carried a torch for Émile. She lived in some comfort in one of the few elegant townhouses in Tranquetaille, the suburb on the north bank of the Rhône opposite Arles proper. She remained a close confidante to Martine, and Smith and Arthur were regular visitors. As if sensing that one of his favourite people was the centre of interest, the dog wandered slowly down to that end of the table and lay alertly down, looking up from the old woman's feet. The point was not lost on the assembled company. With an equally wide grin Émile continued but the smile faded as he drew quickly to the substance of his speech.

"My friends. For nearly half a century I have tried to serve you all. As the senior member of the Aubanet family it has been my responsibility to try to guide you all, fellow farmers on the Camargue, through the ups and down of our life here. This was, as you know, a responsibility given to my family some three hundred years ago and I hope that we have done our job well."

There was a general assent around the table. If there were any dissenters, this was not the time for them to show themselves.

"However, my friends, I am now seventy-five years old and the time has come to pass on the responsibility to the next member of my family. I wish to retire to my farm; to my horses and my bulls. Before I therefore hand the reins, so to speak, over to my daughter I would remind you that you all have the right in confidence to object to this change. You have one week to register this objection anonymously by letter to me. If I receive such a letter, I will convene a meeting of the original twelve families who, one way or another, represent most of those of you living and working here in the Camargue. I would remind you that the last time this meeting was convened was in 1879."

Again, a slight laugh ran around the table. He continued:

"If I receive no such letter, I will assume that you are content with Martine as my successor."

The old man rose slowly bringing to their feet the whole company. He walked slowly down the length of the table and stopped before the seat occupied by his daughter. To general applause he took her hand gently and slowly led her back up the table to his seat at the head, sat her down and then he himself returned to the bottom of the table. It was a literal as well as a ritual handover.

He gestured that everyone should sit down. He stood for a moment looking at each face up one side of the long table and down the other. Then he nodded slowly and then sat down himself. It was done. There were obviously no more speeches and the general chat around the table resumed. Martine reached across the table and took Smith's hand. Now he understood the seating. More than seats had just been exchanged. That he saw, and he appreciated the gentle way that it had been done. Martine was now the boss of much more than just the Aubanet group of businesses. No real surprise there, he thought. Most people knew that was inevitable. What made him much more uncomfortable was that without changing his own seat he had moved from honoured guest to something that seemed much more tightly bound in and it was a feeling that gave him very mixed feelings indeed. As if he knew what was going through his master's mind Arthur wandered slowly up from the bottom of the table. The flow of tasty scraps had in any case dried up somewhat. He finally reached the head of the table and, being a suitably large dog, laid his head directly on the corner, his nose just touching the still joined hands of his master and new mistress. Smith looked down and saw a warning eye looking up at him. Smith smiled down at the old dog. Obviously he understood as well.

The sun above the shading trees remained high and hot as the meal came to an end. One by one the guests left. Smith was amused to note that the new order was already in force. All the guests came one by one first to the side of Martine's chair. The men taking their leave with the traditional dip of the head to just above her hand, held in the lightest of touches. The women gave a small bob of a courtesy, irrespective of their age. It was only then that they made their way to the other end and offered Émile a stronger handshake. Angèle and

Alexei and the girls were last to leave. They came up to say goodbye and the garden became quiet again. By this time Émile and Madame Durand had come back up to the top of the table and sat in a small group with Smith and Martine. Arthur was happier now that all his favourite people were in the same place and lay flat on his side snoring gently. Deveraux and his friend were there as well. Smith was amused that the friend, a very beautiful woman indeed, rose respectfully as Girondou came close. This rather odd reversal of tradition, Smith remembered, was occasioned by the fact that she was actually employed by the man from Marseille as one of his bodyguards. Smith wondered idly whether it was her fearsome reputation with knives that attracted Deveraux who had met her during a previous adventure. Deveraux, he knew, disliked knives however expert he was with them himself. They weren't elegant enough for him. However, he was obviously prepared to overlook this where is girlfriend was concerned.

'Thank you, Martine, for having us here.' said Girondou. 'It is a great privilege and a pleasure to be invited to this most special occasion. I know how many old prejudices and enmities were in people's minds today.'

Martine smiled back.

'I hope that today we have begun to move away from all that nonsense.'

He nodded.

'I hope so too. You can be assured that I'll do everything in my power to make it so.'

'Thank you, Alexei. That means a lot to me and my father, I know. I too will try to make the best of a new start. It is a great opportunity for us both.

'Yes, and yet another thing for which we have reason to thank you, Peter. Without you, none of this would be happening, I think.'

Smith made a vague hand gesture that he hoped would dismiss the sentiment in an insouciant sort of way. It was Martine's giggle that made him see that it just succeeded in looking what his daughters would have described as 'lame'. In an effort to cover his embarrassment he rose rather brusquely to his feet and looked towards the house.

'Well, I don't know about you all, but I need a whisky.'

His proposed escape to the house in search of the drink was cut very short by Martine who waved at one of the staff who were beginning to clear the bottom end of the table. A glass of well-watered and iced whisky was produced almost immediately. Girondou laughed at Smith's unhappiness that was now beginning to turn into anger.

'The only person, I know, who can match you for cunning, I think, Peter. You really are well matched.'

As usual Smith's discontent was instantly dissolved by Martine taking his hand and lifting it to her lips.

'No Peter. It is much more than that and well you know it.'

He did, of course, but he still felt discomforted with this binding intimacy. Not for the first time he felt the need for Gentry's undemanding company and the calm antagonism of the chessboard.

With an understanding grin from Alexei the Girondou family left with Deveraux's girlfriend reminding him of something he already knew; that a bodyguard's job is never over for the day. They were quickly followed by Madame Durand to be driven back by one of the farm men to her rather grand house in Tranquetaille. The elegant town house was one of the few that had escaped the American bombing of August 1944 of the rail and road bridges of Arles that had otherwise flattened most of the suburb on the north bank of the Rhône. Émile and Martine disappeared into the house on some undisclosed business, leaving Smith and Deveraux, each nursing a cool, watery whisky.

The two were very old friends indeed and their relationship went back many years in the service of Her Majesty's Government in one of its lesser known departments. It was a friendship based on complete trust and confidence in each other's abilities; a confidence that had been profoundly tested on occasions. Deveraux's single-handed rescue of his friend from a week spent in a Mogadishu torture cell had been conducted with such unbelievable savagery that the locals still refused to believe that they had not been set upon by a small platoon at the least. Deveraux's personal retribution on the young American intelligence agent who had drunk too much in a town bar and whose bragging had led to Smith's capture was still the reason that he was theoretically not allowed to visit America. Deveraux, of course, came and went invisibly as he wished. The only thought in his mind when he took the young idiot from the same bar, piled him into a borrowed helicopter and dropped him without a parachute out into the

American embassy compound a thousand feet below had been of his friend Smith, naked and broken, completely covered with strips of flayed skin and deep cuts and bruises, chained to an electrified bed spring, surrounded by blood and faeces. Deveraux had hung about high above the compound, face at the cockpit window so that they had time to look up and photograph him. He wanted them to know.

Memories like these came momentarily to each of them as Smith gently touched glasses with Deveraux. He may be been the most skilled and violent killer in the business but he could also play the piano like a God. It was a relationship that represented the only things that Smith really valued; valued above love and all those other things. To Smith trust and loyalty were paramount, and he had often been very hard on the many people over the years who didn't meet his standards. That was the reason Deveraux was his friend. One of very, very few. However, such thoughts were put aside for the moment.

'Well, Dev?'

His companion paused a while to collect his thoughts. Smith liked his briefings very short and condensed.

'Nothing obvious, boss. This event was anticipated so those who don't like the idea of Martine's promotion have had a chance to get used to it. One or two were less than happy but there was no great show of hostility. Oddly slightly more women than men but that's probably nothing more than you might imagine.'

Smith nodded. That was very roughly what he'd seen too.

'Can you give me a list and I'll compare it with mine?'

Deveraux nodded. There followed a companionly silence until Deveraux plucked up the courage.

'You all right, boss?'

Smith was a little startled. It was not a typical sort of question for the man.

'All right, Dev? What on earth do you mean?'

His friend had the grace to look a touch uncomfortable.

'Well. To be honest this isn't quite what I would have imagined when I thought of you in retirement. I mean, I anticipated the little house in town with your dog and books and stuff. Occasional bouts of grumpy gardening. Cooking. But to be frank ...', and he took a deep breath, 'I never quite saw you as, well, a family man.'

Smith frowned at the man over the rim of his elegant cut glass then after a difficult gap threw his head back and burst into laughter.

'To be frank, old chum, it isn't exactly what I had in mind, either.'

He wanted to question his companion a little about his relationship with his new girlfriend. Given that they both shared professions he was slightly intrigued when imagining their pillow talk. But he knew that what was for him idle curiosity might cross an un-defined barrier between them. He also knew that between them Deveraux and Martine's driver Jean Marie had the security of the Mas pretty locked up and that was, for the moment at least, all that really concerned him.

The same topic was on his mind a little later in the afternoon when he took Arthur for a walk around the farm. Head protected himself against the sun with an old Lock straw hat and a large bottle of water fixed to the saddle, he had borrowed a horse and set off round a long route that would ultimately take him back to Martine's little *cabane* where he was sleeping. The straw-roofed converted herders' cottage had been a gift to Martine from her late mother and few people ever went there. Even her father waited to be invited.

Arthur, of course, was delighted with another opportunity to find and kill something, although in his retirement a certain amount of common sense had finally blunted his hunting instinct a little and he no longer exhausted himself within a few minutes of being let loose. Now he trotted contentedly alongside his master until he spotted something that really was within his compass. He had learned about birds and bulls and now just observed them from afar. He knew there wasn't a lot of reward from chasing them.

In spite of best intentions, Smith knew that his attempts at a solitary contemplation of his situation would yield very little. He had never in his life taken more than a few seconds to decide anything. Important for him, at least, nothing was ever gained by endless rumination, the weighing up pros and cons of anything and coming to a reasoned conclusion after hours of thought. Things, at least the sort of things that Smith was usually confronted with, took much less time than that. So he just wandered calmly around the farm looking out for things with his beloved dog trotting in the shade offered by the walking horse.   They stopped from time to time, and Smith dismounted to give Arthur some water and sat for a while. He was reminded of that intriguing puzzle of the ownership of donkey's shadow. The tale went that a Greek peasant hired his donkey to a local tourist. The trip was in the sun and the group stopped for a rest. The tourist tried to sit in the shadow cast by the donkey. The peasant demanded more money as the tourist had hired the donkey and not its shadow.

It was towards the end of his walk that an obvious re-energised Arthur suddenly took off at high speed. Even well into his retirement he still possessed the speed that had brought him considerable success on the race tracks of south east England in his youth. Smith followed the chase across one of the few large grass fields in that part of the farm and was delighted that it ended quite abruptly in a cloud of dust.

By the time he reached the scene, Arthur was laying, panting very hard, beside a very dead Camargue hare. This sort of event, common when the dog was younger, had happened increasingly rarely in more recent years. Camargue hares were also so pretty rare as well and Smith was filled with pride and affection for the old dog. He was also pleased that Arthur had left his victim un-molested and in place. He was never one to carry it back. He was only interested in the chase and the kill, a point of view with which Smith had complete sympathy. The similarity between the dog and its master didn't escape him. He sat beside the dog and his prey and watched contentedly as the dog's breathing became more regular whereupon he gave the dog a very small amount to drink. That done he tied the hare to his saddle, remounted and continued towards home at a much-reduced pace.

It was an opportune scene as it served to remind him of the past how his own personal priorities before his life had been altered now that Martine Aubanet had come into it. He was increasingly of the opinion that something had to change and perhaps today's events might be the catalyst for that.

Having attended to the horse, he took the hare into the kitchen. There is very little meat on a Camargue hare at the best of times, certainly not enough for human consumption if you only have one of them. However, he felt that at least Arthur should enjoy the fruits of his labours. He quickly skinned and gutted it and popped it into a deep pot to stew gently. He didn't feel that Arthur would mind that it hadn't been hung to tenderise the meat or be stewed with vegetables and bouquet garni. The dog's requirements were simpler. In a way, Smith found himself being envious. He poured himself another weak whisky and settled into one of the armchairs with a book and waited for Martine to arrive back after whatever she was doing. Before long Arthur was asleep on the sofa. His perusal of Edgar Wind's Pagan Mysteries of the Renaissance, his current reading, was accompanied by an unconscious frown on his brow as at least a small part of his subconscious remembered Deveraux's remark about domestic bliss.

It was late when Martine got back from work. She was still dressed in her Provençale costume and still looked gorgeous as a consequence; even more gorgeous than usual. She came in and immediately sat on his lap and took a large swig of what was, it should be admitted, not Smith's first whiskey. Waiting, he thought, was a thirsty business. Smith felt he should start.

'Congratulations, my dear, on your elevation. I wish you all the best, of course."

She planted another, slightly lingering, kiss on his lips.

'Thanks. Do you want to eat, or shall we just take a bottle to bed?'

'Well my darling, put like that, I'm not sure if there's a real choice. However, I have to give Arthur his hare first.'

The broadest of smiles crossed her beautiful face.

'A hare. Did he catch one?'

She was genuinely excited and pleased and Smith felt a flush of pride.

'Yes, coursed and killed. Not big enough for us to eat but I've cooked it for him.

Martine leapt off his lap and collapsed on the sofa next to a slightly sleepy Arthur and started to make a great fuss of him; all of which he accepted with a certain canine insouciance. Smith continued after a while.

'You go and have a shower and get the bottle. I'll feed Arthur, shower and join you.'

And so it was. Smith took the meat from the hare carcass and added it to a pile of dog nuts and threw a considerable amount of the stock over the lot. Needless to say, Arthur demolished the lot in very short order indeed. Then it wasn't long before he had showered and joined Martine. She was sitting up against a mountain of linen pillows, dressed in a low-necked, cotton night dress, holding a very large glass of ice-cold crémant in each hand. They drank without the ubiquitous clink of glasses. She knew he disliked the custom. She wanted to be first to speak.

'Thank you, my dear. I know how much you hate these sorts of public occasions. But both daddy and I much appreciated your being there; for more reasons than just the obvious one.'

Smith was quite aware of why it had been important for him to be there. Today saw the promotion of a new member of the Aubanet family to the position of un-elected head of the community of Camargue farmers. There was nothing too unusual with that. The family had held the position for generations. This time, however, it was a woman who was taking on the job and that was a first. Having what was essentially her boyfriend at the head of the table was obviously meant to impress any doubters, especially those who knew about Smith and his history with the family. Secretly, though, as he lay there and sipped his drink, he was somewhat pissed off. But he also knew that this was not the moment to raise that particular matter. Looking a little surprised at his lack of response, she was forced to continue.

'I think it went well. What do you think?'

To be frank, Smith wasn't too interested in a post-mortem. He would have preferred to talk about Arthur's triumph. However, he understood how important the day was.

'I agree. There were a few faces that seems a little longer than others but nothing too significant. Deveraux and I have made a list. It was good to have Girondou there. That made a few of the more traditionally-minded think a bit. No. In all I think it went fine.'

He paused a little before asking what was, for him, a highly significant question.

'So, what's next? You have to forgive my asking. I'm not completely au fait with these regal transitions.'

'Well the next thing is a bit of an extended tour. There are a lot of people who weren't here today and we have to visit them. Also, of course, some of those who came will want an extended talk. It will take a few days. Father and I would be very pleased if you could come as well.'

'I bet you would,' Smith thought. 'Token male; not my sort of thing.' What he actually said after a bit of a pause was: 'Thanks, but I really need to spend some time in Arles, I think. I have some business of my own there. Also, my house needs some work and the garden certainly does. I think I'll let you two go on your grand tour. It's an Aubanet thing, I think.'

She tried but there was no disguising the slight petulance in her voice.

'I would have thought that you could find someone to do the gardening for you. You know that you don't really enjoy it.'

'You miss the point, my love. I have to do the gardening precisely because I don't like it.'

The slight tension was broken as he waggled his empty glass at her. She leant over to pick the bottle from the bedside table and in doing so exposed a particularly enticing flash of pink bottom. The temptation to kiss it was irresistible. Fortunately, she didn't drop the bottle. Indeed, she seem to take slightly longer than necessary in re-attaining the vertical.

Once restored to a sitting position, glasses replenished, he fell to some practicalities.

'You'll take the Sentinal, please, and Jean Marie as your driver. Please come home every evening. I'll ask Deveraux to keep his usual eye on you both although, as you know, you won't see him. No matter what others might say, I want Jean Marie with you when you have your discussions. You must insist on that. I want him in the room all the time. I've no idea how many enemies you have out there, but you're planning a long tour and putting your head voluntarily into the potential lions mouth three or four time a day.'

'Surely, Peter, this isn't necessary. These are our people, after all.'

'Martine, I'm not going to try to persuade you to do something that you know is common sense.   You've accepted all these precautions in the past without argument. If your recent elevation means that this sort of disagreement is going to become usual, then I shan't make any more suggestions'

Smith drained his glass and slid down the bed to a prone position. As he did, he saw Arthur's head looking at them over the back of the sofa at the far end of the room. The dog sensed that someone wasn't completely right. But it was a problem that didn't concern him much and he acknowledged that by lowering his head back to the sofa seat and returning to sleep. It wasn't long before Martine too finished her glass and lay down. She shuffled across and laid her head against his shoulder. This time, her voice was much lower; almost a whisper.

'I meant it, my love. I was very pleased to have you there today. I found the whole thing quite intimidating and I was nervous. Thank you.'

It wasn't that Smith suddenly forgot his misgivings, but it was true to say that a beautiful woman, one of the most beautiful women he had ever seen, dressed only barely in a crisp linen nightdress, leaning her head first against him and then progressively the rest of her, took his mind off the problem somewhat. The wandering hands completed the process.

There he lay listening to the sounds of the Camargue night with the lady who was now such an important part of his life gently snoring into his ear. Arthur also was making a remarkably similar sound from the other end of the room. He felt content for the moment, a feeling made slightly better by the fact that he had engineered his escape from the grand tour. He could spend some time in his house and garden and go back, for a while at least, to his old routine. It was well past midnight and it was still hot. All the windows were open and there was the very slightest current of air through the little *cabane* from one side to the other carrying with it many sounds and smells of the Provençale night. It had been a long and momentous day and Smith just lay on the big double bed lightly holding his companions' hand and went over the events of the day in his mind as he knew she had been. They lay side by side under a thin cotton sheet. Smith was grateful that Martine's antipathy towards modern technology and any form of air conditioning, an antipathy he shared, did not extend to a very sophisticated mosquito repellent system.

Chapter 8: Walks and Wisdom

The next morning Smith watched the black Range Rover drive out of the yard on the first of its appointments. He was happy that Jean Marie was indeed driving them both. He had supplied Deveraux with their itinerary as well as a promise from them not to deviate from it. He would make his own arrangements. He had checked that there was a fully charged satellite phone in the glove compartment and a fully loaded Glock G42 .38 pistol. He knew Jean Marie had a heavier Glock G30 .45 calibrate beside him in the driver's door pocket. It would be transferred to the back of his trousers when he left the car. He checked the rear compartment under the floor still contained another G30 and a Heckler and Koch MP5. There was a time when all this would have been thought ridiculous but a series of adventures over the previous two years had made the Aubanet family realise that times had changed and they themselves had become targets from time to time. Smith had won that argument a long time ago.

As the dust settled, he and Arthur turned towards his own somewhat more modest transport; his very battered old Peugeot. He was amused to see that since he last used it a few days ago someone had at least played a hose over it, removing a little of its usual coating of dust. Arthur, having initially seemed a little puzzled to see the other car depart without him, leapt joyfully enough into the back of the car and they drove down the winding farm drive, lined with poplars and oleander bushes and out onto the route north back to Arles.

His little house was in good order, of course. Smith knew that it was visited by friends of the family from time to time, so it was clean, reasonably stocked with food and the beds and other linen changed and made up. He opened the double kitchen doors onto the garden. Everything seemed to have grown hugely even though it was only a couple of weeks since he had last been here. Secretly he was rather pleased. He was no gardener and the only sort of gardening he liked was pruning. He actually looked forward to setting about the place, secateurs in hand to bring some order into chaos.

The midday sun was up, and the temperature was climbing so his gardening was both slow and thoughtful. In reality his mind was only partially on the job. It wasn't really on anything special as he worked gradually along the two sides of his narrow plot. At this time of year the vine that he had planted when he arrived in Arles and that he had patiently trained and pruned to give a full covering of broad leaved shade to the terrace that occupied half of the narrow garden, was fully in leaf and bore its customary burden of young grapes. It was thick enough to offer full shade to the table and chairs below and consequently the temperature in that shade was good ten degrees lower than in full sun. All the houses in his row on the square had their own gardens, separated from their neighbours by a variety of fences, wires overgrown with ivy and other creeping and climbing plants. The row also went slightly up hill as it ran towards the church of the Major. Thus, his garden lay about a metre below his neighbour's and was bounded by a low wall.

A long narrow wooden box filled with tomato plants ran along the wall to the end on the terrace where a large and enthusiastic, four metre high oleander took over. He thought with some amusement of the perversity of growing tomatoes in a garden in a part of the world where the farms were groaning with tomato plantations. Especially as he wasn't very good at that sort of gardening. The explanation lay in the fact that he enjoyed making green tomato chutney and over the years he hadn't found a local producer who would pick unripe tomatoes for him. It wasn't that they refused. They simply didn't understand why one should do such a thing. Tomatoes were ripe and red, after all. They offered the information that, of course, he already knew; that there were species of tomatoes that were, in fact, naturally green but he failed to make them understand that this was not what he was after. Many of the market stall-holders had said they would pick some for him, but none had actually done so as if being unprepared to commit what they clearly saw as infanticide. Thus if he wanted his chutney he had to grow his own.

The oleander was magnificent in full bloom and was covered in both deep red and pink flowers. This he left alone. Now was not the time to prune it. The other side of the garden was less disciplined as the boundary was provided by a wire fence through which a huge ivy plant had grown. It was this that took much of his attention as it grew massively and threatened to take over completely from the honeysuckle that was also threaded through it. Under the canopy of vine leaves Smith had also planted a climbing jasmine on either side and this too had to be thinned a little. The rest of the garden that ran back to the tall roman wall that separated his garden from that of his neighbour at the back was three metres high and covered with climbing roses. A tall narrow olive tree and a small orange tree covered in fruit completed the garden.

Everything was growing well. It had taken its time to establish. Indeed, his newly planted olive tree, bought as a mere twenty year old in a pot had taken five years before it started to do anything at all after he replanted it in the ground. But he had been told by people who had lived in the row for much longer than he this would be the case. Not too far down from the surface lay some huge Roman cisterns many of which were waterlogged. Once tree roots found that wet layer they would prosper and that had proved to be the case.

After about an hour, Smith had filled two black dustbin bags full of clippings and the day was getting towards its hottest so after a quick shower, he was sitting on his recliner with a cold gin and tonic in his hand and some rather complicated thoughts in his mind. Sitting there where he had sat so many times before, looking out from under the shade at a by now sleeping Arthur at the tranquil small scene he caught himself reminding himself of why he had come here in the first place some twelve years ago and by comparison what had happened since that afternoon three years ago when he had literally stumbled literally over a dead body in the Amphitheatre. Since then his life had been changed completely from the intended solitary tranquillity of a retirement in the Provençale sun.

It wasn't a particularly structured thought process. That wasn't his style. He had never been one for long and detailed analysis either while he had been teaching art history at the University of California at Berkeley nor even when later he had worked from time to time from one of the lesser public government departments that ensured Britain's safety in the world. He was an intuitive sort of man; even impulsive some would say. Usually he saw problems and their solutions came very quickly and very clearly. Even the inevitable wrong decisions that occasionally resulted were put right equally quickly; often violently for Smith. He was a long way from being a tweedy academic with only a profound interest in Roman sarcophagus sculpture; a subject on which he was an acknowledged and published expert. He was a far cry from his friend Gentry who had come to Arles about the same time as he. Gentry was methodical to the point of obsession. It was this that made him the ideal foil for Smith when planning some of the less orthodox and completely undocumented forays into the dark underbelly of international diplomacy. Gentry had lived for most of his life buried in a windowless dusty room in the basement of the Victorian building in south London. He had been Smith's control and friend.

More importantly, Smith sat there again with a vague feeling that things were not quite right. By any standards he was a lucky man. He was still alive and had managed to avoid the customary heart attack and the occasional assassin's bullet without undue difficulty; the former more by luck than judgement. He had met and fallen in love with a ravishingly beautiful and rich local lady considerably younger than himself and had shared a few adventures with her when various bits of his past that he had hoped to be long-buried had pursued him to disturb the tranquillity of his retirement. Much to his surprise and delight she seemed to reciprocate his feelings. As important as anything his beloved greyhound Arthur was still well and fit.

He looked fondly down at the dog at his feet and was amused to see that the old dog was not, in fact, asleep as he had assumed. One eye was slightly open and was watching him steadily. It didn't take Smith long to realise why. Arthur, like his master, was a creature of habit. It was getting past lunchtime and the dog had seen very little sign of it yet. Smith got up and went inside to investigate the fridge. He had already bought a baguette on the way home but little inside took his fancy. There were the usual cheeses and cold meats but little of current interest. Then he spotted something nestling behind a melon. Now he usually had some eggs which, for some unknown reason, he defied convention and stored in the fridge. He didn't do the eggs for breakfast thing too often, but he was partial to the occasional carbonara. This time his attention was taken by a number of things. Firstly, they were in a bowl and not in a grey, expanded cardboard crate. Once he had fished them out, he saw that the eggs were brown, irregular in size and completely unmarked by any inkjet marking denoting batch numbers or places of origin or dated by which people should throw them away in order to add to the supermarket's profits.

Lunch. Within a few moments he had assembled a couple of small cloves of garlic from the bunch hanging outside under the vine, olive oil, salt and pepper, a slice of lemon and some strong English mustard powder made by Coleman's of Norwich in the UK that was a permanent resident of his store cupboard. He crushed the garlic, salt and pepper in a mortar and pestle, added and stirred in the mustard powder and two egg yokes, then the olive oil. He smiled as he remembered that without thinking he was stirring the mixture in a clockwise direction. Years ago, someone had told him that making aioli by mixing in an anticlockwise motion let in the devil. No point in taking chances, he thought.

Smith's version of this traditional sauce was, in reality, not particularly traditional. Original aioli, whose name derives directly from the Provençal Occitan for oil and garlic, was just that; olive oil and garlic. The result was invariably fiery. It was also difficult to make as the two ingredients were difficult to combine. Egg yolk was added as an emulsifier as it had been in traditional mayonnaise. The mustard and lemon were also later additions. Smith's own version also used less garlic than usual in the South of France which is a region that sometimes confuses ability to consume garlic with virility. It was more like a garlic mayonnaise.

By the time he had finished the mixture and taken it and his baguette back into the garden to join a by now completely awake Arthur, he found that he wasn't particularly hungry. So, having eaten a few morsels of dressed bread primarily to reassure himself that he hadn't lost his touch, most of the meal was tossed in Arthur's direction. He was delighted. Sitting perfectly, he caught each aioli-dipped piece of bread that Smith threw his way. Never dropped one.

Smith still couldn't rid himself of the felling that he had a problem. Martine and the life into which he had gradually been sucked, was difficult for him. Perhaps a contemplative dog walk might help. Arles was now at its hottest and many of the tourists who often choked the streets during the summer would either be queuing for a place in one of the very few restaurants that remained open during August, or, having returned to the air-conditioned splendour of their hotel room, sleeping to overcome the effects of yet another dreadful meal. Arles in August was not a place to eat; especially at lunchtime. Spending a great deal of money lessened the chances of disappointment but only slightly. Arthur managed to overcome the loss of his post-prandial nap as a midday walk was an unaccustomed pleasure. So, Smith took his town stick from just inside the front door. He slipped the lead over Arthur's head.

Taking Arthur for a walk might would clear his mind of the storm clouds that were rolling around in it. A momentary feeling of shame came over him as he experienced yet again the pleasure of a very excited dog cavorting about in anticipation of a walk; shame, because this time the dog's pleasure would be found at a very slow pace on the end of a short lead rather than a free casting about over the open Camargue countryside in pursuit of something to kill. It might easily have been just that had he not indulged himself in the selfish wish to escape all that for a day or so. However, the dog's enthusiasm was undimmed even after he had jumped down the four steps in front of Smith's house and found himself in a street rather than a field; something that only deepened Smiths feeling of guilt. In order to somehow make it up to the dog he struck off down the amphitheatre hill towards the river Rhône on one of his longer itineraries. Smith knew full well that it made little or no difference to the dog. He was incapable of making the dog feel remotely tired whatever length of walk was on offer. From time to time Smith's younger daughter visited from London and she was an amateur marathon runner. She took Arthur on fast runs that were measured in miles and he had never seen the dog return remotely out of breath even then. So, having jammed his venerable and somewhat distressed straw hat from Locks of St James on his head, he set out with dog in one hand, his customary sword cane in the other

It was still quite hot although the fierce heat of the day had fallen away to a calm sultriness. The river equally was at its most sluggish; hardly seeming to move at all around the bend on which Arles had been founded. The Romans had discovered it to be the first place they could construct a floating pontoon bridge to cross it, thus opening up one of the last links in their great highway between Rome and Barcelona. Two thousand years later it still remained the first place up from the sea that road and rail could cross. He made his way down to the quay that had finally been completed of many years of desultory work along the full length of the river. Now people could

111

walk along most of the length between the Antique Museum to the west and the river boat dock to the north; a distance of a kilometre or two.

Unfortunately the quay had been discovered by the many tourists who now filled the town and having spent fifteen minutes, avoiding people and children, all of whom seemed to want to stop and make a fuss of the greyhound and avoiding the enormous amount of dog shit that seems to carpet the walk, he got fed up and climbed the steps up to the road level for the bridge that crossed the river into Tranquetaille. He was confident that the tourists, interested only in taking pictures of themselves with their telephones standing in front of something recognisably more important, wouldn't venture across in any great numbers. The famous early twentieth century travel writer Karl Baedecker once described Tranquetaille as not worth crossing the river to visit and some of that feeling remained. It is true that the suburb on the north bank of the river suffered particularly from the American bombing directed inaccurately at the road and rail bridges in the late summer of 1944. However, it still contained a few places that had not been hit and where you could get a sense of the elegance that was once there.

Smith was no great romantic, or so he thought. He didn't believe in the supernatural or in anything mystical or external. He was essentially a pragmatist. Educated in his younger days by a succession of very hard-nosed, left-wing, German, Jewish, refugee academic art historians in the rigours - and rigours is what they were - of always

112

questioning everything, of taking nothing for granted unless you have worked it out for yourself, he had followed that approach to life pretty closely. Before that, five years in a very old fashioned English public boarding school that happened to be in Edinburgh had also taught him self-reliance of a more muscular sort. Classics and Rugby. Both required muscles.

The river was like the rest of the town, sluggish. The flow was so slow that it seemed almost to reverse in the eddy caused by the south bank of the great curve on which the town of Arles had been built where the Rhône changed from its course south to west before falling into the Mediterranean through the Camargue delta. Almost without thought he turned across the small road bridge that link Arles to the south to Tranquetaille.

Immediately he got onto the bridge he found himself surrounded by fewer people and his spirits lifted accordingly. So much so that half way across the bridge he looked down to the permanently moored river boat that housed arguably the worst restaurant in the town. It was with a benign sort of contempt - still contempt, of course, but at least benign.

Pre-ordained or not, however, he realised then that without a conscious decision his steps were taking him towards an elegant town house located slightly back from the river close to the cemetery that had somehow miraculously escaped the attentions of the American Fifth Airforce. The street around it had been rebuilt in the plain and functional concrete with which much of Arles had been reconstructed after the Second World War - his own house amongst it - but the house they approached was rather grand. A solid but ornate front door in dark varnished oak with brightly burnished brass fittings was flanked by tall windows, two on each side. Above were two more stories, each with two windows on each side; windows that became slightly smaller in height as they rose up the stone elevation. In reality it was Arthur who knew first. Being a retired racing greyhound, he was used to walking on a lead and would normally do so perfectly, never allowing the loose curve of the lead between his slip collar and his master's hand to tighten at all. However now he allowed himself a most uncharacteristic light pull on the lead as he realised before Smith where they were going. They were headed for one of his most favourite people.

Like Smith, Arthur gave his loyalty very sparingly. A life on the dog tracks of East London had taught him not to make friends casually. Smith, of course; Martine, obviously; Gentry up to a point. Few others. But the person they were going to call on now was right up there with the best of them. It was with a joyously wagging tail that he waited for the door to open after Smith's gentle knock.

Madam Durand's somewhat wizened ninety-year-old face smiled broadly at the sight of her guests. She waited patiently for Smith to bend down to complete the ritual of placing three kisses on alternately presented cheeks. The hand that was not holding Smith's dropped to the dog's head and his eyes closed momentarily in contentment.

'Come in, please,' she said, 'I've been expecting you.'

Smith released Arthur's collar and he immediately bolted past them both and disappeared. Smith waited for his host to pass into the cool interior of the rather grand house and followed her into her sitting room at a slightly more leisured pace. The dog had already taken station on the dark green upholstered chaise longue that was his customary place. He lay, head raised for the old woman to join him, whereupon he would lay his head in her lap and go to sleep.

'Do the honours, if you would, my dear. You know where everything is.'

Smith nodded and went into the kitchen at the rear of the house. The window that faced south gave onto a huge and perfectly tended garden full of sharp contrasts of light and shade and much colour. The back of the house was kept cool by the shade of a variety of different pine trees. The kitchen was surprisingly modern and, naturally, spotlessly clean. He noticed that a silver tray was already prepared with two cut glass tumblers and a bowl for ice and a small glass jug that matched the glasses. It also carried a half-full bottle of Smith's favourite whisky; the simple blended supermarket brand. The fridge yielded ice and a bottle of Perrier water. He was pleased to see there were none of the usual indigestible nibbles that so often accompany social drinking outside Britain. He filled the ice bowl and the jug filled with Perrier - Madame did not allow plastic bottles in the main rooms - and he returned to find, as he knew he would, Madame seated at the chair end of the chaise with Arthur's head in her lap. The dog had fallen sufficiently asleep in the short time to have started soring very quietly. She was looking down at the elegant head smiling contently.

Smith crossed to a side table in the beautifully furnished drawing room, put down the tray and poured two drinks. His was his usual long with ice and Perrier. Hers was neat on ice in the American fashion. He set hers on a small table to the side and then sat across from her in a high-backed wing chair that was surprisingly comfortable given the usual French predilection of acutely uncomfortable formal furniture. They raise their glasses towards each other and smiled.

"Cheers,' she said.

'Santé, Madam,' was his reply.

She waited for him to start. It was, after all, he who had come unannounced to visit her.

'You were expecting me, Madame?' said a curious Smith.

She nodded.

'Yes, ever since the lunch at the Mas de Saintes I knew you would come to see me. Although I will admit I didn't think that it would be quite this quickly.'

He looked at her. How on earth could this old woman know something that until a few moments ago he had not known himself? He kept silent. She would tell him if she wanted and it proved she did.

' I was watching you at lunch, Peter. Watching you very closely, in fact. You certainly didn't notice because I was probably not one of the ones you were watching - thank goodness. You were on duty, as it were, as was your friend Deveraux. You were doing what the Aubanet family should continue to be grateful for. You were protecting them. There is no reason why you should have noticed me particularly. But I noticed you.'

It was with a slight feeling of brittleness that Smith asked.

'And what, pray, did you observe?'

Hearing the slight tetchiness in his voice she raised her hand in an elegantly defensive little gesture.

'I observed, my dear young man, that you were troubled.'

He frowned slightly, not with any anger, but with a feeling of disappointment that his feelings had been so easily read from the far end of that long table. She continued.

'I observed that you were troubled, and I surmise there were a number of reasons for your unhappiness. You were concerned that around that table there were some who would not greet the news of Martine's succession with great joy, for a number of different reasons that need not concern us here for the moment. Then, you and your friend were looking at the way people reacted to the news and were making mental notes.'

'True Madame. That is precisely what I was doing.'

'But, my dear Peter, there's a different and perhaps more serious reason for your concern.'

It was the inevitability of hearing something that he didn't particularly want to hear that made him break the moment by getting up to replenish their glasses. Arthur opened one eye and followed him with it until he has taken his seat again. She mentally squared herself to say something that might not be well-received no matter how good were her intentions in saying it.

'I think, Peter, that although you remain in love with Martine and she with you, you are troubled because all this transition further strengthens the hold of the whole Aubanet family and their lives here have over you. You're feeling even more trapped than you felt before and you don't like it. You value your independence, but you fear that doing anything about it will hurt Martine. Above all you are troubled because you feel that these very thoughts are in some way disloyal and loyalty, I know, is the only thing you truly believe in. You are honest enough to know that you need help with this dilemma, but you don't feel that you can talk to Martine about it, not yet at least. Your relationship with your old friend Gentry seems to be at a pause; hopefully not for ever, though. In any case I'm not sure how useful a council he would be concerning matters of the heart.'

Smith was feeling pretty solemn at the way all this was going but even he couldn't resist a slight smile at this last observation. She noticed, of course.

'That's better. So, who do you turn to talk about this? Well, me of course, and if I am as wise as I am old then you have come to the right place. I am much complimented too. So of course I was expecting you.'

Not for the first time this old woman had seen very clearly. She was completely right, obviously. He was also pleased that she was there to help him. He looked directly across at her and said in something of a stage voice to rob his description of any offence:

'So, old woman, what do I do, for you're completely right?'

Her first answer was to hold up her glass for a top-up.

'And this time, young man, kindly remember to put some whisky in it. Your last effort wouldn't have deranged a gnat.'

He paused before adding a very small amount more to her glass and an extra ice cube to the ones already in it.

'And what would Martine say if I gave you too much whisky and made you, er, ill?'

She tossed her head back and laughed.

'You mean if you killed me? She would be very unhappy with me and also with you. But she would understand and forgive us both.'

'Yes,' he replied, 'I do believe she would.'

There was a silence in the room as he waited. Affairs of the heart weren't exactly his forte either.

'It is as obvious to me as I'm sure it is to you. You must talk to her. She is a wise woman and all this stupid business about who runs the Camargue won't stop her knowing about your feelings.'

Smith was surprised.

'Stupid, Madame?'

She suddenly became very firm.

'Yes, stupid. Medieval, insensitive, irrelevant, dangerous. It is a dreadful irony that the first time in all those centuries that finally a woman can change the entrenched historical stupidity of generations of this bull-rearing, male-dominated monocracy, the whole system has finally become irrelevant. Yes, stupid is the right word. I have talked many times with Emile about this and told him that he has failed to put this right. Finally, there was a man in charge who had only a daughter and he could have done something, but he has done nothing. He has just passed the buck on to Martine. Much as I love him, and you know that I have always done so, I have a small contemptuous place in my heart for all this.'

She stopped to take a sip of her drink.

'Martine will be the last, thank God. She knows it. The transition will be difficult. It would be easier for her if you were here to help. But she won't ask you. She values your freedom too just at the moment when she has lost hers. That is love for you. When this tour of hers is over you should sit and talk. That is my advice. Sit and talk.'

She was right, of course. And in that instant, he made up his mind without realising it.

'You've given me something to think about, Madame, and I thank you for it. If you know me as well as I think you do, then you will also know that I both understand and agree. Whatever happens I will let neither of you down.'

'Peter, my friend, it never occurred to me to think otherwise. That's the reason you have always been welcome here and always will be.'

He made as if to get up. It was dark outside now and it was probably time to leave. However, she stopped him with a gesture.

'Please stay for a little longer, Peter. There is something else I want to mention to you before you go. Pour yourself another drink. No more for me though.'

He did as he was bidden and before too long was sitting again; this time rather intrigued.

'There is one matter. I'll try to explain but it is something that you will have to take on for I cannot. Firstly, a question. How many people around that table were enemies?'

Smith was slightly taken aback with the directness of the question. However good it was.

'Deveraux and I put question marks against four particular individuals - all men as you say - who seemed less than joyful at what was going on.'

She interrupted him.

'Let me guess. Cordiez, Maneschi, Baroncelli and Brun.'

Smith was astonished. She was completely right.

'How ...?'

'Later, perhaps. You are not the only one who is good at this sort of thing and I have been observing these men for a lot longer that you have. However, I should add to that another piece of information that I am sure you don't know. Neither does Martine.'

Smith waited with some anticipation before she started again.

'Two weeks ago, I was visiting some relations in Le Cailar. We were sitting at dinner all together, my uncle and aunt and their children. They have three boys. I was telling them that on my way to them, my nephew was driving us, we were almost forced off the road by some huge black car that was driving much too fast for our country roads. It came past us at high speed, barely moving out of our way. It was a miracle that we didn't end up in the ditch. I said how very selfish some of these tourists are - especially the ones from Germany. Whereupon the little Georges, my little great nephew piped up.

'Great grandmamma, was it big and black?'

'Yes,' I said. 'It was.'

The boy was quiet to a moment and then he spoke again.

'I know the car. It's been here for a few days.'

'What do you mean?'

'I've seen it before. It is a Mercedes S600. It had tinted dark windows, armour-plated sides and glass and run flat types - you know the ones that will continue to work even if they're punctured.'

'What on earth are you talking about?' his mother interrupted. 'The boy is completely nuts for cars and German cars in particular. I sometime think that he knows the make and specification of every car made since the last war.'

I saw the young man swell slightly with pride.

'Have you ever seen this car here before Emile?'

'No grandmamma. It didn't look like a tourist to me. Normally tourists drive too slow not to fast in Japanese four-wheel drive towing caravans or old Volkswagens with bicycled hanging off them. This was different.'

'And...?' She encouraged the boy who obviously had more to say.

'Well, next day I got together with some of my friends and most of them had seen it around in various places. One or two had seen men getting out. They were well dressed in suits and were visiting some of the farms here.'

At once I sensed something interesting.

'Georges, can you do something for me? Can you talk to your friends again and try to make a list of dates, times and places where you have seen this car? Can you also tell me how you know about this car? You seem to have been quite close to it?'

Georges scoffed.:' We had a very close look at it when it was parked outside old man Baroncelli's place. We saw the AMG badge and the big quadruple exhausts. Also, the window glasses were marked with the word "gepanzert" which means armoured.' 'I was astonished to think that my little grandson could find out what a German word meant. But he was delighted to help me of course and within a day I got a list.'

She handed a piece of paper across to him. Sure enough it contained a list of ten places over three days where the car had been sighted. Most importantly of all it contained a registration number. Smith looked across at her. She nodded. All four of the names she had identified from the Aubanet lunch party were on the list. He didn't think about it for long. In these situations, he seldom had to. He pulled his telephone from his pocked and having asked permission of his hostess with a slight raising of the eyebrows, he hit 2 on his speed dial list. A very surprised Gentry answered but was forestalled from a further inquisition by his caller.

'Gentry? Smith. I need urgently the owner of a black Mercedes S600, registration HY 675 HT.'

To give him credit Gentry didn't hesitate. He just rang off. There would be time for a more traditional conversation if necessary later. If Smith wanted something urgently enough to call him now, then it really was urgent. They sat in silence until the telephone rang again after no more than a minute or two.

'Sebastien Moroni. Resident of Toulouse.'

'Can you find out more about him?'

'Of course. I know a little about him already.'

'And?'

'Let's just say he is the Toulouse equivalent of your friend Girondou.'

'Ah. Thank you, Gentry. I'll call you.'

'Good. Not before time.'

Smith ignored the sarcasm. Smith rang off and immediately hit the third speed dial button on his phone. Girondou, as usual, answered before the second ring. Smith often wondered how he did that.

'Peter. Nice to hear from you. Have you ...'

'Later, Alexei, please.' Smith cut him off. 'Have you heard that some guy called Moroni from Toulouse seems to be touring the Camargue, talking to farmers who don't like the Aubanets?'

There was a long silence before the man from Marseille spoke again and this time the voice was very, very different. If the sandpaper on the bottom of a parrot's cage could speak, the Smith was in conversation with it.

'You sure?'

'Yes.'

'Then we need to talk. Soon.'

'I thought you might think that, Alexei. Tonight I have plans but perhaps tomorrow?'

'Yes. Lunch? My place?'

'I'll be there at one.'

Again, the call ended without any of the usual pleasantries.

Smith made a final call, this time to speed dial 1. Martine answered. He cut her a little short.

'My dear. I miss you. Can we eat together tonight? Perhaps at your cousin's place.'

To give her credit, there was no hesitation.

'Of course, but only if I can sleep with you afterwards.'

He chuckled. It was a condition that was easily met.

'The restaurant at 9? Oh, don't drive yourself.'

'Of course,' she replied. 'Bring Arthur.

He closed his phone.

Madame Durand sat with a satisfied look on her face.

'That's better, young man. You're a lot more interesting when you're not being all introspective and soppy. I prefer the man of action. I know that Martine does too.'

He looked across the room at this frail little old woman with his dog still firmly asleep on her lap - or at least pretending to be.

'You're a devious, scheming old bat.'

She grinned broadly.

'I know.'

'And, I love you for it,' he said.

'I know that too,' she replied. 'Now leave me and go talk with her.'

This time they got up for real. Arthur was, of course, reluctant but followed them to the front door. As they went out of that elegant front door, he turned to kiss her. This time most familiarly only once on one cheek. She smiled broadly with pleasure. He half turned.

'Emile and Martine are lucky to have you looking after them, Madame.'

She nodded in agreement.

'There are more ways to be a good wife and mother, Monsieur, than just by being married.

So it was that, having got home, he watered Arthur only for he would be well fed later. He showered, changed into something respectable and found himself walking into the little café in the Roquette, the old fishing and ship repair quarter of Arles. It was there that Martine's cousin had his restaurant. Like many of the smaller Aubanet enterprises it was not run on entirely predictable lines. It was, without doubt one of the best restaurants in the town; the best as long you don't like your food looking like Christmas decorations and courses accompanied by long lectures from pre-pubescent waiters with skin conditions. Martine's cousin was a cook without compare and living evidence that you needed no formal training nor to be festooned with Michelin stars to cook well. The restaurant was hidden away in the maze of tiny streets and alleys that threaded themselves through the quarter. It took no bookings, accepted no credit or debit cards. Many of the people it fed were locals with no money and, as a consequence, were charged nothing. Visitors were sometimes turned away from an almost empty restaurant without explanation; usually to their outrage and the utterance of promises of inevitable doom at the hand of TripAdvisor. It often closed its doors when only half full. Occasionally it didn't open until past eleven. Sometimes not at all. There was a sort of culinary Darwinism at work. The people who wanted to feed and felt welcome knew when it was open and that was enough.

Smith went into the little restaurant and again let Arthur off the lead immediately. The dog was a more welcome guest than many of the humans that entered the place and he disappeared like lightening into the kitchen where he knew many delights awaited him. He wouldn't emerge until they left and then so full of food that he could hardly walk home.

As always Martine was there before him and walked down the narrow room to greet him. She looked completely devastating. A white silk blouse unbuttoned to some distance below her breasts. On closer inspection, for that is what it merited, it wasn't unbuttoned in the conventional sense. There were no buttons. A short, tight black skirt cut enticingly above the knee. Dark but not opaque stockings or tights - Smith hardly dared guess which. Black Louboutin court shoes of a positively vertiginous height. As usual her only jewellery was a small silver Croix de Camargue on a chain. This time it hung well down into her cleavage. Clearly whatever effect was intended it worked. Smith could only guess and enjoy the result. She smiled and said with characteristic directness.

'I thought I would remind you what you would be missing if you upped and left me.'

He held her very close.

'Little chance of that my love. Little chance.'

She held him equally tightly.

'Good, because I love you more than I can say.'

The high romance of the moment was somewhat spoiled by the fact that Smith, looking over her shoulder, could see Martine's cousin, his wife and numerous kitchen staff and assorted other family squashed together in the kitchen door grinning at them.

Tonight, was a bouillabaisse and it was inevitably one of the better he had tasted; fishy and meaty at the same time; mercifully free of miscellaneous bits of unidentifiable of fish, empty but pretty shells, molluscs boiled into a state of not-so-fine leather, floating green stuff, croutons and other bits of rubbish that tourists habitually demanded in their expansive versions of a majestically simple dish. Nothing floated around aimlessly on the rich brown surface from which rose an aroma unlike anything else. The greatest soup on earth was served simply with slices of baguette and small bowl of rouille.

As is the correct way, the cooked fish was placed separately on a small side plate; just a few pieces of Rascasse rouge and Grondin. These were enough to remind the eater where the broth had come from but not enough to divert him while eating it. Smith marvelled at the balance of it all. As with much Provençale cooking it is all too easy to get things wrong with too much of things that should be used in intelligent moderation. The garlic, so often abused in some Provençale sources was there in the rouille as it should be but just sufficiently to taste. The same could be said for the saffron; real in this case unlike in most restaurants that ring the Vieux Port in Marseille. The fish had been gently cooked through but not too much and Smith could still taste the difference between the two species.

As usual while they were eating, they hardly spoke. Both disliked making conversation when there were more important things to be done. But once they had finished, Smith brought her completely up to date. She listened calmly and by the end of his story he had become a little concerned. She remained completely calm; serene indeed.

'You really ought to look a little more concerned, my dear. These are serious matters.'

She nodded with a mischievous twinkle in her eye.

'Of course, as is the bouillabaisse. But in both cases I know the right man for the job. However, for tonight, I want to enjoy this evening with you. I spent a considerable amount of time making myself look as sexy as possible and I refuse to let all that effort go to waste on talk of gangsters, criminals or anything else. There will be time to discuss all this other stuff later. What I wanted to say to you, Peter Smith,' and she reached across the table and took both his hands into his, 'is that I love you completely and without reservation. I would do anything for you and, indeed, anything with you. It is important that you know and believe that.'

If he imagined a muffled round of applause for the kitchen, then it was probably just that; an imagining. So, they let their meal settle while she bought him up to date with her day's travels and the itinerary for tomorrow. He noted that amongst places she and her father were to call at the Cordiez farm, but he decided not to break their agreement. In any case she now knew what was possibly going on and needed no advice from him to keep vigilant. In any case Jean Marie would have been with them and Deveraux would be around somewhere in the background. He thought that perhaps he might brief his friend then immediately thought better of it. Deveraux knew something was wrong when he saw it and having an unbiased view from him would be useful.

It was near midnight when they finished their conversation. They took no pudding or coffee, just a glass or two more of the rich red wine from the family vineyards on the banks of the Rhône. They said goodbye to their host, collected a reluctant and extremely replete dog from the kitchen where he had obviously fallen asleep and headed for the door. Directly outside was the Aubanet Range Rover with its rear door being held open by a smiling Jean Marie. The competition to be the first to hold the door for Madame was an old one between the young man and Smith. As proper gentlemen they both slightly averted their eyes as Martine's very tight skirt made a completely elegant entry into the high vehicle somewhat difficult. Smith was pleased that the car was there for even the short journey back to his house. Trying to make Martine take security seriously was an uphill struggle and he remarked on that while Jean Marie open the rear hatch for a very sluggish Arthur to hop up with slightly less than his usual grace. She replied with some asperity:

'Security be damned. It's these bloody heels.'

The car dropped them off at the house and disappeared into the night. It would return in the morning. Without much discussion they headed up to his little first floor bedroom and got quickly ready for bed. Smith used the bathroom first as he took less time and by the time he was in bed, Arthur had climbed up onto his customary place on the small sofa in the corner of the room. A little later he was joined by Martine and they just lay quietly, naked in each other's arms. They both knew that Smith's reservations about the future were fading fast and didn't need any more talking about. So, there was just a mutual contentment as they drifted off towards sleep, bodies intertwined, his arm around her with her head resting on his shoulder.

Or so he thought as he felt a gentle but sharp prod in his foot. Clearly his love was not completely without clothes and Monsieur Louboutin had joined them in bed. Inevitably it was another hour or so before he was allowed to sleep.

Chapter 9: The First Rescue

As he drove steadily along the road from Fos sur Mer and Martigues towards Sausset-les-Pins and Girondou's house, Smith thought that the south of France was no different to almost anywhere else in that more and more CCTV cameras were appearing along the autoroutes ostensibly to monitor the traffic and make the roads safer but actually to catch speeding motorists and raise money. Their installation in French towns tended to lag behind other countries, especially in the UK but the roads were catching up fast. Most of the new cameras along the AutoRoute were linked to number plate recognition systems and he was amused to see number plates of transgressors flashed up periodically on the overhead gantries to warn the offending motorists. His rather clapped out old Peugeot could hardly trouble the authorities even if it wished. However, he noted the cameras as he reached somewhat perilously across to the glove compartment and pulled out his phone.

'Hi Deveraux. All OK?'

It was a stupid way to start a conversation. Both of them knew it. Deveraux would have told him if there was anything odd going on. Smith sighed:

'Sorry, Dev. Something seems to be happening that you should know about. How is the royal progress going?'

'As, you say, nothing to report.'

'What do you think of their protection?'

'Looks fine to me, gov. Jean Marie is pretty good these days, thanks to our coaching and the other man doing the driving looks reliable. He can certainly drive a car well. Rather un-French in that regard.'

Smith smiled to himself before continuing.

'Have you seen a big black Mercedes from Toulouse while you've been travelling around: AMG, armoured, run flats, all the grown-up bits?'

As usual, Deveraux was concise.

'Yes, four times in two days. Thought it was rather odd.'

'Do you think that Jean Marie can cope with the rest of this tour? I think tomorrow is supposed to be the last day of this royal tour.'

'Certainly.'

'Then please could you transfer your attention onto the Merc as soon as you can pick it up. Inside should be a big cheese from Toulouse, probably a number two, a driver and a guard. I want to know where they go. I'm particularly interested if they cross the river and visit anyone between there and this side of the Étang de Berre.'

'OK.'

Few drivers of cars and lorries would be observant enough to notice that these cameras were still there after they turned off the main road onto the D5 for the final few kilometres of his trip. In fact, there seemed to be more of them rather than fewer. So it was that with admirable restraint that he refrained at waving to the cameras as he passed. The feeds from most of these cameras went into Girondou's private system and unwelcome visitors were identified and dealt with long before they reached the rather imposing gates that gave onto the long drive that wound down the hill towards Girondou's house overlooking the sea.

He always enjoyed this trip from Arles to Marseille. It went from the fertile plain of the Crau and turned south through the eastern edge of the Camargue before entering the very different industrial world of the oil refineries and shipping that took up most of the land that surrounded the north side of the Étang de Berre down to and including the sprawling expanse of Marseille proper. All this was Girondou's power base; the centre of an area of influence that extended across the entire length of the south coast to the Italian boarder and north to Lyon east of the Rhône. It illustrated the contrasts that made this part of the world so seductive to him. He loved the fact that within an hour of his house he could be in the depth of the Camargue, the great stretches of beaches along the Mediterranean, the mountains of the Alpilles and into the foothills of the Luberon.

Martine had left to resume her grand tour early enough for Smith to pay a call at the shop of Madame Leblanc, the fabled Arlesian chocolatier to buy a box of her eye-wateringly expensive chocolates that formed his usual present to Girondou's wife and two daughters. It amused him to buy something fattening that clearly made no difference to the three exceptionally attractive and slim women. After a little over an hour's driving he turned into the open gates past

135

the little rustic-looking gatehouse where its usual occupant, an old man in a open necked Provençale shirt and battered straw hat, raised a hand in greeting. He felt, rather than saw, the two lowered steel bollards set into the ground and could be raised in a fraction of a second and would stop a truck at speed.

He smiled at the man as he slowed and waved back. Smith was relieved to see that the cheery old gatekeeper had raised his left hand and he tried to forget that his right was out of sight, poised just above a button that would fire a pair of belt fed, L1A1 heavy machine guns located in oleander bushes fifty metres down the drive and aimed to converge at the very spot over which he was driving. The combined impact of 20 C44 12.7 mm rounds per second hitting anything would be more than effecting stopping anything that might escape the bollards. That rate of fire equated to slightly more than 1 kilogramme of armour piercing steel travelling at almost three thousand kilometres per hour each second.

The man that stepped out from the shade of the rambling villa to meet him was not the usual relaxed, beautifully dressed, urbane Alexei Girondou with whom a number of adventures had brought him close. The greeting was a quick handshake followed by Smith's immediate question.

'Angèle and the girls?'

'With Angèle's parents in Grasse - and before you ask, Henk and some others are with them.'

Henk van der Togt was an ex-special protection group soldier from Holland who had been made head of Girondou's security detail. Whatever Girondou wanted to talk about it Smith assumed it would serious. They sat together under the vine that covered the veranda in front of a spectacular view of the great curve of the Mediterranean that had so entranced Cezanne a hundred or so years before. On this occasion neither of them was particularly looking at the view. A cold lunch, very modest in comparison with previous meals with the Girondou family consisting of a variety of meats and cheeses, fruit and other constituents of a picnic. It was unfortunate that although the two ate sporadically they paid as much attention to the food as they did to the view.

Girondou was obviously worried about something and that feeling crept across the table to Smith. He had seen the gangster nervous before. A couple of years before his wife had been briefly kidnapped as part of a previous attempt to unseat him. The problem had short-lived thanks to Smith's intervention that left the kidnappers more damaged that many could credit. Smith was very fond of Angèle. This time in spite of being immaculately dressed as usual - pressed slacks, crisp open-necked shirt, pale cashmere sweater loosely knotted by the arms around the neck, Gucci loafers complete with the obligatory tassels - Girondou looked uncomfortable. He looked drawn and sleep-deprived and Smith could see that he had cut himself shaving; twice. It didn't take a genius to work out that whatever all this was, it had been troubling Girondou for some time. The man was preoccupied to the extent that conversation was difficult. Smith decided to move things along.

'Let me take a wild guess, Alexei; a guess at why you are sitting there with a face as long as the Rove Tunnel. This Moroni character is roughly your equivalent in Toulouse. He's trying a takeover; not too amicably I would guess judging by your newly-discovered inability to shave safely. He has also found that your recently acquired *entente cordiale* with the Camargue farmers has resulted in you coming uncomfortably close to his territory. Presumably before it was a combination of the farmers who disliked you Marseillians and the River Rhône had kept you two apart. You have known about this for some time, hence the absence of your immediate family, sent off presumably in your opinion for their own safety. However recently the change at the top, as it were, that sees Martine replace her father has caused some ruffled feathers among some if the more traditionally-minded farming families and now Moroni is looking for some allies. I gather he is currently doing a bit of a tour drumming up some local support, presumably by promising to restore the status quo or money or both.'

Girondou looked uncomfortable and angry. Smith got slightly angry as well. The man was a friend and Smith didn't expect this sort of treatment from his friends. He decided to go in hard which was a dangerous tactic given who was his lunchtime host.

'What is odd, Alexei, is that normally you would take this in your stride. Hostile takeovers, as they are known in the world of

138

business, must be a regular occurrence for you. You would normally swat this Moroni away like an annoying mosquito and with about as much effort. But there you sit, looking like something the cat dragged in in spite of your usually polished exterior. You're worried more than you're prepared to acknowledge, and you're not prepared to talk about it. Yet you've invited me to lunch on the strength of a single name mentioned in a telephone conversation. And that in particular worries me.'

Girondou stirred at last.

'Why should you be worried about a lunch invitation from me, Peter? There've been many such previously.'

'The lunch is dreadful.'

At last a glacial smile crossed Girondou's face.

'Sorry about that. The cook's ill.'

There was no point is going further with this. It was pretty obviously bollocks. In any case, Smith was beginning to get a bit bored with the mystery.

'OK. Enough of this,' his anger rising as he continued. 'You either tell me what you want or I'm going home. There are a number of things that would be more enjoyable than having lunch with you today, Alexei, including tidying my sock drawer, as they say. If you want my help, then I suggest the first thing you do is to get your family back from whatever Alp you've sent them to hide from all this as quickly as possible. This is the most secure place for them not exposed in the middle of the Sound of Music countryside surrounded by cows wearing bells. I can sure as hell protect them even if you think you can't. You'll recall I've done it before. Then you are going to get some better bodyguards than the idiots that I can spot lurking in your shrubbery. You also need to start being straight with me. I surely won't give up on Angèle and the children, but I might on you.'

There was a very long gap as Girondou got increasingly uncomfortable under Smith's unwavering gaze. Finally, he looked across at his friend.

'Peter. I need your help. More importantly, my family needs your help. I have a slight feeling that I'm going to get it whether I want it or not. But you must understand that, for the moment at least, I can't tell you everything.'

Now it was Smith's turn to think quickly as he decided what to do with Girondou's silence while doing what he had to protect Angèle and the girls who he regarded as an extended family. He felt somewhat in loco parentis while Girondou was somewhat out of commission. He made up his mind and started to make some fast plans to get them back under his protection. Girondou seemed completely useless at the moment. The first question was easy.

'Give me their location; address and GPS coordinates.'

Girondou hesitated and then consulted his phone, wrote a note and passed it over to Smith.

'Christ, Alexei. You put that on your phone? Jesus. OK. How do you talk to them?''

'Er, I just call them.'

'Ordinary mobile or satellite?'

'Ordinary.'

'Do you mean they've got their phones switched on?'

'Yes.'

'They're not even using sat phones.'

'Er, no I don't think so. Henk said it wasn't necessary, I think.'

'Fuck, Alexei. What the hell's happened to you? Whatever is behind all this shit had better be good. Good enough to make you forget almost everything I've taught you.'

Girondou just seemed to sag in his chair; shrink a little and just said nothing.

Smith pulled out his phone and called Gentry.

'Gentry, I need a long-range helicopter to pick up Girondou's family from the Alps somewhere and bring them back here. As soon as possible.'

'That's about a five hundred mile round trip, old chap. You'll need a big bird if you want it done fast. A Cheyenne.'

'And...?'

'It just so happens..'

'Just set it up Gentry, please. Girondou will pay. Change to your satellite phone and I'll text you the details. Quickly please.'

'Only the three. Anyone else?'

'They can walk home, for all I care. And that includes van der Togt. What the hell he was doing allowing them to keep their phones on, I don't know.'

Suddenly a thought came to him.

'No, on second thoughts. Bring Van der Togt back as well. I want a little chat with him. You'd better send a couple of good people along as well, David. The fact is that given his prime responsibility is to guard Girondou in the first place, I want to know what the fuck he is doing up there in the mountains anyway.'

The next call was to Deveraux.

'Dev. Drop Moroni for the moment. Get over here to Girondou's house and bring some equipment, if you would. We'll also need some people. About six, I would think. Good people. Secure sat phones as well. We need to police Girondou's house for a while.'

Next Martine.

'Peter, darling. How nice.'

He couldn't help smiling.

'Martine, my dear. Girondou's in trouble. I need you and your father to get back to the Mas immediately. Stay there and I will telephone later. I'll brief Jean Marie. Something's going on and I don't think your safe gallivanting around the countryside until I know better what is going on. The rest of your tour of inspection will have to wait a day or to until we've sorted things out a bit.'

He finally returned his attention to Girondou who remained virtually lifeless.

'So where are they, Alexei? Really.'

'I sent them away, Peter. For their own safety.'

They both knew that this wasn't the answer to the question that had been asked. So, Smith just sat impassive and waited. He was interested to note that there was a palpable gap before Girondou actually answered. The man was obviously reluctant to share something. Smith filed it away for future thought.

'They're in the Alps.'

'I know that, you idiot.'

'At my house in the Alps.'

'Who exactly is with them?"

Henk, of course and two others. You don't know them. They're Henk's people.'

'Staff?'

'A house keeper and a gardener. Both have been with us for years.'

Smith knew that this wasn't the time to point out that in his view long service was no guarantor of loyalty. More likely the contrary. Girondou seemed to be remarkably uncertain and he felt that some unusually carefully handling was required. He tried to adopt a conciliatory tone although he actually wanted the strangle the man.

'Alexei. You obviously think that they're at risk and you've sent them to safety. I won't ask about security arrangement there. I'm pleased, at least, that Henk's with them. But really, Alexei, don't you think that your family is better protected here than six hundred kilometres away in a foreign country?'

Girondou nodded miserably.

'Yes, I suppose you're right, Peter. As usual. Perhaps I wasn't thinking clearly.'

The urge to strangle the man grew and it took a considerable effort for Smith not to lose his temper. Instead his tone became even more gentle - dangerously so for anyone who knew him well.

"Alexei, I suggest we get them back here as quickly as possible. Whatever you are trying to protect they from we can do it better from here.'

Girondou just raised a hand limply and dropped it lifelessly back onto the arm of his chair.

'If you think that is best, Peter.'

Smith found himself on the point of vomiting.

'Is Angèle on her usual phone?'

Girondou nodded. Smith pulled out his mobile and called her.

'Angèle? Peter.'

'Hi Peter. How are you?'

'Concerned, Angèle. I'm here at home with Alexei. I really think it would be better if you came home as quickly as possible. I haven't got to the bottom of what is going on but I'm sure that back here in Sausset is safer for you and the girls than on top of an Alp far away from anywhere.'

'Really, Peter. We are quite safe. Henk is with us and we're enjoying ourselves.'

There had been a time or two in the past when doing exactly what Smith said and when he said it had been the difference between life and death for her. He reminded her of that. After, she raised no objection.

'All right, Peter, what do you want us to do?'

"Get yourselves packed and ready to leave. A helicopter will come within a couple of hours and pick you and the girls. Henk as well. It will be a long-range machine and probably military, so it will be fast, noisy and unheated. Make sure you are all wearing your Alpine kit, have some spare cushions and, if possible, ear plugs or iPod with earphones. OK?'

'Yes, of course.'

"OK. Now I'll call Henk and tell him.'

Fortunately, she was quick to reply as he was on the point of ringing off and calling the Dutch bodyguard.

'Peter. Thank you."

'Don't be ...'

'No. Thank you for being there. There is something wrong and Alexei doesn't seem to be able to deal with it. He needs someone and I'm pretty sure that's you.'

'That's what friends are for, Angèle' he replied and rang off. Actually, he wasn't sure.

Henk was next. He and Gentry had been responsible for recruiting the young Dutchman from the Dutch Close Protection Group to head Girondou's security staff some time ago. After some fairly muscular training, both physical and mental, the man had become more than competent at his job. He has also become quite close to one of the Girondou daughters or so Smith had heard to his distinct disapproval.

'Henk? Smith.'

There was a silence on the line. Smith smiled slightly. At least the man had learned something.

'In about ninety minutes a helo will come and collect Madame Girondou, her two daughters and you and bring you back to Sausset-les-Pins. It will probably be a fast military machine without too many mod cons so please make sure that everyone is comfortable and properly equipped for the trip. When you arrive here, I want a full debrief. Understood?'

The man sounded more reluctant than surprised; slightly grumpy, even.

'Perhaps, Monsieur Smith, I should talk with Monsieur Girondou. I work for him, after all.'

'Don't piss me off. Henk. You really don't want to do that. You know exactly who you work for even if Monsieur Girondou doesn't.

146

Just get the family back here safely. That's your responsibility and I'm the one who will hold you to it. I will meet you and if you don't get them back here unharmed and unworried, you better not come yourself. Stay with the helo when you land. I'll meet you.'

Arrangements in place, he turned to his host who had remained seemingly motionless at the table.

'They'll be back in about four hours, Alexei. I think I'll just do a bit of a tour and check things over here.'

Looking at the man sitting miserably in his chair he wasn't tempted to offer any sympathy as he left.

'If I were you, I would lay off the booze, Alexei. You family will be back soon and I doubt whether Angèle would want her children met by a drunk father.'

Without waiting for a reply, he got up and started out for a long walk around the estate. In truth he just wanted to get away for a while. The morose and uncommunicative gangster was not the best company. He also had the feeling that Girondou wasn't being entirely straight with him and that pissed him off more than anything else.

Girondou's little piece of heaven occupied much of the hillside immediately to the east of the little village of Sausset-les-Pins. The view towards L'Estaque was spectacular. It was pretty close to the one famously painted by Cézanne. As he wandered the many tracks the criss-crossed the hillside, he easily located the people who were following him. He had been at that sort of thing much longer than they had. As an estate it was as near as possible impregnable. Anyone coming in by road would be spotted very early. Apart from the one landing pad below the house, there was nowhere else to land an aircraft. The house was roughly in the centre so an incursion on foot was equally difficult. He sat on a rock, surrounded by the usual assortment of bushes, indigenous to the region. It was a hot, south-facing slope so while the area nearer the house was watered so that large oleander and rose bushes flourished, out here further into the naturally arid dryness untended wild olive trees and Kermes oaks shared the spaces with smaller clumps of juniper, holm oaks. Nature had filled in the spaces with rosemary and thyme, cistus roses and Senecio daises; artemesia too. It was as typical a chunk of Provence as it would be possible to imagine.

He tried to assemble some thoughts although in reality there were precious few to assemble. So far, he had heard that Girondou was under some pressure from an attempted coup from his westerly rival who seemed to be making a play via some discontented Camargue farmers. Girondou was obviously concerned, worried even, far, far beyond what one might have expected. He had sent his family away in a hurry without thinking properly about what he was doing. That was about all of it. Not much to go one. Another stray thought drifted in. It took him a little time to put his finger on it but what was slightly troubling him was that he was feeling slightly troubled. He just stared out across the bay and waited for some sort of clarity. Actually, he was kidding himself. He never needed to think about very much about anything. What was wrong was that his life seemed to be slipping away. He didn't think he was dying. He knew all too well what that felt like. No, it was just that things were happening in his life and they seemed to be increasingly nothing to do with him. Or maybe what was when he just wanted; or thought he did.

He had retired to Arles some years ago to do just that; retire. To spend his time walking his dog, cooking in a ham-fisted but talented way, reading what he wanted and writing scholastic articles that would never now be published. The odd book, too. Perhaps the internet had made that sort of thing so much easier. He remembered with a small sniff of nostalgia the days when to consult a library you had to visit it. If you wanted to look up their holdings of a particular book or periodical in their catalogue you had to stand in front of it and thumb through the pages yourself. He remembered fondly that great multi-volume catalogue of the then British Museum Library what was alphabetical only insofar as gaps had been left on the huge pages for new entries to be stuck in with little bits of paper and white glue applied with a short, glue encrusted brush. The effort in time and money made the actually discovery of the book all the more precious when it happened. Or maybe it just did now looking back. It had taken more than two years to put together the starting bibliography for his doctoral research. It had taken visits to at least half a dozen countries. Actually visiting the library in question was the only way to find the book. The internet has made such visits almost redundant. Now the experience of visiting those great reading rooms of legend, of breathing the air of those utterly magnificent spaces is ignored by almost all but the old and the sentimental like him. Now they are just lens fodder for the cold and castrated view of the camera of Candida Hofer. Experience the book without having to read it. That is the way of things, these days.

He knew he was meandering along some old paths and was enjoying it. But his earlier mood returned all too quickly. Now other things took his time but, being honest with himself, it was time that no-one but he had decided to invest. Martine, Girondou, the Camargue were all part of his life now and that was by his choice. There was no point in fretting about it. It was what it was. Perhaps it was rather selfish to do so. Only Gentry and Deveraux remained from the old days. He realized somewhat guiltily that he had begun to forget that. Older loyalties should be much harder to forget.

His backside had at last become used to the rock and the discomfort had stopped. He called Gentry. He knew that he would be monitoring the flight.

'They'll be with you in about three quarters of an hour.'

Smith was surprised at how long he had been sitting there lost in thought.

'Thanks, Gentry.'

There was a gap before a decision was made with surprising ease.

'Business as usual, I think, Peter. Business as usual,'

It was surprising how much relief could be packed into the two little words: 'very well.'

'It's an EC 725 Super Cougar.'

'Christ, Gentry. I thought they were all still in service with the French Air Force.'

'They are,' came the rather dry response.

'Send the bill to Girondou.'

'Oh, I will. Don't worry. Oh, one other thing.'

'Yes?'

'They're supposed to be on some sort of training sortie and that doesn't usually include dropping off the radar for a quick landing. They'll come in fast and low and won't stay long.'

'Very well, Gentry. And thanks. Oh, by the way, could you go around and feed Arthur? I didn't think I would be away this long.'

Gentry rang off, Smith made to get up. He had in mind to tell Girondou. But then he relaxed. Why bother, the thought. He would know soon enough. He gestured to the man who has spent the last hour behind a bush some fifty metres away. By the time he had arrived he had almost got over his embarrassment at being spotted.

'How many of you are there in the grounds?'

'Six, monsieur.'

'Get three of them and bring them to the helicopter landing pad as quickly as possible. Leave the others doing whatever they're doing.'

It was less than five minutes before they were assembled. The landing pad was actually quite small; a circular piece of level concrete with a white cross painted in the centre. He was reassured that the ground around, whilst not actually cleared, lacked the sort of larger bushes that could conceal a short-range ambush or sniper.

'In a few minutes, Madame Girondou, her daughters and Henk van der Togt will arrive on a military-looking helicopter. They'll come in quickly and they won't stay long. You are to escort Madame Girondou and her daughters directly to the house and stay around the house until you see me. Mr. van der Togt will stay with me for a time and then we will join you.'

He turned back to the first man.

'Contact the gateman and tell them to shut the gates and raise the barrier. It's to stay that way until I say so.'

Just over half an hour later he heard the dull throb of the approaching rotors as well as a shriller whine of the twin turboshaft engines. Sure enough it came in fast, swooping over the house down the hill from the north literally brushing the treetops as they came. Just before the pad it reared up and stalled to a hover and immediately seemed to fall from the sky. It hit the ground with an undignified thump. The door was flung open and the four passengers almost fell out of the aircraft as if pushed. A few bags were unceremoniously flung out after them. A moment later the door was slammed shut and the machine sprinted back into the air and vanished on down the hill making a fast curving turn to the west. The helo had been on the ground for less than ten seconds.

Smith was first to the group and put his arms around the three women and waited until the air had stilled after the helicopter departure. As soon as he could he spoke.

'Angèle, please take the girls and up to the house with these four men. Find Alexei and go inside. I'll come up for a chat in a few moments.'

He was immediately struck by the fact their greeting was a good deal less affectionate than usual. Solange, in particular, had to be held in their usual communal hug by her mother.

'Sod it,' he thought to himself. 'It might just be the trip. A military helicopter is not best known for its comforts.'

Turning to the tall Dutchman he said: "Just stay here for a moment, would you, Henk?"

He made sure that the family had started up the hill towards the house before continuing.

'Henk, Monsieur Girondou and I thought that for the moment it would be better to have the family together here. For the foreseeable future, could you set up a strong perimeter. I'd like to ensure that the family is secure for the moment. No trips out and strict security around any visitors.'

The Dutchman seems to bristle a little as if he didn't like being told what to do. From the very beginning when Henk had first been recruited by Smith and Gentry to help reinforce Girondou's security it had been clear who was calling the shots and it was interesting for Smith to note how things had seemed to change a little. Normally he would not have been too concerned. Girondou was usually more than capable of organizing his own security. But currently things were not normal, and someone needed to be looking over the man's shoulder. Henk's seeming reluctance get too involved with Smith could just be excess loyalty to his boss. He had not been once of Smith's people in the first place. But given Girondou's current fragility he was more than usually vulnerable and therefore Smith decided to take more than usual interest.

'Mr. Girondou has a few things on his mind at the moment, Henk, and I will be taking a few things on for him. So please do what I ask.'

Ignoring the dark look, he went on and pushed the point home.

'I have already informed the men.'

He waited until the bodyguard had turned somewhat gracelessly and started to make his way until the hill before talking out his phone to call Gentry. He gave his friend a quick but complete resume. Gentry's reply was succinct.

'So, if I had to guess you want a good hard look at Girondou to see if anything more is going on in his recently troubled life. You also want me to take another vetting on Henk van der Togt and line up a replacement should one become necessary. You want me to bring Deveraux up to date as you will be too busy and continue to fiddle about in this slightly odd business about the Camargue manoeuvrings of our friend Sebastien Moroni.'

Smith couldn't help but smile. Gentry was, as usual, dead right. He waited until his friend rang off and then imagined him climbing the narrow stairs to the rooftop glass box that comprised his office to set to work. He climbed back up the hill and arrived back in the house to find the family together and was pleased to see that Girondou had tidied himself up considerably and had finished what looked to be a substantial cup of coffee. The three women looked surprisingly unruffled considering their recent flight but all three looked up at him expectantly. Actually, they all looked to be in a bloody bad mood. To be honest he really didn't know what to say to them apart from the obvious but perhaps that would have to do in the circumstances. He started with bending the truth a little.

'We thought that it would probably be a good idea if we kept you at home for a bit. There are a few bits and pieces that we need to clear up and we need to be sure that you are safe and sound.'

Chapter 10: A Night-time Perambulation

It was Smith's favourite time for dog walking. For much of the summer daytime it was too hot or the streets were too crowded. Many tourists bought their dogs with them as well and most didn't seem to bother with leads. They also didn't bother much with collecting their dogs' messes as they walked either. Tonight, Smith couldn't sleep. It was very hot, even at 1am and rather than just lie there he decided to go for a walk. During the winter this was not an unusual time for him and Arthur to go for a wander around the town. The winter was easier; fewer people and fewer dogs. So, he got out of bed, threw on a pair of old cotton trousers and a shirt and collected a surprised but delighted Arthur from his slumber on the sofa at the foot of his bed. Arthur was always up for a walk irrespective of the time. This time the quarry would most likely be cats rather than Camargue rabbits, but it was all the same to him. Smith also paused by the front door to collect a walking stick. It was rather an elegant short stick with a shaft in carbon fibre and a Tamboti knob made by Burger in South Africa. Apart from its design, Smith valued the 18 inch bade that was fitted into it. Going for a walk around the town without a jacket with a Glock stuffed into the back of your chinos was not a particularly subtle thing to do. The stick also helped to keep over-interested dogs at bay.

He decided to walk down past the Arena and to the Cavaliere gate. Most of the quarter inside the Roman city wall was occupied by Arab families and, ironically, that made it less hazardous walking at that time of night than other parts of the town. The families that lived here were very tight knit and fathers and grandfathers exercised more that the common amount of discipline. Further out to the north of the Place Lamartine and heading on up the road to Avignon, the area was a little wilder. Here low-rise buildings were interspersed with large mass-occupation concrete blocks of apartments festooned with washing and satellite dishes. But these quarters of Griffeuil and Stalingrad were still also predominantly Arab.

Rather than go for a long route he decided just to wander around the place Voltaire a the many little streets that criss-crossed the quarter closest to his house. It was an area that been very badly hit during the American bombardment of the Rhône bridges in the summer of 1944. These streets were a mixture of very old building that had been patched up after the bombing and newly built concrete structures put up quickly in the fifties and sixties. By this time of night, of course, everything seemed closed. In fact, restaurants and even bars had been closed to the tourists for a long time. Smith had observed for some time that there was a tendency for restaurants and bars to close earlier and earlier. When he had first come to Arles in his childhood, people never started to eat much before eight or nine o'clock and restaurants and bars were never closed until after midnight. Now people wanted to start eating at six or just after and be in bed by ten thirty it seemed. Perhaps it was something to do with more children being on holiday, Smith guessed. In any case the restaurants were happy to make their working day shorter and not to pay the overtime for late working that the new laws demanded. However, the bars where people might migrate to after eating also started closing earlier so by about eleven thirty the streets were pretty nearly empty. In other parts of the town, this had led to them being left open to drug dealers and thugs. But here in the Arab quarter the streets were almost self-policing. There were also people still to be seen. They were just wandering around chatting in small groups or sitting outside their front doors, enjoying the sultry night. One or two recognised him, or rather they recognised Arthur and waved. A number of the families had in the past told him about relations back in Algeria who used to use greyhounds for hunting in the North African deserts.

He passed through the place Voltaire for a final time and was beginning to make his way back up towards the Arena and his house up the Rue Augustin Tardieu and passed the rather grandly named Cybercafe which was, in reality, a little internet, telephone, Western Union shop, of the sort that were often unofficial social centres in parts of southern French towns and cities. It was also one that never seemed to close as, even now, it was brightly lit and filled with people. Outside a group of old men sat around a small table drinking tea.

'Arathar!'

The cry came from one of the tea drinkers and Smith saw it was one of the Arabs who he regularly saw on his night perambulations around this part of town. It was a man who had long ago taken Smith and Arthur into his house to show him proudly a

158

faded photograph of his grandfather and father standing proudly in the desert near home with a brace of pale greyhounds and holding pair of very dead desert hares.

The man was waving at him.

'Come and joins us, Monsieur Smith. It is a long time since we saw you on your night time walk with your beautiful dog.'

The man had become a friend to both of them years ago. He obviously loved the dog and took great pleasure of telling Smith many tales of hunting with his father and grandfather back home in Algeria before the war with France that had so shattered that county after the Second World War. He was now well past his own eightieth birthday and was a man of respect in the local community. He preached in the little mosque buried away in the warren of streets behind them. Smith had always enjoyed talking with him, especially when the conversation finally went beyond the beauty of greyhounds and onto the issues of the day. His companion was one of wisest and most moderate people he had ever met. Privately he believed that the almost complete peace in which the large Arab community in the town lived with their fellow Frenchmen was due to this man and his immediate followers. He sat at the table with the old man who had risen courteously to greet the Welshman. He offered his hand and kissed Smith on the cheek.

'As-Salaam-Alaikum.' he proffered.

'Wa-Alaikun-Salaam,' replied Smith.

There followed a considerable amount of time spent making a fuss of Arthur. More tea was brought and a plate of *griouech*, small twists of pastry coated with honey and sesame seeds.

'It is good to see you again, my friend.' said Smith. 'It's been much too long, and I apologise for that.'

The old man hardly paused from his chosen task of feeding a considerable number of the *griouech* to an ever-attentive and grateful Arthur as Smith continued:

'And I think you better stop that before the poor dog becomes as fat as one of your salukis.'

The Arab straightened and looked at him with a twinkle in his eye.

'It is never particularly good, my dear friend, to attempt to appear ignorant when those in your company know that you are not.'

The small group of men around the table smiled. They all knew and trusted this Welshman and knew how fond was their leader of this man and his *alsuluqi*.

Finally, Arthur lay at the feet of his benefactor who slipped off his sandals and rested his feet on the dog who dozed off.

Smith asked after the man's family and listened with interest to a fast run through of the recent history of a family that seemed to run into hundreds. It was a concise history that would have done credit to one of Gentry's briefings. As the imam seemed also to be related to half the people in the quarter, Smith was soon au fait with most on the public goings on of the quarter. After a while their two companions made their excuses and left. Sheik Nasir turned to Smith.

'It is indeed a gift from Allah that you pass this way today. I wanted to speak to you and I was thinking of paying you a visit. Do you think that it not too late to ask you if now on your way home you would accompany me to my house for a short visit for there is something I wish to discuss with you in confidence?'

Unlike his dog, Smith was fully awake.

'Of course, my friend. Lead on.'

After gently waking a slumbering Arthur and putting on his sandals, the imam rose, and the unlikely-looking trio moved off up the road. They quickly turned through a low archway and entered a small courtyard where the imam had his house. Smith had been there before, and he again found himself in the familiar little sitting room.

'Please make yourself comfortable, my friend,' said the Imam. 'I'll be back in a moment.'

Smith caught sight of the photograph that had been the subject of their first encounter. He was looking at it again with sufficient intensity that he didn't hear his host returning. When he turned, he saw that the man had prepared the inevitable glass of tea for himself, but he was holding out a weak, well-iced whisky to Smith. Smith smiled his thanks.

'Sometimes I envy Christians,' said the old man as they sat together. Arthur hopped up on a small sofa and returned quickly to his interrupted sleep. He had clearly decided that this was to an unusually broken night as far a sleep was concerned, and he should get some whenever the opportunity presented itself. The imam smiled gently at the dog.

'They really are all related, these greyhounds. Ours were either killing or sleeping. Perhaps that is the way of Allah. I hope not but sometimes I do wonder.'

He paused for a while before addressing business.

'Firstly, Peter, are you sure you are still all right to talk. It is really very late – or perhaps early would be better.'

'Please. I'm fine. This is just one of those nights that sleep doesn't seem to be happening. Please go on.'

'Well, apart from acting as imam in this part of Arles, I also have the same responsibility for the village of Mas Thibert in the Camargue.'

Smith remembered the little village situated about half way to Port St Louis from Arles on the east bank of the Rhône.

'Well I had a somewhat disturbing conversation with someone the last time I was there. I don't know whether you know that at the end of the Algerian war in 1962 there was a huge influx of refugees from North Africa by people who had supported France; the so-called *pieds noirs*. Particularly the Harkis who had served as military auxiliaries with the France army. There were many thousands seeking to come to France and their right to come had been part of the Évian Agreements that had finally ended the war and granted independence to Algeria. So, it was all a bit of a panic. In fact, the French government had to re-open many of the internment camps that had been used for Spanish Civil War refugees in the thirties and Second World War internees by the Germans. Places like Rivesaltes and Bourg-Lastic and many others. Conditions were dreadful, and the France government didn't seem to know what to do with them all. There had been more than a quarter of a million Muslims serving in one way or another in the French army. Well, after a while the government tried a new policy of settling groups of Muslims in smaller communities and Mas Thibert was chosen. It has developed into something of a success and grew as a farming community helped, incidentally, over a lot of years by your friends, the Aubanets.'

Smith had heard about this little piece of Camargue history, but he hadn't heard about the Aubanet family's involvement although it didn't particularly surprise him.

'How did the Aubanet family help?'

'Well,' the old man said. 'When the Harkis arrived – there were about four or five hundred or so – the conditions were initially almost as bad as in the internment camps. The housing that was put up was very poor quality. In addition, these were military men not farmers. Some of them had no idea what to do. Denis Aubanet, Emile's father, and some others helped them learn how to farm on the marsh and they supplied materials and labour so they could rebuild their houses. It was an act of great kindness considering they were all Catholics although I suppose those were more understanding times than now. People hadn't come to hate the Muslims then as they seem to nowadays. In any case this was the basis of the current respect that exists at Mas Thibert between the two communities, although it must be admitted there is still a bit of resentment about those early conditions towards the French government that did very little to help.'

'So, what did you hear about?'

The man looked a little sheepish as if he wasn't used to carrying tales; which, to be fair, he wasn't. He was a member of the Muslim church, or, at least, a senior lay member of it, and presumably not given to tittle-tattle. But this was obviously something that was troubling him. Why he had chosen to unburden himself to Smith was another question, of course.

'There is a rumour amongst my community in Mas Thibert that the Camargue beaches are about to be targeted by refugee smugglers.'

Smith managed to keep his face straight and waited for the man to add more information. There was some but not much.

'I believe it's only a rumour. I don't think that anyone has actually seen anything. But the rumour is that the refugees are coming from Algeria which, as you know, is their homeland. They naturally have strong opinions about it.'

Smith became a little suspicious.

'And why, may I ask, do you think you should mention this to me?'

The old man looked a little uncomfortable at this point.

'Well, Peter not only are you very well connected with what is going on in the Camargue but you seem to have, er ... a certain reputation, shall we say.'

'And what sort of reputation would that be, Sheik?'

The imam raised his hands in an embarrassed and somewhat defensive gesture.

'Peter, please don't misunderstand. I am not trying to be rude. But I am told that you have helped people on occasions.'

His voice faded away a little as he found himself embarrassed by the way the conversation had gone. Smith was also not prepared to play the game much longer. He may have a liking for this man who seemed to do a lot of good in the Muslin community with a very moderate and humane approach to the community's problems. However, Smith didn't think that gave him the right to make insinuations. His reply bypassed the problem.

'Surely you should take your suspicions to the police? They're the right people to sort this out if, indeed, there is a problem at all and it's not just another wild rumour.'

The imam just raised a hand slightly although it was not clear what the gesture meant.

'Perhaps,' continued Smith, 'some of your flock are involved in the scheme, or maybe their families back home might be.'

His companion looked shocked.

'No. no, Peter. I really don't think so.'

'Given the amount of money that might be on offer in this sort of business,' Smith replied dryly, 'I wouldn't rule anyone out, if I were you. In any case I really can't imagine how I might help you. Go to the police, as I said.'

The imam looked a little sad.

'Unfortunately, some of my flock don't particularly like the police very much.'

Smith started to get up and take his leave, his voice hardening.

'Then, my friend, I would suggest that the problem is yours rather than mine and that of your flock, as you call them. Perhaps this might be a chance for your flock to come a little closer to the police and to find that they are not all the pigs that they might think.'

The imam looked ineffably sad as he shook Smith's hand.

'That might be difficult,' he sighed.

'Difficult or not,' replied Smith, somewhat firmly. 'It's your job, I would have thought.'

After their host had given a farewell pat to the dog and a more ritualised one to Smith, the two of them left the little house and they made their way up the short climb to the place de la Major and home. It was past three and Smith just lay back on his bed to pass the rest of the early morning, running the conversation through his mind again. He must have dozed off, of course, but by the time the sun was up he was fully awake with the same questions buzzing around his head that had been there when he had finally dropped off and they were still troubling him when he woke. He reached for his phone.

166

'Morning, Gentry. If you are at a bit of a loose end this morning, could you do a check on someone for me.'

'Of course,' came the reply giving no indication of whether he had been woken or not. 'Who is it this time?'

'Sheik Nasir, our local imam. Lives at 13b Rue Augustin Tardieu. Properly known, I believe, as Nasir ibn Salman ibn Amin al-Farsi.'

If Gentry was surprised, he didn't sound it.

'Urgent?'

'Not particularly. Have your Weetiebangs first.'

'I'll call you.'

The morning was taken up with domestic chores. Although he could perfectly well have taken Martine up on her regular suggestion to arrange for someone to come in and muck him out from time to time, he preferred to do it himself. It wasn't that he enjoyed it, or anything like that. Actually, he hated it. But it was his house and it remained his alone. While he now regularly shared it with Martine, it was still his. She hadn't moved anything in other than a few clothes in his wardrobe and a surprising number of tubes and bottles and other unguents into his bathroom, all of which he felt were completely unnecessary if appearances were anything to go by. By the same token he had only moved a very similar selection of stuff into her *cabane* where they also co-habited from time to time. He would have claimed that there were many fewer of potions but that, of course, was not the

167

point. So, the house was vacuumed, bathroom cleaned and polished and laundry in the machine. Arthur obviously thought that his master was overcome with something and took refuge in the early morning sun on the terrace where he could have nothing to do with it.

Such an unusual burst of domesticity merited a period of recovery, so he settled next to Arthur with a glass a whisky and his current project; an article for some obscure American academic journal on the subject of dog symbolism on Roman sarcophagus sculpture. It had started when he was asked to review a thoroughly mediocre book that an over-enthusiastic young American, ink hardly dry on his PhD certificate, had penned on some newly-discovered sarcophagi buried in the deepest storage of the Museo Nazionale in Rome. The sarcophagi were not "discovered", of course, but judging by the illustrations that took up most of the book – the author clearly thought that words were less important than pictures – the coffin had just lain in storage for a century or two in well-deserved obscurity. It was a difficult book to review without being too rude. However, one of the illustrations had caught Smith's eye. It was of a sarcophagus illustrated with the scene of the famous hunt for the Calydonian boar by the Greek hero Meleager. The work was in very bad condition, but Smith could see that decoration, as usual, included many hounds of the large mastiff type. Most sarcophagi showing hunting scenes, as popular subject for the Romans, carried numbers of dogs as part of their decoration. It did, however, unmistakably also include a greyhound. Greyhounds were often part of Roman sarcophagus decorations, but this was the first time Smith has seen one included in the Calydonian Hunt. His interest was piqued and the result some considerable time later was a much longer piece of the many different dog iconographies that were to be found in sarcophagus programmes. One of his old editors from his days as an art historian wanted to publish it and now he was faced with a publisher's deadline and a careful proofing job neither of which he relished. However, as he sat at his terrace table concentrating hard, he did, at least, find the concerns of refugees and gang bosses fading from his mind for a while at least. Arthur, who one would have thought would have taken a particular interest in the subject, showed none but just continued to snooze and catch up on what had been a thoroughly fragmented night's sleep.

Smith's stomach had just begun to remind him that he had not yet eaten when Gentry called back.

'You know. I don't know how you do it.'

'What?'

'Well. Only you can have a perfectly innocent friendship with an elderly neighbour who is a pillar of the local society and an imam to boot and find probably the only one in the whole of the South of France who was full-blooded infantry general in the French army and ex-head of the OAS Intelligence unit in Algeria. His military life consisted of stints as a lad as a Harkis in Free French Army in Algeria during the Second World War, landing with the Allies during the Operation Dragoon that liberated the south of France in 1944, fighting in Indonesia, commanding a full regiment at Dien Bien Phu, no less.

He then joined with the French Army during the whole Algerian War and just managed to out before the FLN captured him and burnt his ass for good.'

'Shit,' was Smith's reply.

'Quite,' was Gentry's.

'Just so you know who you are dealing with, down there drinking over-sweetened tea in that little café in the place Voltaire, the man holds the Legion d'Honneur, the Ordre de la Liberation and the Médaille Militaire with enough bolt-on salad and other decorations to make Idi Amin proud on his day.

After a while Smith recovered sufficiently to ask a question.

'Whose side is he on?'

Gentry took the question seriously although it was a moot point as to whether it was meant that way.

'Well, one assumes he's on Allah's, given his current day job. But nobody gets that many gongs without remaining on the official radar. I would suggest the question is not whose side is he on but how retired is he. Christ, he's probably got more contacts on both or all sides of the great moral divide than I have.'

'Humm. So why would he tell me about a pretend rumour about Moroni's refugee project when he probably knows it isn't a rumour at all. And why me, for God's sake.'

'Ah, my old friend. I'm afraid you're going to have to ask him yourself. If it's any help I can give you a phone number to a phone that he doesn't have.'

Smith made a note.

'By the way, what rank was he when he was kicked out?'

'Général de Division. Which probably means he actually wasn't kicked out, as you rather delicately describe. More likely someone rather high up the system and very conscious that he was dealing with a serious and influential Arab rather than some dumb squaddie, reminded the good Sheik that he was well past the three score years and ten and perhaps he might like to think about retirement.'

There was a silence before Gentry continued.

'Just in case you're struggling with the mental arithmetic, that means he made it into the higher echelons while he was in his early sixties. Not bad for a little Arab boy from Ouargla.'

Smith looked down at the piece of paper in his hand for a time after he put the phone down on Gentry. For the life of him, he couldn't see what the man was playing at. Only one way to find out, he thought, and dialled the number. It was answered almost immediately.

'Yes?'

'Good morning, general.'

Again, there was a gap during which two and two were put together to make a very great deal more than four.

'Ah, Monsieur Smith. It appears that what they say about you is true, then.'

'Unlike you, mon general.'

A genuine laugh came across the ether.

'Touché, Peter, touché.'

'Perhaps we should talk, my friend; and soon.'

To give him credit, it took the old man very little time to get up to speed.

'I am heading out to Mas Thibert for a meeting later this morning. Perhaps you would like to come with me. You could meet a few people and, of course, we could talk as we go.'

'OK. That sounds good.'

'I will pick you up in an hour. Please bring Arathar. Perhaps we can find something for him to chase while we talk. I know many of my flock would be happy to see him.'

'You mean many of your forces, don't you?'

An amused voice came back to him.

'Forces, flock. There is little difference sometimes, my friend, especially for us Arabs.'

The Arab had a Honda SUV. Big, ugly but serviceable and indestructible. There was no dog grill however. So no sooner had Arthur hopped up into the back via the tail gate than he continued to hop over the back seats and lay down full-length over them and pretend he wasn't there. Sheik Nasir just smiled slightly. He obviously had time for dogs. It was a little time before they struck up a conversation. In fact, they were well down the D35 that would take them south from the town to Mas Thibert before Smith ventured:

'So, what do I call you, Sheik or General, or is that a matter of what hat your wearing?'

'Oh, I only wear a taqiyah, these days, so sheik or imam will do. And what do I call you, may I ask.'

'Oh, Smith just about covers it.'

He nodded and frowned a little and it wasn't just because of the sun that was streaming in through the windscreen as they headed south.

'You seem to have found out a lot about me in a remarkably short period of time, Peter. I won't ask you how, of course, but I would be interested to know how much.'

'Enough, I think,' replied Smith.

'Then your sources are a lot better than mine, for I have found virtually nothing of you. Nor apparently am I likely to.'

Smith remained silent and just watched the outskirts of the town gradually change into the Plan de Crau. The road they were on ran down the east side of the Rhône from Arles to Port St Louis on the coast where the river finally empties into the sea. It also marked the beginning of a highly fertile irregularly shaped strip of land that extended around the top of the Étang de Berre as far east as Aix en Provence and many miles inland. It was markedly different from the salt marsh of the Camargue. The land was highly fertile and was able to produce a wide variety of fruit and vegetable crops for which the region is famous. It was also the road that led on towards Martiques and Istres and into the territory that was Girondou's own. The area around Mas Thibert was therefore good farming country and relatively prosperous by Camargue standards at least. Most of the farms were

173

small and their produce was sold locally either through the two weekly markets in Arles or Port St Louis or further afield in Salon de Provence or Aix.

The village itself was split by a canal that ran beside the main road and most of the village was across a single bridge to the east. Before long they stopped in front of a house that looked out onto the small football field. Inside there was a small group of Arabs who got up respectfully as they entered. Tea was served, and the discussion started.

As an information gathering exercise, the conversation was worse than useless. They all told the same stories; yes, they had heard some rumours about trafficking refugees from Algeria. No, they hadn't seen anything themselves. They hadn't any information about who might be involved. No, they hadn't actually been approached by anyone in particular. No, they hadn't reported anything to the police. Yes. They were very unhappy about the possibility as they were law-abiding people. No one spoke without a glance in the general direction of the imam. They all confirmed that they had heard of Smith and understood that he was trusted by their imam and was a man of respect in the area. But no, there was very little they could tell him.

The meeting came to an end – or at least the bit of it that was supposed to involve Smith – and he left them to it while he took Arthur for a walk around the village. It wasn't different to many of the small Camargue settlements; clusters of small, single- and two-story houses with white painted walls and red pantile roofs. A few shops and the odd office and a couple of cafés completed the pictures. Smith saw that the village, apart from being separated from the road by a canal of the sort that criss-crosses much of the Camargue, it was also bounded by another, second one running parallel some five hundred metres distant. Thanks to a helpful map by the side of the road he discovered these were called the Canals d'Arles a Bouc and de Vigueirat respectively. He walked to the second canal and turned south presuming that before too long another lane would join and enable him to complete the square and regain the village.

It wasn't long before he saw a figure coming towards him also leading a dog and as he got closer it proved also to be a greyhound. Smith tightened his grip a little. Arthur was not particularly sociable when it came to other dogs. It was one of the characteristics that has attracted Smith to Arthur in the first place when he had found him in a greyhound rescue centre in Deptford one of the tougher parts of East London some years ago. Alone amongst a distressingly large number of dogs waiting to be re-homed, he occupied a single kennel. These were the lucky ones, however; ones who had been successful enough in their racing careers to be kept past their retirement on sentimental grounds or in the hope of further earnings at stud. Many, many more were just put down and buried in a big hole in the ground. There is little romance in greyhound racing.

The man drew near and the natural affinity amongst dog lovers, especially one that love the same breed, started the conversation. The man was an Arab and dressed in the traditional *thawb* and was bare-headed in the morning sun. Pleasantries and compliments were exchanged about the dogs while to two animals in question just stood quietly and observed each other. The man came to the point of this chance encounter.

'Monsieur,' the man said. 'You came with Sheik Nasir, I believe, and you talked about this rumour about immigrants.'

Smith wondered for a moment how this man knew when he hadn't been at the meeting. However, he quickly realised that it would have been pretty certainly common knowledge. Smith just nodded. He also realised that this was the main reason for this coincidental meeting of greyhounds.

'I'm pretty sure that no one admitted actually to knowing anything specific'

'You could say that,' replied Smith.

'Well they are lying. A number of us have been approached including me. I got a visit two days ago by a man called Chirosi. He was driving a Mercedes SUV with Montpellier plates.'

'What did he want?'

'Well it was a little confusing really. He didn't seem to know much about the geography of this area. He was looking if any of us had farms that connected with the beaches. It was all a bit daft, really. Most of us farm on this side of the Rhône and there are no sea beaches around here. You have to go through Port St Louis before you get to the Plage Napoleon and there's no farming down there either. It is still owned by the salt companies, I think. Most of us just shrugged and left him to it.'

'Did he mention anything about illegal immigrants?'

The man shook his head.

'No. He just asked about the farms. But I'm not surprised to hear the rumour. I can't think the man was looking to buy our farms or anything like that. In any case we only rent our land.'

Now this was news to Smith.

'Oh, who owns the land around here?'

'Well, most of it is owned by Sheik Nasir. I think he had owned it since he arrived in the area.'

Now Smith really was interested.

'And when was that. Can you remember?'

The man laughed.

'I was born here so I'm not the one to ask but I get the impression that he arrived here very soon after the Harkis were sent here from the camp in Rivesaltes near Perpignan. That is where most of them came from, including my parents in 1962 or 3, I think it was. These were bad times. It was hard for my parents to be imprisoned in the same camp from which so many Jews had been sent to Germany during the war. Especially as they had been loyal to France. There is still a lot of resentment about all this amongst the old people.'

'And you say the Sheik Nasir came here at the same time?'

'I really don't know exactly. All I know is that he owns a lot of the land around here. How he got hold of it I have no idea. However, I

177

know that many of us here would be very unhappy if our countryside was used to smuggle refugees from our homeland. We would be prepared to help prevent it if necessary. We are honest men trying to support out families by honest work.'

Smith was now more than interested.

'So, what you are saying is that although a number of your friends have been visited by the man Chironi, he didn't actually mention the refugee plan to you.'

The man nodded.

'Well can you remember who did?'

'I think it was Sheik Nasir.'

Suddenly Smith got a smell in his nostrils; the sort of smell he got when something wasn't quite right. He needed to talk to Gentry again and thus started to end the conversation.

'Well, thank you, my friend. It was nice talking to you and to meet your beautiful dog.

He held out his hand to the man who took it but seemed a little reluctant to let it go immediately.

'Monsieur, I have told you this because I know about you a little. I know of your reputation here in the Camargue and I also know that you are both a man of honour and of action. I would not want Sheik Nasir to know that I have talked to you about these things. Although he is my imam, I don't trust him. Nor do many of us who work here; the younger ones, at least.'

Smith nodded and smiled at the man.

'Rest assured, monsieur, our conversation will be only about the undeniable beauty of our dogs.'

'The man looked relieved.

Thank you for understanding, Monsieur Smith. My name is Sadik al Asri by the way. If I or my friends can assist you further, please ask us. This little place is our home and we will defend it against anyone if needed.'

He bent to say goodbye to Arthur and then turned and left. Smith watched him go thoughtfully before he too turned and retraced his steps along the canal bank, not before retrieving the small slip of paper that his erstwhile companion had slipped through the collar of Arthur's slip lead and put it quickly into his pocket. Before reaching the road that led back into the village, he called Gentry again.

'Can you find out exactly how our humble imam escaped Algeria and, more importantly when? Also, how did he end up owning half the land around Mas Thibert?'

'Yes. How is the nice little harkis hamlet?'

'Bloody hot,' was the only reply.

By the time he had returned to the village centre, he found the imam standing by his car with a small crowd around him. He was obviously anxious to leave so before long they were speeding back towards Arles.

'I do hope I didn't keep you waiting. I met an interesting chap on my walk with another greyhound and we spent a very nice few minutes swapping dog stories.'

179

'Of course, my friend. We Arabs are all dog lovers. However, I'm sorry if I may have misled you. Perhaps this whole refugee smuggling thing seems to have been something of a red herring, I believe, you English say.'

'Perhaps,' Smith agreed, 'A red herring is exactly what we Welsh say,' giving the man a very long, hard stare as they parted.

\----------------------

Gentry's next report was concise.

'He got out pretty sharpish after the Oran massacre in July '62. In fact there is a thought that he was actually there. He was an Arab officer in the ORO which is the intelligence bit of the OAS and there is some evidence that he remained part of the organisation during the sixties which puts him slightly in the terrorist bracket from time to time. He was actually under a sort of rather relaxed house arrest in Arles until De Gaulle's let many of them go. However, although obviously he was never an FLN man, it is a little difficult without a lot of deeper probing to answer your original question to find much about whose side he was actually on. As you might remember, sides and loyalties were somewhat blurred back then as they often are in civil wars, and they didn't get any clearer after the French officially left Algeria to the Algerians. You will recall that the OAS got pretty nasty towards their one-time colleagues; assassinated a lot of them on French soil as I recall. Nearly added De Gaulle himself to that list too. Nasir's connection is slightly unusual as the OAS were predominantly white and French and they didn't take lightly to Arabs on the payroll.

He must have had something they needed or maybe they just wanted to keep an eye on him. My guess was he was a colonial loose end and the powers that be decided that the best way to keep him quiet was to give him some land in the Camargue around a community of his own people and let him become their imam and live off the rent until he pops his cloggs.'

'Not on the dark side, then?'

'My guess is no. As I said, things got pretty confused in the sixties between Algeria and France, but he has always fought for the home team even if he did stray into one of its more extreme departments for a while. I can't see him siding with the criminal fraternity, thought. Too many gongs for that. But, of course, you never know.'

'Hum. Thanks Gentry.' he offered before ringing off.

'Red Herring,' he thought to himself. 'Maybe he was succumbing to his own conspiracy theories and that was all it was.'

Chapter 11: A Game of Chess

Gentry's beautiful book-lined study was in its summer mode. This basically meant that the logs in the huge fireplace weren't alight. The shutters were still closed, and the varnished mahogany bookcases were illuminated with picture lights hung above them. A pair of rather battered leather armchairs stood in their usual places on either side of the fire and a buttoned leather Chesterfield completed the square. Smith knew from experience that the Chesterfield was unspeakably uncomfortable but that didn't deter Arthur from making a bee line to it and settling down with a satisfied grunt.

The room housed some of Gentry's stock of books. In theory Gentry was an antiquarian bookseller but he went to great lengths not to sell anything to anyone who had had the persistence actually to get in front of the door to the house. 'Front' was not quite the right description as the door itself was buried in an internal courtyard at the dark centre of an old five story house lost in the maze of little streets and alleys that were situated between the Arena and the Rhône. Outside on the street were no signs or plaques to guide the determined shopper. It was actually quite difficult to find an actual door. Also there were a great deal more layers of extremely high tec security that a casual passer-by might imagine. Of course, what none of these intrepid potential book buyers knew was that the very last thing that Gentry wanted was actually to sell anything to any of them, however rich. Smith had no idea why Gentry kept up the pretense. He had always assumed it was something to do with tax but had no real idea why or how. Smith had, in any case, only a tangential relationship with tax himself.

The game was laid out as usual on a stunningly elegant Sheraton inlaid chess table, an armed dining chair by the same maker on either side. Each side sported the usual refreshment Single Banff malt for the host, well iced and watered supermarket blended scotch for Smith. Both looked equally at home in their antique Treveris cut glasses. Some time ago Smith had asked Gentry why he preferred drinking from German glasses. He replied that he hated glasses that weighed more than a ton and were made out of glass so thick that you could keep bullets out with it. He preferred his glasses cut, certainly, but lighter and thinner. The old Treveris water glass by Villeroy and Boch during their Saarland days fitted the bill perfectly. Smith found he agreed. They may be on the small side but they were more than adequate for sipping during the course of a game of chess when imbibing a large amount of alcohol was not a usual priority. Without much ado they sat and started. Smith saw that Gentry had even remembered that it was his turn to play white. They habitually alternated.

The game progressed oddly. Usually the game was, as is usual between serious players, between two intellects rather than between two players. Gentry was methodical and logical; taking risk-free positions and building without danger. It was not that he was obsessively defensive. He was as capable of attacking strategies as anyone. It was just that he preferred to develop his attacks cautiously without taking unnecessary risks and that for Gentry, meant without any risks.

Smith, on the other hand, was much more impulsive. He preferred the unconventional and often relied on making things up as he went along, often at a faster pace than his opponent. When Smith lost, it was often because of this impulsiveness and Gentry knew it. What he also knew was that if it was called for Smith was perfectly capable of methodical, theoretical chess backed with a seemingly endless repertoire of famous openings and strategies. It was just that he enjoyed his chess played less sedately. It was this knowledge, that when necessary Smith could be as conventional as he, that Gentry had always feared his old friend, in life as well as in chess. Someone who could be achingly predictable at the same time as being completely unpredictable was a formidable opponent as many had discovered, often to their cost.

For many years they had used most of the simple openings or at least some of the more usual. Ruy Lopez, of course, and the Sicilian and French Defences. These were the basics and still offered some of the most flexible variations for further play for amateurs and professionals alike. Both Smith and Gentry were very competent amateurs, but neither would claim to be more than that. They had no great use for some of the more esoteric openings that usually grew out of grand master play. Their love of chess was based as much on the sort of friendly debate that existed between colleagues than any intense rivalry between competitors. In any case they usually held a conversation as they played; not something a serious chess player usually does. But the game often helped them concentrate on a different matter in hand. And so it was tonight as Gentry, playing white and therefore choosing the opening gambit, started the famous three pairs of moves, e4 e5, Nf3 Nc6, Bc4 that lead to the fourth and possibly oldest recorded of these famous openings, the Italian Game. It usually led to lively and imaginative encounters between them with Smith often shading the result by taking some unpredictable directions.

As usual they played in silence for a dozen or so moves until the game settled into a pattern and they could turn to other things as well. The game was played with Gentry's original 1849 Staunton set.

The initial speed of play had slowed a little while both men thought a little more carefully about how to develop their middle games. Gentry had continued to lead quite aggressively with the Evans Gambit which Smith accepted, and the game looked set for a lively second half. Smith started the conversation.

'Well, where do we start'?

'I've got quite a lot of information for you but none of it really amounts to a solid explanation of anything really. Let's start with Henk.'

Smith nodded and just waited.

' I went all the way back to his initial vetting when he joined us three years ago and traced it all through until today and there are no obvious difficulties. You rightly found out that he tends to be a touch squeamish about the messier ends of the job - in fact somehow he has managed to avoid any significant violence at all. Obviously, no fatalities other than the shots on Beauduc Beach with you which a slightly unusual given that working for Girondou usually involves some. He's done the rest of the job competently and there have been no complaints. The only other thing of note is that he has got rather close to Girondou's daughter, Solange, recently. It seems that Girondou doesn't seem to object. He probably thinks it's good protection.'

Smith frowned a little.

'I can't say I'm completely happy. I know he and I haven't really got on particularly well, but I don't really like his attitude at the moment. I am also a bit uncertain about why Girondou sent him with the family or at least why he went. I'm not even sure who sent him. He knows as well as anyone that his sole job is to protect his boss irrespective of how much he fancies one of his children. He said to me that he was just following Girondou's orders. Girondou was not particularly certain but he gave me the impression that Henk himself suggested it. It would be typical of him to agree to the idea given how much he loves his family.'

Gentry nodded.

'Something you're going to have to figure out, my friend.'

Smith agreed silently. He had had a bad feeling about the man. Perhaps he would set Deveraux on the job. The game had slowed as the conversation took over.

'Moroni next. It certainly seems that he might be making a play for the territory. We know he has the territory from the Rhône to the Spanish border and north as far as Lyon. He's tried expanding north in the past but the Paris gangs have put a stop to that and, of course, the Spanish are having none of any cross-border shenanigans. East is the only opportunity and is also the richest territory in France. However, it is hardly possible to see Girondou being dislodged.'

Smith looked grim and made his next move with slightly more force than usual. Gentry peered down at the board to tell if his opponent had made an error. He hadn't.

'In his present state I don't think he could pull the skin off a rice pudding. Maybe this is the opportunity Moroni is waiting for.'

'Any idea why Moroni is mucking around in the Camargue?'

'Again, not really, unless it is about this people trafficking business. That would make some sense. Obviously, Martine's takeover of the top job isn't universally popular whether from male chauvinist piggery or from general ambition. It could also be noted that while Toulouse is the centre of his empire rather as Marseille is of Girondou's. However most of the rest of the patch is widely spread over the farming country of the south-west and there was never the independence of the Camargue to deal with. Maybe he's sees a way in to Girondou's territory or he just wants to see the possible effect of this new founded alliance between his rival and the Aubanets.'

There was a bit of a pause while Gentry thought about his next move and Smith got up to replenish their glasses.

'Finally, there is the question of Girondou himself. He is certainly behaving oddly at the moment and there are a number of rumours locally, but they are no more than that. Girondou's businesses range over a huge selection of activities and I doubt whether anyone other than he actually knows all the details. He doesn't seem to have a number two. It may just be that he over concerned with something in particular that no one else knows about.'

'It's certainly very unusual. I tried to have a word with Angèle when I was at the house and she was as unhelpful as Alexei. Something of a family conspiracy I feel.'

'And to what extent, old friend, are we actually interested?' asked Gentry trying to adopt a more practical line. 'Surely if they don't want to tell us then maybe we shouldn't get involved? None of our business and all that.'

Smith concentrated for a while on the chess and Gentry found himself pedalling quite bad to keep up. Smith's anger often came through onto the chess board and when it did, he didn't take any prisoners. He felt less than interested in interfering in his friend's business especially if that friend made it plain that he wasn't welcome. But he certainly wasn't prepared to forget about it. Girondou was acting entirely too strangely for that. But his priority, as always, was

Martine and the whole Moroni story was of more immediate importance.

'Let's see what more we can find out about this Moroni man first. Do some real digging, not just about what he's up to now but some background. Who are his colleagues and so on. He must have some sort of command structure. Perhaps we can find a weak link. I'll get Madame Durand to get her little circle of juvenile spies to continue to do some more poking around the Camargue. They at least can keep an eye out for who is going where and when. If Moroni is trying something of an approach that way, then Martine is at risk and I don't think she is in any position to deal with Toulouse gangsters.'

Gentry had made a move and snorted slightly.

'I have a feeling that those Camargue farmers are more than capable of taking care of themselves, but it is better to be safe than sorry.'

Smith decided to change the subject a little.

'I noticed the new locks.' Smith ventured not being completely happy to let his companion off the hook so easily. Gentry smiled gently.

'Noticed?'

'Heard, actually,'

Gentry nodded. Yet again he knew that his old friend was ahead of him. There were at least three electrically operated locks between Gentry's inner courtyard and the street outside and each had to be opened manually by Gentry himself. He had indeed changed all three since his last adventure with Smith. They both knew why. Bigger and American. To be honest he had no idea whether an electrically-operated locks could be hacked but if anyone could do it, Smith could. The bloody man had heard the difference as each had clicked open.

'Yes, given that we seem to have escaped relatively unscathed from the forces of evil last year that included some rather formidable bent GIGN commandos and certain unsavoury elements of some back offices in the Elysée, I thought I might beef the system up a little.'

'Very sensible.' Smith commented dryly.

As was his habit, Gentry set himself to summarise.

'Your man Moroni seems to be muscling in on Girondou's territory and is choosing the Camargue as the place to start and you're worried about Martine. Let's see if I've got this picture right. This unpleasant man from Toulouse is setting himself up against the equally unpleasant man from Marseille who you seem to think is not as unpleasant as other major high-level criminals because he is your friend. The chosen battlefield for this clash of criminal masterminds is your beloved Camargue where your amourata has recently ascended to the unofficial but nevertheless very real top job against the wishes of a number of the more powerful but traditionally-minded landowners who believe, as have they forefathers for many generations, that it is no job for a woman. You have decided to defend the ladies honour and position as well as that of your friend Girondou - although the extent to which he has any honour to defend in any traditional sense is best described as 'moot.' You intend to do this without actually discussing it with them and at the moment, at least, you are going to do this on your own.'

'You are here,' Gentry continued 'because you need the sort of information that I can provide when required. You are pretty sure you can supply all the rest yourself. I understand why you want to do this. I'll help, of course. You will go ahead anyway so I might as well watch your back as usual.'

The game ended in a draw which was less deserved than it might have been if either man had been taking it more seriously. The whole of the Girondou family saga getting into some sort of collective pet was a pain in the arse Smith thought. Gentry was quite right. Perhaps it wasn't his problem after all.

By the time he and Arthur had got home it was past midnight. The town was again warm and the night was still. As he walked past the Amphitheatre he found memories of the past coming back. He had been visiting Arles on way or another since he was a boy, first with his father and then on his own. He remembered the days when the town was full of tourists with the cafes and hotels all doing enough trade in the five months of spring and summer to keep them going through the autumn and winter. But even here things were changing. Only a decade or so ago his present route home would have led him through streets well-populated with visitors. Now it was different. Visitors were increasingly day-tripping and had therefore left the town long ago. Many also came to the town nowadays on huge river barges down from Lyons. They tied up at a smart new wharfs three or four deep.

191

There the visitors slept, ate in on-board cafés and drank in on-board bars all paid for in advance with their tickets. They ventured into shore to file in close groups behind a tour guide, each electronically plugged into their leader to be told what to look at and what to think. Their entry tickets to the monuments were also part of their holiday pre-payments and the most they might spend in the town were on cups of coffee and a postcard or two. By now they were all fast asleep onboard. A further cohort of visitors occupied the town's campsites and were also asleep in their mobile homes having consumed a self-cooked meal. Even at high season the town's hotels were often only half full and the town's bars and restaurants had started to run out of customers by 10 'o clock. Smith's trip home was made through deserted streets. Even the cicadas seemed to have given up and turned silently to bed.

By the time he mounted the last of the hill to the top of the Hauteur as the highest point of the town around the Amphitheatre was called another thought had occurred and, having decided that he was far from tired, he settled into a chair on his terrace for a final whisky and a further cogitate. Arthur was content to lie at his master's feet and snooze. After a while he picked up his phone.

'Good evening , Boss.'

In spite of the hour there was no hint of annoyance or even surprise in Deveraux's voice.

'Dev. Do you have an hour or two free tomorrow? If you weren't busy, I thought we could have lunch and a chat somewhere.'

'That would be nice, boss. I gather that Madame Aubanet was going to spend much of the day going around some of their grain and rice storage businesses. These are very easy visits to protect. There will be lots of people around and Jean Marie is more than capable of doing the job without my skulking in the background. Where do you want to meet?'

'There is a nice little restaurant just out of the town centre near the Alyscamps called Le Jardin de Manon. About 1?'

With a casual 'see you there', the conversation was ended.

Chapter 12: Food for Thought

Deveraux and Smith sat together in the corner of the garden of the restaurant Jardin de Manon. It was midweek, and the summer temperature meant that the few customers occupied only half of the tables. Arles had many restaurants of note if not actually quality and Martine's family ran one or two of the better but more anonymous ones. They tended to be for locals rather than visitors. But the Jardin de Manon had long been a favourite. Smith remembered its twenty years before. He had been walking past the house situated in an unfashionable place just near the Alyscamps, the roman necropolis outside the town walls when he was drawn to loud music and louder laughter. No sooner had he investigated he was drawn in to a party that celebrated the opening of a new restaurant. The toddler Manon had been running around in the garden while a crowd of friends, family and well-wishers clinked glasses and chatted. Now Manon had grown up and was a tall elegant woman practicing medicine in Montpellier and the restaurant remained at the top of his list and he was a regular. It held a relatively modest single Michelin knife and fork rating but it has held that for almost all of its life; always a sign of quality.

He looked across the table at his companion with an expression that came near to affection. Deveraux had been a long and loyal friend. Just as Gentry had been Smith's more intellectual companion in organising and planning much of his life when it was necessary, Deveraux had been his very strong right arm. He had proved over and over again to be utterly courageous and loyal. More than once in some odd part of the word he had come to Smith's aid with total disregard to his own safety. The fact was, of course, that the service had been mutual too. In what is euphemistically called "the field", their employer regularly placed them in extreme peril confident that if anyone would get the job done and survive, these two would. They also knew that if the price of success was their lives, they would pay that too for their country.

'Something odd is happening and I'd like to do something about it.'

Deveraux knew full-well that an explanation would be forthcoming so his sipped contentedly on his Pastis and waited. He obviously knew enough about the background. It wasn't before the first course, a bull beef paté, had arrived that Smith had started his explanation.

'Something's going on, Dev, or perhaps a number of somethings. There seem to be an odd series of events that, to date at least, seem to be disconnected. My belief is that they are not but only some seem to be accessible to us, for the moment, at least. We have Girondou and his immediate family acting like idiots and keeping silent. They are all wandering about looking like death warmed up. We have Girondou's great rival Moroni from Toulouse making periodic visits to the Camargue and talking primarily but not exclusively, to farmers who seem to be less than happy with Martine's succession to the top job.'

Deveraux nodded slowly.

'I can't see us doing much good by getting involved in the Girondou / Moroni spat even if our attentions were welcome - which for the moment at least, they don't seem to be. According to Jeanne this rivalry has been going on for ever and this time seems no different to all the others.'

Smith remembered that Deveraux's new girlfriend worked as part of Girondou's protection staff.

'My concern is the Camargue connection because that could have a fairly direct consequence on the Aubanet family. I have no idea how Moroni could use some local farmers' dislike of the family to his own advantage, but something is going on and whatever it means, I don't think it's particularly good. As for Girondou, I agree that his business is not our affair, at least directly, but I like the man and I wouldn't like to think that I was doing nothing when he actually needs some help even though he's too pig-headed to ask for it.'

The meal had moved on to the main course which was lightly grilled fillets sea bass and red mullet with a simple salad and new potatoes. Both men paused their conversation while they ate.

'So how can I help, boss?'

'I think that we need some more information to start with. I've got Gentry delving into the two gangsters. Perhaps there's something in either their backgrounds or current businesses that will help explain things. I'd like you try to find out some things on a more focussed level. Firstly, I have had a slight reservation about our friend Henk almost since the time I set eyes on him, but I originally put that down to the fact that he wasn't one of us. In spite of coming with a full Gentry vetting he has always been a little reluctant to get properly involved in the way we normally require.'

Deveraux smiled.

'You do tend to have slightly more exacting standards than others, boss.'

Smith shrugged slightly.

'Perhaps. But I'd like you to take a closer look. Perhaps that girlfriend of yours can help. She works with him after all. I want a check on his relationship with Girondou's daughter Solange. That seems to have popped up out of the blue rather fast right about the time that Girondou went off the rails and I don't like the fact that neither Gentry nor I were told about it. Everyone seems to have forgotten that although he works for Girondou, he is one of us and I don't like free-lancing.'

'OK. Anything else?'

'Yes. I want a detailed account of Moroni's visits around the Camargue. We have a nice little source of primary information from Madame Durand's network of car loving kids. I want to try to find a way of knowing what he is talking about and why it's just to these particular few.'

'Wouldn't Madame Aubanet be better placed. She, after all, knows these people personally.'

'The main reason for my wanting to get involved at all is that all this might add up to a danger to Martine. We know that some of these farmers are not terribly happy with her taking charge and they would probably hide things from her or her father. Also, Martine is not exactly practiced at this sort of thing and would probably give more away than she learned. This whole thing may simply be a false alarm or normal run of the mill stuff and I don't want to worry her before I have to. No, I want to get into this rather quietly. If you think you can trust Jeanne maybe she can help. As I said, the other matter is Henk. I am getting increasingly uncomfortable with the man. He's becoming an unknown quantity and, as you know. I don't like those.'

'Well Jeanne works with him every day. She is probably best placed to spot anything unusual.'

'OK. But make sure she doesn't take any risks. I've got Martine and her father coming round to the house for supper later to talk a bit about this. Perhaps you could drive them in from the mas and join the conversation?'

Having got back from lunch, he decided that further gardening was not on his list. The afternoon was hot and sultry, and Smith decided to put the whole thing out of his mind for a while. There was going to be enough conversation about it this evening. He spent a little time tidying the house for his guests then sat in the shade of his grape vine in his garden with Michael Baxendall's intriguing little book 'Painting and Experience in Fifteenth Century Italy' in one hand and a very weak cold whisky in the other. It was one of the books he traditionally read every year, along with Thomas Mann's Magic Mountain and Kenneth Graham's Wind in the Willows being amongst the others. During his time as an art historian, he was much influenced by Baxendall's then revolutionary ideas that art of a certain period should, as far as possible, be viewed and interpreted using the ideas and social mores of the time in which it was created not from our own. It was quite a useful approach to life in general he had found. As usual he got lost in the book and the afternoon slipped by. He wasn't expecting his guests until considerably later and he was looking forward to having some time on his own. So, it was Arthur who heard the car before him. In fact, it always was. But using some sort of doggy mechanism that Smith never understood he only recognised the Aubanet Range Rover and the pizza delivery man. Both were recognised some considerable distance away and for the dog both held the promise of pleasure. For him too he thought. He started to get up slowly to join a thoroughly excited greyhound at the front door to discover that he had been beaten to it by Martine who let herself in. It was a good deal earlier that he had imagined she would arrive, but it was a pleasure to see her, as always. Oddly, however, she was carrying a large picnic basket rather than shopping bags. Having given him a somewhat perfunctory kiss on the cheek she plonked the basket on his kitchen table and started to unload a series of plastic containers of the Tupperwear variety.

'Well,' she started by way of explanation, ' I wasn't going to waste hours cooking a wonderful meal when everyone was just going to be talking over the top of it. So I raided our freezer. Actually, I'd forgotten that there is some really rather nice stuff lying forgotten in there. I've brought a rough selection of what may or may not go well together. It's a bit hit and miss because labelling stuff was never my strong point.'

'I'm sure it will be great, my dear,' Smith mused inconsequentially. He did actual agree about limiting conversation when there was good food to be eaten but as he knew that Martine cooked or at least helped to cook regularly for dinner parties at the Mas he couldn't imagine that her guests were forced into silence while the ate. There must be another reason, so he waited.

'I came early as some of it needs to thaw out a bit more, so it gives us a bit of time to get started.'

'On what?'

She turned to him with a look at astonishment on her face.

'Why on each other, of course. I told you I intended to spend this evening making love to you and as you've mucked that up slightly by inviting guests and the fact that you might be tired later on, I thought we'd get a bit of a start now.'

Emile, driven by Deveraux, arrived a couple of hours later. The four were finally assembled around the table in Smith's little garden. Smith. Martine, Emile and Deveraux. The first part of the meal was

200

taken up by a general review of the last few days. Both Emile and his daughter had been pleased that the general reaction to his handing over to Martine had been very positive. She was well known and liked, of course, and her knowledge of the Camargue and its traditions and customs was highly respected. In general, they felt things had gone well. After a while, however it was Smith who took on the discussion.

'Emile. There are four Camargue families that I want to ask you about. I'd like to learn a little about them and to know why they might oppose you and why particularly now they should seek an opportunity to do you and Martine damage. These are Brun, Maneschi, Baroncelli and Cordiez.'

Emile rather reluctantly finished his plate and gently laid down his knife and fork before addressing the question.

'Well, three have reasons to dislike the Aubanet family somewhat but they tend to be different. I certainly don't immediately see any reason for it to be particularly serious. You should try to understand that we are not talking about a big happy family. There have been rivalries between the families here for centuries. It is just that for important matters, maters that concern the general wellbeing of the farmers or their collective security, these rivalries are usually set aside. Take Laurence Brun, for instance, it is all simply a matter of business. The Brun family has a major interest in the rice business here on the Camargue. As you know there has been rice growing here since the sixteenth century if not before. It was used primarily as cattle food and planting it was also a method of stopping the land naturally reverting to salt marshes. Production received a big boost between the wars when it began to be cultivated for food for with the help of immigrants from French Indochina. But it was only really after the Second World War that Marshall Plan money from America was invested and rice production really increased. Two groups of rival producers were created. The Aubanet group was created as a collaborative for the farmers that wanted to get involved in the crop and the Brun group was wholly-owned by the family. They have been fierce rivals ever since. Perhaps competitors would be a better word. Our group is smaller but we have the better land. The Bruns have made many attempts to take us over but so far the members of our collective have remained reasonably loyal. I don't really see anything personal in this. My relations with Laurence are always very cordial when we meet. It's just business I suppose.'

'So, Laurence Brun's presence at your recent lunch was a peace offering, as much as anything?'

Emile nodded and smiled rather sadly.

'Yes, it was although, I am not sure how much of a success it was. It was Martine's idea and well-intentioned, I think. But I also know that family. If there is any opposition to us it is certainly not political or personal. Their business is their obsession, I'm afraid.'

Martine just looked a little unhappy at the knowledge that her attempted peace-making was not a success. She just shrugged as the old man went on.

'The Maneschi family is perhaps the simplest. They have been here for as long as we have and have always resented the fact that the farmers have always voted for us to act as their guardians. This has been a constant source of discontent for every generation. The family is Italian in origin not French and even the branch that has been here for so long has always maintained its Italian connections rather strongly. There were also some rumours about their wartime allegiances. You will recall that Italy was an occupying power here in the south. They played a very minor part compared to the Germans and were stationed just really between Marseille and the Italian border. But the memory of these things tends to linger as you know without any real justification. That, as much as anything, explains the reluctance of many local farmers to trust them now. I don't think there is anything personal against us particularly.'

'The Baroncelli family is much the same but the resentment is of a slightly different origin. Folco de Baroncelli-Javon, despite the name suggesting Italian origins again was, in fact, pretty fundamentally local. His parents came from Avignon and the family had originally settled in Provence at about the same time as ours did in the fifteenth century. At the beginning of the twentieth century Folco became a farmer as well as a writer and moved to Stes. Maries de la Mer and started raising bulls and became more and more interested in local folklore and tradition. He helped organise the Courses Camargaise and well at the Nacioun Gardiano, the brotherhood of *gardiens* and the Félibrige, the society founded with Frederic Mistral to perpetuate of Provençale language. In fact it's possible to think that much of the present-day external appearance of Camargue that we offer to tourists and visitors is due to him and his family. However, from the beginning many farmers objected to this and still do. They felt it was an intrusion into their lives and it certainly offered a picture of local life as a sort of tourist attraction which many though was cheap and undignified. Actually, Baroncelli wanted to be seen as the king of the Camargue and made this a very public ambition and in general he was not completely popular because of this. After the war the family continued to farm in a small way but pursued a much less public profile. I invited them for historical reasons really. I certainly don't think that there is sufficient animosity left to be significant. Indeed, this local animosity has diminished as presenting a somewhat folksy view of life here to tourists and become an important source of income. People have got used to it, as they do, and tourism is now an important part of our income. There may have been some residual historical jealousy but nothing very significant. I feel.'

Smith smiled inwardly at the thought that tourism was very far indeed from the Aubanet range of business interests, but he left the thought unsaid. Emile took a long sip from his wine as if he was gathering strength for something more difficult.

'The Cordiez family is a slightly different kettle of fish. Franco Cordiez is a small farmer and, in my view, a more than unpleasant man. The family have been like this for generations, apparently. The exception is the son Robert whose education into the profession of a bullfighter has led him into a wider group of people which has been much to his benefit. His father has always been one of those people with a chip on his shoulder and I am sure that I'm not the only person who has difficulties with him. I invited him primarily because of the son. This is a big year for him and his family and perhaps it might serve to bring the family in closer to us all. However, to be frank I can't imagine any real personal animosity towards our family; just a general discontent aimed at the world in general, I think.'

The old man had clearly come to the end of his monologue. Their table was cleared with no one electing to have a pudding and they simply sat on each with a glass of wine to hand.

'So,' said Emile. 'Are you able to tell us what all this is about? Something is clearly going on and it seems to involve us. I know you usually like to do things very much on your own, but I think we have a right to know.'

He was, of course, perfectly right and Smith knew it was the right time to tell them both what he thought might going on.

'Well, of course, you're right but I can't really make much sense of it. In fact, I not really sure if there really is anything to understand. You know, of course, that Girondou's great rival in the south of France is Sebastien Moroni whose power base is in Toulouse.'

Emile nodded.

'Yes, of course. But rather like Girondou and probably for similar reasons he has tended to leave us alone. '

205

'Well,' Smith continued, 'In the last week or two either Moroni or some of his people have been seen paying house calls on a number of your inhabitants; mostly farmers but not exclusively. The only common factor seems to be that the people visited are some distance away from your closest friends. We have just talked about four of the more typical but there are others. There is obviously something going on, but nobody seems to know what. Moroni's timing so near the handover of things on the Camargue to Martine might just be coincidental. It might not. If you add to that the fact that Girondou who one would have thought would be most interested in what his rival is doing edging nearer his own patch is present occupied by an extreme of melancholia together with the rest of his immediate family. Certainly, I can't get any information out of him. It has been suggested, not without some justification, I might add, that it is none of my business. I don't suppose if either of you have a clue as to what is going on?'

There was a respectful pause while they waited in vain for a contribution from Emile but then it was Martine who answered.

'Well I can't guess what is happening with the Girondou family, of course. They seemed perfectly fine at our lunch. But I could offer a few suggestions as to why either Girondou or Moroni might be interested in getting a foothold in the Camargue. The Camargue is a huge open space of more than 900 square kilometres with very few roads and is notoriously difficult for getting around. It is also very difficult indeed to police. If I ran the sort of enterprise that needed

206

secret places to meet or hide things it would be ideal. If I needed some seventy odd kilometres of unobserved and un-policeable deserted coastline import or export anything from drugs to nuclear weapons as you will remember all too well, it is ideal. A perfect spot for a criminal enterprise I would have thought. Ever since the end of the Second World War there have been attempts to annex the Camargue by Moroni or Girondou or their predecessors and we have always resisted them. Everyone here knows that my father would never allow any of this business to get a hold here, nor will I, and so I would have thought that anyone who opposed my father would be a natural ally for Mr. Moroni. Perhaps he thinks there would be enough uncertainty around because of my take over to offer an opportunity. The fact that we have at last been able to form a good relationship with Girondou, largely through your efforts, Peter, means that Moroni is now our only significant enemy. If, as you say, something has happened in Girondou's life which weakens him so dramatically then this is obviously a good time for him to make an attempt.'

Both men knew that she was right. The whole Mediterranean coastline had become increasingly populated and policed and criminal access was getting to be impossible for much of it. Access to the secure areas of the Camargue would be highly valued. Especially so if Girondou's empire could be added as the same time.

'OK,' said Smith. 'If this is some sort of threat to the residents of the Camargue then clearly, we need more information about what is going on. We need to find someone who has been approached by

Moroni but who would not necessarily support him. At the moment we don't know how many there might be. I just picked four who we spotted as being potential malcontents at your lunch and who we knew had received visits. There are almost certainly others.'

There was a general pause while people considered the options. It was always difficult to plan for something that hadn't happened yet and might not be happening at all. In the end it was Smith.

'I think at the moment we just have to be vigilant. Keep an eye out. As usual the Camargue farmers will know what is going on, and perhaps, Martine, you can enlist some of the ones who are loyal friends and are closer to you and Emile to help keep an eye out for unwelcome visitors and who they might be visiting.

Chapter 13: Confessions of Alliance

The farm was nothing to write home about. It had never been. It was one of the smaller ones of those bordered the lagoon. It was buried deep in the salt marshes with a corresponding lack of fertile arable land. Making a living had always been a struggle. A few pigs, some grass land to fatten other people's livestock. Cordiez had long had to rent himself out as a labourer on other people's farms. His own wasn't enough to earn a living. His wife had left him; unable to cope with his continuous bad moods. Passing tourists ogled the views over the farm. They see the glistening waters, the little banks and mounds, glittering little pools of water, tufts of spikey grass. They see the pink flamingos, little bulls grazing gently in fields, pines bending in the wind, scudding hawks and clouds. No-one looked around to see anything you could actually live off. Tourists never did. Like all tourists they were on holiday and imagine that everyone else is too. They just took their photographs, felt the heat and went back to their big houses and their credit cards in Stuttgart or Manchester, in Cincinnati or Adelaide. All his life he had had nowhere to go and no money to go there. But now, finally there was a glimmer of hope with this man from Toulouse.

It had been the usual hard day. He had been working off the farm for much of it so now he was home he had to try catch up with his own work. It made for a very long day indeed. His late supper was the remains of a stew that he had made some days ago. He wasn't particularly interested in food and certainly couldn't care whether or not he ate the same thing for days on end. The stew had been a big one and had lasted him a good few days. Tonight was the last of it. However, his son was coming home later to stay for a few days and that would mean not only another pair of hands around the farm but also a new and possibly different stew. The boy was quite a good cook and he usually made some stuff for the fridge and the freezer when he was at home. He was very conscientious in his visits and in spite of a busy schedule he came home regularly especially when he was fighting far away, and his father could afford neither the time nor the money to come to watch. They would sit together, and he would describe the fights in detail. His father was intensely proud of his son and now that his wife had left him, these visits were some of the few thing left that gave him pleasure. However tonight he had news of his own as well.

So, it was late when the two had eaten and sat together at the table to talk. Between them there stood a new, unopened bottle of whisky and two glasses.

'Gosh, dad. Have we come into an inheritance we didn't know about?'

'Can't think what you mean.' said the older man in a pretend rough voice. 'Can't I celebrate my famous son coming home if I want to?'

Robert laughed.

'Of course, you can, dad. I just don't often see a bottle of whisky in the house. That's all.'

'Well I have had a little bit of good luck recently. But first have a glass and tell me your news first.'

'Well the fight in Istres went well but you know that as you were there. It looks like I might get a fight in Nimes next Easter after the *alternative* is past. I think that I might be cheaper than many of the others, I suppose. We know that they are struggling a bit there.'

'They should pay the proper rate like everyone else. They know that they'll sell a lot more tickets with a local lad fighting. Don't let them off, if I was you.'

As usual the older man was right, so his son just smiled before coming back to the mysterious surprise.

'Come on, now, dad. Where is all this new cash coming from?'

'Well, I met this guy from Toulouse who offered me a business proposition; a well-paid one at that.'

'And?' Robert urged.

'Well, it isn't exactly completely legal.'

The son laughed again.

'Very little that makes any money for the likes of us is these days.'

'They want to use a bit of our beach for a spot of smuggling and they are willing to pay handsomely for access to it through our land.'

'Just access. I mean they don't want us to do anything. I mean, if they get caught, we can just deny we knew anything about it?'

Franco nodded.

'That's just about the size of it. They do all the work. They tell us, of course, when it's going to happen, so we don't barge in on anything by mistake and they pay us each time they have a shipment'

The son shrugged.

'Sounds OK to me. How much are they paying?'

'Oh, we haven't agreed that completely yet but somewhere in the region of four or five thousand euros a time.'

'Wow, that's a lot of money to pay us for doing nothing! What sort of thing are they smuggling?'

The father had anticipated this question and had tried to decide how to answer it. He knew that if he told the truth the boy would certainly not like it at all. He decided to try being vague.

'Well they probably don't want to go into too much detail, but I think it's a mixture of things. The usual, I suppose.'

It was the lack of precision that caught the youth's attention. It was very unlike his father. He would certainly have found out exactly what was going to happen and how much he was going to be paid.

'Come on, dad. You would never negotiate like this. You would have got it all nailed down otherwise there wouldn't have been a deal.'

He knew that he couldn't get away with lying to his son. He knew him too well. Perhaps he could get away with a little white lie.

'Well its five thousand a trip for ordinary stuff; fags booze, drugs and so on. But they might be a few special shipments where we would be paid, er, double.'

'What? Ten thousand! For what. What could possibly be worth that much just to use our farm that borders on the beach?'

The father's voice became much more uncertain.

'Well they did say that from time to time they might be bringing in people.'

'People? What sort of people?' the boy was getting insistent.

'Oh, I don't know.' He replied, his voice getting angry. 'How the fuck should I know.'

The boy went silent for a moment while he worked it out. His father just downed his whisky in a single gulp and quickly poured himself another.

'Fuck, dad. It's refugees, isn't it? These people are smuggling illegal immigrants. I read about some of this further west along the coast, but they kept on getting caught. They've come here for a bit of peace and quiet for their filthy trade. That's it, isn't it?'

The father just nodded and took another drink.

'No, dad. You can't do this. Its one thing standing by and getting paid a few euros for closing you eyes to a bit of booze or even drugs. But this is very different. If you get caught, you'll be in jail for the rest of your life.'

Cordiez senior was immediately on the defensive.

'I don't see anything wrong with it.' He spat out angrily. You could say we are giving them a chance of a new home. They're fucking refugees for Christ's sake. They must be fleeing from something.'

'Don't tell me this is all philanthropy, dad. You and your new friends are just cashing in on other people's misery. Good God, man. If you get caught and you inevitably will you know how sharp-eyed people are around here, the people here would never forgive you. They'd chuck you off the Camargue.'

The old man rounded on him.

'And what favours has the bloody Camargue done for me in my life? Tell me that. Fuck all. This is a good opportunity to get some serious money and get out of this fucking place just like your mother did.'

Robert knew that this was getting out of hand. He also knew that it was his father that his mother had left not the Camargue but saying that would just escalate matters. He adopted a more conciliatory tone in the hope of calming his father down; never an easy task at the best of times.

'Look, dad. I really think you should think again. Please. I don't think it is a good idea.'

But Franco Cordiez had his temper up and was not for persuading.

'This is my business. It's also my farm and my life and I'll do whatever I want to. You have no idea how shit life is here, day in day out. You go gallivanting all over the place killing your precious bulls and hob-nobbing with all those stuck-up pricks that you call friends. You wait until something goes wrong. You see how long they stay around. This is my first chance to make some proper money and I am going to do it whether you like it or not. If you don't like it, you can just piss off back to your bull friends or to you mother and leave me alone. Now if you don't mind you can keep your opinions and your advice to yourself. I've got some farming to do.'

With that he got up, took the whisky bottle by the neck and went out into the night, slamming the door behind him. Robert sat for a long time at the table alone just staring into space his whisky remaining on the table in front of him, untouched.

Chapter 14: La Chassagnette

He was more intrigued than anything else. He certainly had no reason to be particularly concerned. He knew better than most people how good he was at taking care of himself. He also was slightly amused to see that however good this person was – and he had to admit the person really was quite good – his experience did not extend to avoiding the ill-advised strategy of following someone who was walking slowly over farmland on his horse with a dog in tow. Even taking account of the fact that Arthur was what is known in doggy circles as sighthound: a dog whose instinct was to hunt things he could see rather than those he could smell. Arthur's sense of smell was in perfectly good order particularly when in even remote range of one of a variety of Arles restaurant kitchens with which he was increasingly familiar. He could pick up the scent of Boeuf en Daube from a distance that would do credit to a Labrador.

Like his master, Arthur showed no particular signs of anxiety. He had also decided that this was at worst a curiosity and certainly not something worth getting all het up about. His mind was still set on the possibility of a hare of which there were still a few to be chased in spite of the high heat of the day. The memory of a recent triumph was still fresh in his doggy memory. They were passing over one of the dryer parts of Emile Aubanet's manade and it was there that he had occasionally found one. To him it was a small annoyance; an irritant, part of whose irritation was that it was not passing. The bloody man had been there ever since they had saddled the horse and set off.

While there had been many and various times in Smith's past when he had been followed, he had to admit that it had never been when he was on the back of a horse. It was a novel experience. It could, of course, be someone playing a game of some kind; a joke. Deveraux was perfectly capable of such familiarity, but he was, Smith knew, already occupied with a trip to the rather cumbersomely named new Museum of European and Mediterranean Civilisations in Marseille with his new girlfriend. In any case had it been Deveraux following neither he nor Arthur would have known. Deveraux was altogether too good at that sort of thing. Jean-Marie might have used him for practice without telling him. He had a habit of doing this from time to time and Smith had always approved. It reminded him of the relations between Inspector Clouseau and his faithful manservant Kato although he would never have dreamt of telling Jean-Marie or even Martine. Taking the piss out of the French was something to be avoided he had found and Peter Sellars had given a masterly performance at that in the film. However, Jean-Marie was escorting Marine to some business meeting in Nîmes.

It goes without saying that you usually tail someone when you want to know where they are going. And for this to be important enough to invest a number of tedious hours of your life, the person you are following has to be going somewhere important. Smith was going to lunch; on his own and that, he thought, didn't really count as important. It might have been to him but he couldn't really see why it might be important to anyone else. He wasn't meeting anyone of any importance either. In fact, he was going to a local rather famous restaurant called La Chassagnette and had decided to ride there by a relatively direct route across country rather than arrive by car with all the restrictions on alcohol consumption that that usually requires. Most of the route was either over Aubanet farmland or that of its neighbours and by now he was well known by known to all of them. The restaurant had become rather grand since he was last there and even grander since it opened some twenty-five years ago. The food had recently gained a single Michelin Rosette or "star" as it is consistently referred to in spite of the symbol in their famous Red Guide not looking remotely like a star. He was having to fend for himself for lunch so he thought he might give it a go. Given the restaurant's importance – self-importance, Smith wondered – he did call ahead to book and to make sure they had somewhere to accommodate his horse while he ate. The person who answered the phone sounded less than enthusiastic although Smith could not decide whether that was because of the horse or because he only wanted a booking for one. The attitude changed very quickly when he decided to drop the name Aubanet into the conversation. Yes, monsieur, both you and your horse will be very welcome. He hadn't the courage to tell them about Arthur. However, the trip was a solitary one for lunch and for the life of him he couldn't see why he should be followed to that.

It did occur to him that there might be another reason for someone following him and that was the person just wanted to talk. It was an unorthodox approach to be sure, but one never knows. Looking at his watch he saw that, having left a generous amount of time for his trip, he was running about fifteen minutes early. In a gesture that startled both his slowly ambling horse and Arthur trotting along at their feet he swung around and stared to re-trace his steps at a brisk trot. It was not before long that he came across a rather startled man on a grey Camargue horse.

'Monsieur Cordiez, good morning.'

The man recovered quite quickly. It was the young bullfighter to whom he had been introduced at Gimeaux. He tipped his hat.

'Good morning, Monsieur Smith. A lovely day to be out for a ride.'

'Yes, it is. Something of a coincidence that we seem to be going in the same direction. Are you heading for La Chassagnette for lunch as well?'

The man smiled.

'Unfortunately, no Monsieur. It's a little out of my price range.'

'Well perhaps after your upcoming *alternativa* perhaps things might change.'

'Perhaps, Monsieur, perhaps.'

Smith was conscious of the time and wanted to push things along somewhat.

'So why were you following me?'

'Monsieur, I wanted to talk to you.'

'Well this is a slightly unorthodox way of going about it I must say. However, what do you want to say to me.'

The young man shook his head a touch angrily.

'I need to speak with you in private, Monsieur Smith.'

'Well, why don't you join me for lunch. Don't worry it will be my treat.'

'Much as I would like to, Monsieur, there are too many people here in the Camargue who would recognise me.'

Smith thought for a while. Martine would be away until late tonight and he had intended to go into town for a game of drafts with his new friend Marcel Carbot. The old man had become a fierce opponent at the game since they had met a year or so ago and he much enjoyed his games. He would normally then stay at home as the games tended to go on until late.

'Look, I will be staying in my house on the Place de la Major tonight. Perhaps you can come there after dark. Say about eleven,'

The young man thought for a moment and then agreed.

'Good. I'll see you tonight. Now perhaps if you will excuse me I have a lunch to get to and Arthur will certainly appreciate not having to look over his shoulder all the time.'

'He is a fine hound, Monsieur,' he said as he wheeled his horse away.

'Yes. I know.' replied Smith as he did the same.

The Aubanet factor was apparent as soon as he got to the restaurant. He was greeted by two young men dressed smartly in dark trousers and white shirts. One took the horse away around the back of the extensive range of old farm buildings to be put into a shelter for an hour or two. The other man looked slightly uncertainly at Arthur, a glance that Smith intercepted. Most French restaurants are perfectly happy to admit dogs but those with pretentions to greatness and well-heeled American clientele often were reluctant. There seems to be a well-established convention that dogs are dirtier than humans. It was a convention that Smith had always found to be precisely the opposite of the truth. Smith indicated a preference for eating outside and that he would like a table next to the house towards the end of a long bamboo shade that ran the length of the main building. There were a number of long tables each seating up to fifteen or twenty as well as smaller ones dotted around. The place was obviously set up for groups. A number were already occupied by early diners and he noted a considerable interest at his somewhat unorthodox arrival. He felt a certain frisson of pride to see how easily a fine Camargue grey horse could upstage a car park full of Porsches and Ferraris.

'Would this be satisfactory, Monsieur Smith,' said the man indicating a table near to the wall of the house.

Smith appreciated the fact that instead of being offered a tiny table for two at which solitary diners in fashionable restaurants were usually seated, he had been offered a table for four with more than adequate space underneath had Arthur been the sort of dog who likes lying under tables. The young man smiled at him with a conspiratorial gleam in his eye.

'It's where my dog likes to sit when I eat, Sir,' he offered by way of explanation as he walked away.

Smith looked around and his memory went back to when the young chef Jean Luc Rabanel saw the possibilities in a large vegetable garden and established a reputation for good food and wonderful vegetables. He was a good chef, soon to become a very good one and after number of years Maître Jean Luc decided that the 15km required of his clients to drive into the Camargue was limited his business and transferred into the town in pursuit of the gold card trade. His successor was now in charge and the restaurant had just won its first Michelin rosette. This, to Smith, usually means an increase in the chef's self-absorption often to the detriment of giving people a good meal.

The waiter had brought a menu and Smith saw that there were various fixed menus based on a number of different courses in succession, each with a wine chosen by the house to suit the food. Alarm bells were beginning to sound in Smith's mind, but he had also heard that the food was remarkably good, so he decided to put some long-held prejudices aside and trust his hosts. Judging the price, it had better be good. However, first things first. After a suitably long delay before another waiter took any notice of him, he finally got one to his tableside.

'I shall have the full menu découverte please but first I would like a large glass of very cold Crémant. Can you manage that? Oh, and a bowl of water for my dog.'

The waiter looked somewhat stunned at the departure from what he was obviously expecting. So much so that Smith had to ask.

'Have I asked for something that is impossible?'

'Er ... no, Monsieur.'

He clearly didn't regard getting bowls of water for thirsty dogs to be part of his responsibilities as a waiter in a Michelin starred restaurant. A bit beneath him, Smith thought.

'Good, then I would like the Crémant and the water immediately, please. I came here by horse and both I and my dog are extremely thirsty. If you don't have a large glass for the Crémant, I will have two of your usual -sized ones. Thank you.'

The man left looking more than a little bothered.

Smith remembered that almost throughout its life the restaurant had been known for its own vegetable garden and most of its menus had reflected this over the years. It was one of the first local restaurants to go "bio", something for what Smith had little time or respect, and vegetarian, something equally that Smith neither understood or cherished. However, he noted from the menu that apart from a separate vegetarian menu, something that would not delay him unduly, he saw that the main menu page showed an interesting departure from the norm. Usually the description of a main course of, say, lamb would start with some rather exotically-named lamb

223

preparation that might or might include a sauce, then go on to list the vegetables that would accompany it with the long-winded description finishing with whatever the chef had decided to heap on the side of the plate.

On this occasion the order of events had been re-arranged and the vegetables held sway. Thus, long and detailed descriptions of vegetable preparation, cooking and embellishment were followed by a brief coda that mentioned the meat or fish very briefly and seemingly rather grudgingly. Thus, references to tuna, bream and pigeon were buried in detail of three of the five main courses, each surrounded by plethora of vegetables dressed up as if they were prima ballerinas. These three courses were separated by two further vegetable-only courses where the stage was left open only to the ballerinas. All this was introduced by a fully vegetable starter / amuse-bouche. Creations based on fruit formed the two-course pudding. No wines were mentioned but a "wine flight" was offered, chosen by the house as, presumably, the client was incapable of doing such a thing.

This didn't auger well in Smith's view but he forced himself to remain faithful to his resolution and see what came.

The first thing that happened was his original waiter, the one with the dog, was the one who bought a large wine glass of crémant and a dog bowl full of water. Clearly the other waiter had been somewhat disconcerted by Smith telling him what he wanted rather than the waiter telling his customer what he was getting. It was a distinction that Smith had often come across in "better" restaurants.

Both man and dog drank deeply of their respective drinks and settled in to wait for the theatre to begin.

Indeed, it was a wait. Smith spent time surveying the restaurant and his fellow diners most of whom were like him, waiting for food. After a while the second waiter appeared with a small plate of beautiful arranged - perhaps poured would be a better way of describing it - velouté of bitter herbs, fondant of kohlrabi, and leaf foam. Smith found his heart sinking. Clearly teeth were not necessary for this meal. If that was not bad enough the young waiter started to recite what was an obligatory lecture on what he had just placed in front of his customer and why he should be in awe of it. Here Smith drew the line.

'Young man. Please bring me my food without the lectures. If I have any questions about the food, I will ask. All right?'

The young man in question looked slightly desperate and left unable to reconcile a head chef who insisted on his clients being made to understand how and why his food was so wonderful and a client who just wanted to be left alone to eat. When the course was due to be changed he noted that the burden of waiting on his particular table had been passed to Smith's original waiter which resulted in the meal going much faster than those around him and with much less controversy. The courses came and went, each looking more beautiful than its predecessor and each defying Smith's attempts to find the actual fish or the meat when it was buried in a baroque entanglement of exotic vegetables. He found himself unable to distinguish the myriad of different "taste sensations" that littered his plate. Much to his surprise he remembered his school days and the ability of the school kitchen to render green vegetables to a tasteless mush. At least you knew what was what. Even the first of the two puddings had the potentially straightforward taste of and apple *mille feuille* submerged under an explosion of rice pudding flavoured with a strong lemon and basil ice cream. Poor old apple, Smith thought. Apple pie in any of its somewhat simpler forms was one of his favourite puddings and it was a dish at which the French were pre-eminent. Small glasses of wine also came and went with each course. Each was completely unremarkable and one or two were actually unpleasant. Smith left at least half of them untouched after an initial tasting.

He called for his bill. When it arrived it was slightly over one hundred Euros and even paying in cash left the restaurant at a loss. Obviously so few people used real money any more that there was a difficult scramble while someone located some change. Yet another member of a staff that seemed to outnumber the customers arrived at his table and asked how he had enjoyed his meal. Conscious of the fact that he had mentioned the Aubanet family he smiled bravely and just offered: 'memorable.' It was a verdict that satisfied them both.

As he just got up to leave a large American got up from the table beside him and approached.

'Please excuse my intrusion, Sir but I wonder if you could answer a question for me?'

Smith smiled in a friendly way at this unexpected contact.

226

'Of course. How can I help you?'

'Well, my wife and I,' he started gesturing at an elegant but rather pink-faced lady still seated at the table, dressed in a rather gratifyingly old-fashioned floral cotton dress and wide-brimmed hat. 'Like you we have been eating our lunch but unlike you whenever we want to attract the attention of a waiter for some reason we have failed. They all vanish for hours on end and when they appear, other than to change the plates and give us another lecture, they all seem to be looking in the wrong direction. You, on the other hand, seem to have found a waiter who comes when you want and does not give you any lectures. How did you do it?'

Smith appeared to take that problem seriously.

'I think, monsieur, it might be because I have a dog and I arrived on a horse.'

With that he offered them a charming smile and turned away, Arthur at his feet, with a gay "bon appetit" thrown carelessly over his shoulder.

He reclaimed his horse and gave his waiter who had escorted him around the building to the stables a large tip.

'Thank you for your help. I appreciate it.'

'I am delighted to have been of assistance, Monsieur Smith. Please give my best wishes to Madame Aubanet. She and her father are friends of my parents. My family farms near Salin de Badon. My name is Roger Dumaine. I am sorry that your meal was not to your taste.'

227

Smith looked down at the young man from his horse. Arthur had been slipped a few morsels on the way to the stables and now clearly had a new best friend as he was standing next to him looking up expectantly.

'Please don't worry, Roger. I am probably not the sort of client that the chef is looking for, in any case.'

'Next time you go for a walk, why not try coming in our direction? We still have a few Camargue hares on the farm and my mother cooks better than this,' he said with a casual jerk of his head back towards the restaurant.

Smith smiled and nodded his thanks as he rode away.

'Perhaps I will, young man. Perhaps I will.'

It was about four in the afternoon before he got back and found that Emile was out and Martine hadn't returned. So, conscious of his draughts game later that evening, he put himself and Arthur into his battered Peugeot and made his way back into town and to his house.

They played the Polish Game on a board ten by ten squares with twenty pieces each over the dark squares only. In fact, the Polish game is the most widely used throughout Europe including Poland in spite of the fact that it is called French Checkers in that country. They played to the normal rules whereby pieces can move and capture backwards as well as forwards and captures must be made if they are possible even if they are to the disadvantage of the player. Pieces that are not taken when they should be are "huffed" off the board. Pieces

228

can be "Queened" on arrival at the opposing back row even if they have not taken an opposing piece to get there. Queens can slide over any number of squares.

Occasionally to ring the changes the two occasionally played an additional variation popular in Turkey and Friesland that allows Queens to move orthogonally as well as diagonally.

The two had been playing off and on since Smith had helped out in solving the mystery of the murder of Marcel Carbot's grandson on the beach at Beauduc a year or so ago. Their games were hard fought, serious affairs. Polish Draughts was a serious game in France; that country having held the world championship many times during the early years of the championship and the old man was a dogged opponent. Smith knew that he was the worse player by some distance. But rather in the same way that he tended to win more games on chess that he should against Gentry by being unorthodox, he managed just to hold his own against Carbot by breaking rules rather more than by playing to them. The difference being that while Gentry was always mildly annoyed at Smith's flouting of usual chess conventions to win, his French opponent was highly amused when defeated by similarly unconventional tactics.

Carbot also enjoyed a chat so it wasn't long before Smith asked:

'Do you know, by any chance, the family Cordiez, Marcel. I think they farm somewhere near Salin de Badon?

Carbot took his time before replying. He was moving one of his pieces and that merited a considerable amount of contemplation. However, once the move was made he was perfectly happy to chat, presumably in the hope that it might break his opponent's concentration.

'Of course,' came the unequivocal reply. 'Everyone knows that family.'

His tone was less than warm but Smith thought it best to wait.

'Don't get me wrong. The children are fine. The young Robert is a delightful young man and a very talented bullfighter. But that's probably due to the fact that he has spent a lot of time during his education and training in the company of others. In any case you don't get very far in the world of bull fighting if you are unpleasant and *mal élevé*. The father is a pain in the arse, just like his father was.'

'In what way, Marcel?'

'Well, nothing specific. It's just that he never has a good word to say to anyone. He's always complaining about something; criticising others and generally being miserable. As a result he's not particularly liked in the area. People just tend to avoid him. As I said, his father was just the same.'

'But reliable. Nothing particularly odd about him other than not being particularly nice.'

The old man shrugged. He obviously wasn't particularly interested in the Cordiez family. Smith went back to the game and had to work quite hard at holding his own. His opponent had advanced his central pieces in the conventional way and had built a position that left his own four home pieces still on their squares. His opponent was also manoeuvring for some pair trapping to achieve this. It was a favourite tactic. Without a few creative sacrifices, Smith could see that he could be a Queen or two down very soon. This was a significant danger given their habit of using the orthogonals as well as diagonals for Queens. However, Smith was on a slightly different mission this evening than just to avoid defeat at the hands of this old man. Carbot knew a lot about what was going on in the countryside. Like Madame Durand, he kept in touch. His next question was rather more direct.

'Have you heard anything about a man from Toulouse called Moroni, I think he's called. He seems to be poking around the Camargue?'

There was a brief shake of the head. Carbot was concentrating on the game.

'No. I can't say I have but I can ask around if you like.'

The game progressed, and the old man was doing most of the winning. However instead of his normal attacking strategy Smith found himself out-manoeuvred in rather an elegant blocking strategy. A traditional but somewhat underused method of winning at draughts is to get your opponent into a position that he cannot move. Smith could see it coming but refused to ask for a draw. Even then he was pretty sure that the writing was on the wall.

'Well done, you crafty old bugger. That blocking thing is something I've never been able to master.'

The old man was obviously pleased.

'Thank you for the game, Peter. It was nice to see you again. I'll ask around for you about this man Moroni, but I don't hold out much hope. My connections with the Camargue as less now since Jean-Claude was killed.'

His glance went up to the mantel piece where photos of both his son and his grandson in military uniform were mounted silver frames each decorated with a diagonal black ribbon and topped by a line of medals.

'You are certainly not forgotten by the Aubanet family, Marcel.'

The old man's face brightened.

'No. You are quite right. Madame Aubanet comes to see me sometimes. It is always nice to see her.

Robert Cordiez arrived promptly at 11.

'Monsieur Smith. Thank you for seeing me.'

'Well, I hope I can help. Can I offer you something to drink? Wine,? Whisky?'

The man smiled slightly regretfully.

'Unfortunately, just water please. I'm in training.'

'Well,' he said after they had sat down. 'What can I do for you?'

'Monsieur, I want to ask for your help. I know you a little and, of course, I know something of your reputation. I have a family problem that I cannot solve.'

Smith's heart sank. He really didn't want to get involved in this man's family problems even though he was obviously well connected to the Aubanets. The recent events at Gimeaux showed that. He just set himself to be a polite audience and think up some good reason for not getting involved. It didn't take long for him to change his mind as the young man spoke.

'My father, Franco Cordiez, seems to have made an agreement to help a man from Toulouse called Sebastien Moroni to import illegal immigrants using our family farm which borders onto the Beauduc beach as a landing place. I think that they have offered him a lot of money to turn a blind eye to this when they are landing these unfortunate people.'

A lot of things fitted together in Smith's mind very quickly. However, he tried to find out more.

'I assume that you are sure?'

The young man nodded.

'Perfectly.'

'Have you told anyone else about this?'

'No.'

'And what do you want me to do for you.'

Robert Cordiez looked very uncomfortable.'

'I want you to stop him.'

Smith didn't like to suggest that there were a wide variety of ways of stopping this little plan but, he had to admit to himself, not too many that would allow the son to remain anonymous.

'Presumably you have talked with your father and tried to dissuade him?'

'Yes, but he is determined to go on.'

'I also assume,' said Smith, 'they're offering a large amount of money.'

'A total of twenty thousand per shipment if it is successful.'

Smith whistled to himself. That was more than enough to tempt the hand of an unsuccessful Camargue farmer.

'Have any of these a landings taken place?'

'I don't think so. Not yet.'

There was a silence while Smith stopped to think. This certainly explained Moroni's trips to the Camargue. He would certainly be more likely to recruit people who were anti-Aubanet. They would keep quiet. The project had to be stopped, of course, and that should be a responsibility for Martine not him. But he was concerned about the boy.

'Robert. If I get this stopped, then sooner or later your father will find out that it was you who let the information out. To date you are the only person he had told. Are you prepared for the consequences of that?'

'I thought a lot about that before I came to see you, Monsieur Smith,' replied the man rather sadly. 'My father is a difficult man but he's not a really dishonest one. I am pretty sure that the money turned his head. Actually, I have a good relationship with him. I am pretty

234

sure that will survive even though he will be mightily pissed off for a while. He's already calmed down after our first argument about this.'

'OK. Are you prepared to tell me when there something is scheduled?'

'Yes.'

'All right. We obviously have to wait for there to be an attempted landing to do anything. Mere threats, I suspect, won't do anything. If we can stop one while it is in progress than Moroni might take the hint and give the whole idea up or at least take the grubby little game elsewhere. I need to talk to some people but as soon as you hear any details then let me know and we'll do something about it. Let's exchange mobile numbers and you can text me when you have any news.'

Cordiez got up to go and offered his hand.

'Thank you, Mr Smith. I know my father is not an easy man to get on with, but he has very few friends and certainly none that would help him in this. As I said, I don't think he is a bad man. He is just a bit misguided and is easy prey for people like this man Moroni. I would be very grateful for your help.'

With that he left leaving Smith with a good deal to think about.

Chapter 15: Sharing the Secret

He had arrived at the Mas des Saintes in time for lunch. It was just the three of them, Martine, Emile and himself sitting around one end of the long kitchen farm table. The cook had the night off and he wasn't sure who had done the cooking. They had a cold pistou soup followed by pissaladière, followed by cheese and fruit. It was all washed down with the usual un-labled bottles of wine from the Aubanet vineyards along the lowest banks of the Rhône. He didn't like to tell them that his preference was for hot rather than cold soup, but he had to admit that at least this was thick enough not to see through. He drew the line at soup when you could see the bottom of the bowl. But the vegetables were done perfectly and the pistou had obviously been made less than an hour ago. It was delicious. The pissaladière was the traditional onion tart from Nice with a good thick, politically incorrect pastry made of bread dough and topped with anchovies, olives and slightly caramelised sweet onions.

He kept silent while Martine brought him up to speed with the remainder of her visits around the Camargue. She did seem to have visited most people and, with a few exceptions, it had all gone well. He was relieved that it the grand tour seemed to be over. From a security point of view, it had been a nightmare, but he was forced to admit that this was a little bit of the world where she would be as safe as anywhere. For the last few days Emile had not accompanied her. He was in a hurry to try to retire to the joys of his farm and the tending of his beloved bulls although he too had been out most nights, invited personally to the houses of some of his closest friends and allies. These were families who for a number of generations had made up the core of his support; loyal families who had both benefited and contributed to the success and survival of the farmers of the Camargue. They just wanted to say their own personal thanks to him, quietly and in private. When they both had finished, he felt that it was time to add his unwelcome news to the party.

'I'm afraid that I've found out what these mysterious visits from the bad man from Toulouse are all about and you were right, Martine. Sebastien Moroni is recruiting people to help with his plan to use the Camargue beaches for smuggling illegal immigrants. He has been talking with people who, for some reason or another, aren't happy with the status quo and those who have farms that give some sort of access to the stretch of beach between Piemanson and Stes Maries and between Stes. Maries and Le Grau du Roi. Now I don't know all the people he has been talking to but I do know one; Franco Cordiez.

Suddenly Emile Aubanet looked much more than his seventy-five years. He just sat back in his chair and sighed deeply gently shaking his head.

'I thought it would come to this sooner or later. Our beaches have been used by smugglers for centuries. Martine is right. They are ideal. Somehow, we look at the past with a certain amount of romance. Centuries ago it was spices and silks from the east, then it was tobacco and spirits. During the war we got people in and out that way. Many of the British OSS people were regularly landed from submarines off the coast and by fishing boats and we sent escapees out that way too. The Germans found it impossible to police the area. You need to have been born here to know your way around. All this, as you point out, Peter needs the support of the farmers. In fact, it has often been the farmers that have mainly done the smuggling. More recently, however, people have tried to bring drugs in here from time to time but we have been able to stop most of that. For some reason here, at least, drugs are a dirty business, much more so than cigarettes or booze, and there is little support for the idea. Now, I suppose it is refugees. God only know what it will be next. I reckon we'll just have to stop it ourselves like we have always done.'

Martine turned to Smith.

'What do you think we should do, Peter. We obviously can't let this happen. It is vile and disgusting to trade on people's misery.'

'I think you have to understand one thing before making any plans at all. Things have changed because life has changed. There is obviously a big difference between a small amount of contraband moving into the Camargue two hundred years ago and what is going on now. Then it could be regarded almost as a sport, playing games of cat and mouse with revenue men who were trying to collect the taxes due rather than anything else. These days with drugs and now people smuggling not only are the financial stakes so much higher, but the people involved are very, very different. Men like Moroni are playing for huge stakes; millions and they will happily kill anyone who gets in their way. He doesn't do business by talking to people. He does business by sticking a sub-machine gun into their faces and pulling the trigger if they don't do what he wants. With respect, this is no longer a problem that a few principled farmers can solve. Men like Moroni can afford to pay people like Cordiez twenty thousand dollars every time they land a group of refugees and all Cordiez has to do is give them free passage across his land. He doesn't even have to do anything; just look the other way or, at most, guide them away from the beach and the roads. This is a vast sum for a man like Cordiez. In a year he could become one of the richest men on the Camargue – in terms of cash at least. That is probably all he can see at the moment. I suspect that the morality of the whole thing doesn't bother him in the least. All he can see is the money solving all his problems.'

Again, there was another silence while they took it all in.

'How did you find out, Peter; that it is Cordiez, I mean.'

'His some came to see me. I certainly don't know whether Cordiez is the only one who has signed up to this. There may well be may be others. To be practical, the only people who Moroni would really be interested in are the ones, like Cordiez, whose land is on or near the coast. I don't know how many that would be. Emile can you think how many that it?'

The old man frowned in concentration.

'Well, between Piemanson and Le Grau du Roi, I would imagine about twenty or thirty.'

'And how many of those are doing well enough to resist the offer of a hundred-thousand dollar addition to their income?'

Emile just snorted.

'If you just look at the farms that have no other income, then most of the farmers would be tempted. But especially the ones near the beaches. There is very little arable land there. Much of it consists of salt pools and marshes. Even the land that might be suitable for rice is difficult to get to for planting and harvesting machinery. That's the reason for the popularity of nature reserves. It is a way of getting government money for land that is impossible to use. So the answer to your question is most of them I think.'

'Well, if we are going to plan anything, we have to make some assumptions and by that, I mean take a few guesses.'

'Go on, my dear,' said Martine.

'Well we don't know whether it is just Cordiez who has accepted Moroni's shilling. There may be others. But looking at it from Moroni's point of view he would want to have a trial run. He will have to arrange not just the landing but also getting the immigrants off the beach and inland before anyone sees him. Now no matter what scheme he dreams up to do that, someone is bound to see what is going on. As far as I can see it is impossible to move around these parts without anyone spotting you. Thus, in time Moroni will have to make arrangements with a number of people spread along the coast so he can change the landing point and keep people guessing. How long is this stretch of coast, Emile.'

'Oh, about sixty odd kilometres if you take Stes. Maries out of the picture.'

'Plenty of space to ring the changes. But I do believe that he will have a trial run and I think that Cordiez's farm will be the first. At least, that's my best guess.'

Martine now joined the conversation in earnest. It was as if she understood that her father was reluctant to get too involved in this.

'You seem be suggesting that we have to let at least one of these operations happen before we can try to put a stop to it. Can't we do anything before and stop the suffering for these poor people.'

'I don't see how we can. Unless there is actual evidence that something is happening, we're almost powerless. We can't just go around telling people not to get involved. They would just deny anything we might suggest. If we confronted Moroni, he'd laugh in our faces or do a lot worse. These people play for very high stakes indeed and they won't be put off by much that you or I can threaten. Moroni would prefer to put a bullet in your head rather than waste time talking to you.'

'But if we wait until something happens, then what will we do if, as you say, these men are armed with machine guns? Presumably there will be a lot of them. We can't do anything.'

Smith had to agree but he had the glimmer of an idea.

'There is a way, perhaps. I need to talk to Gentry to set it up. If you give me a little time I'll come back with a suggestion or two. In any case Robert Cordiez said he would tell me if something was being organised. So, we may have a little time to lay plans.'

Lunch was finished, and Martine headed for her office to look after some of the increasing amount of paperwork that seemed to follow her these days. Emile went for his customary afternoon nap and Smith took Arthur for a stroll finishing up sitting in the shade on the veranda on the side of Martine's *cabane*. Having formulated his thoughts, he called Gentry.

He brought his friend up to date.

'Well,' he said at length, 'That certainly explains some of the odd comings and goings in your part of the world. It doesn't shed much light on Girondou of course.'

'To be frank, Gentry, I'm getting less and less concerned with everyday life in the Girondou household. If he decides that he wants my help he can bloody well ask for it. For the moment, I am far more concerned with sorting this little problem out. It seems to have landed right on Martine's doorstep; literally as the Cordiez farm is only twenty or so kilometres from here.'

'Well I agree that you can't do anything much until something happens. The only way dissuade Moroni from pursuing this whole thing is by making sure that you intercept an actual shipment. And the problem with that is there are likely to be a lot of baddies with a lot of guns and a lot of innocent civilians. Sounds a bit complicated to me.'

'I agree. So, I was thinking of a different approach. Perhaps we might persuade the proper authorities to get involved. Sort of delegate the problem to people best equipped to deal with it.'

Gentry smiled to himself.

'That's an alarmingly conventional suggestion coming from you, dear boy. I presume you are thinking of the army or police. Did you have anything more specific in mind?'

'Well actually I have. You remember that chap Messaille?'

'Ah yes, I certainly do.'

'What's he doing now?'

'Hang on.'

There was a silence while Gentry presumably consulted his computer.

'Ah ha. Well since you gave him the Beauduc thing a year ago, his career has had something of a lift. When we last met him, he was the regional commander of the PACA area gendarmerie. Thanks to his success that you handed him in rounding up the terrorists and the rotten eggs in his own GIGN, he is now up there in Paris and is something quite senior in the Operations Directorate of the Gendarmerie National. He's not the boss. That is a full *Général de corps d'armée* - Lieutenant General to you and me. But when we met him he was a colonel. Now he seems to be a *Général de brigade* - a Brigadier General - so he's obviously getting there.'

'Do you still have his private mobile number.'

'Yes I do or if it has changed I can get the new one.'

'And can you check whether he still has that tasty not-so-little Swiss bank account? I want to attract his attention again and although the fact that we have proof of his little nest egg from last year should do the trick, up to date information is always useful.'

'Ah I see what you're getting at. Just hand the whole thing over to, as you put it, the proper authorities.'

'Precisely. And get a few more brownie points with Messaille and his irresistible rise to the top in the process.'

'OK give me half an hour.'

It was twenty minutes only.

'I've got his number and yes, although he changed banks, I've got his new one. It looks as if he still does a few little jobs for your friend Alexei Girondou as there is now a good deal more in it that last year.'

As usual Smith continued to be surprised at Gentry's contacts. How he found this stuff out was beyond him.

'I know the original file on Messaille came from Girondou but give that our friendly gangster seems to have difficulty communicating with his own family let alone us, how the hell did you find out this time.'

'Trade secret, old man. Actually, my contact isn't Girondou. It's his accountant. The unofficial one. He gave me the stuff on Messaille last year and I have been keeping in contact with time to time. Doing the odd favour, here and there. You know how these things work. Perfectly simple.'

'OK clever clogs. I want you to set up another meeting for me with Messaille in two days' time. Same place, same time as the last one.'

'Sure. I'll set it up. Given that he may now be part of the gendarmerie elite in Paris, it may be slightly more difficult to persuade him to come south at such short notice than the last time. He's probably got an appointment with his tailor or polishing his medals or something.'

'Just remind him we know about the new bank account. That should do the trick.'

'You're very probably right. However, given that the man is now a Paris-based General and might be even more reluctant to come than before, I'll have a couple of friends to get there an hour or so before your meeting to make sure that Messaille doesn't try anything clever and brings some chums of his own.'

'Thanks, and please put all this into a briefing for Messaille. I suspect that he doesn't want to stay in my company for any longer than he has to.'

There was a WhatsApp message on his phone. It just said "5 minutes". It was just enough time to get a very cold bottle of crémant and a pair of glasses out of the fridge, take it out onto the veranda and open the bottle. Arthur woke from his slumber in the shade immediately and rushed out into the year to greet the mistress of the house. She kissed him, downed the glass in one and held the empty out

245

to him for a refill. All as she collapsed gracefully into the cane chaise longue.

'God, that tastes good. It was one thing running the business but now I get people bringing complaints and difficulties as well. I tell you I have learned more about the personal lives of half the Camargue families in the last week or two that I have in the whole of my life. Father never told me about any of this.'

Smith laughed.

'Perhaps he thought that you'd turn the job down if he did.'

'You're very probably right, my love.' she said as she made a not insignificant dent in the second glass. 'Now tell me about your plans.'

He did, of course, including the upcoming meeting with Messaille.

'He won't like that, I think. People get very pompous when they go to Paris. It's a well-known fact. Something in the water, I'm told.'

Smith looked sharply across at her. Cracking English-style jokes was not her usual style. Perhaps the crémant was working faster than usual.

'Oh, he'll come all right. What I've got on him would have him bounced straight off his peacock throne in Issy-les-Moulineaux onto his arse in La Sant prison just up the road. Shit they might even re-open Devil's Island for him. No, he'll come all right.'

'So, you get the gendarmerie to mop the whole thing up.'

'Yes, that's the general idea. They do the dirty work. God knows they got enough fire power these days to handle the beach operation no matter how many people Moroni has sent in. They can intercept the refugees well out to sea before they are anywhere near the France coast and treat them as humanely as is appropriate under the circumstances. Moroni gets the message to keep away from the Camargue. You and your father are not implicated in any way. I'll ask Messaille to find some pretext to get Cordiez out of the way. He is, after all, only guilty of greed and, given the sort of life he's had, he can be excused a little, I feel. I'd like to find a way of getting to Moroni too given what is happening in Marseille, but we would run the risk of confusing the issue for Messailles. He is, after all, only a policeman.'

'Good.' she said approvingly. 'I would be pleased if we could keep Cordiez out of it. I can't help thinking that he is a little misled about all this. He may not think us as part of his family, but he is part of ours.'

'That,' thought Smith to himself, 'is sentimental claptrap.'

'Just bear in mind, my dearest, that he may actually be the unpleasant bastard that everyone who has met him, seems to think he is. Some people are actually like that.'

Chapter 16: Messailles Again

It was a direct re-run of the same scene of just over a year ago. The ill-named Café de Paris was situated almost next to the Cavalièrie Gate at the north edge on the old Roman town wall. The food was very basic but their beer or their Pastis was as good as anywhere else. It was also one of the main watering holes for those more inclined to the National Front than the Communist Party which Smith always thought was ironic as the café was situated in the middle of the large Arab quarter that runs northward from the Arena. Basically, it's a perfectly comfortable, anonymous drinking café where few people if they were locals would ever dream of having a meal other than a croissant. It suited Smith perfectly and he was a regular.

Again, as before, Smith let Messaille arrive first, but the man was noticeably more relaxed this time. He knew what this was all about and understood no matter how annoyed he was at being ordered to do something by the anonymous Englishman, it was probably likely to be a personally fruitful meeting. Messailles was in civvies but still managed to look thoroughly out of place. Unbidden, the owner brought a coffee to the seated gendarme who took out a copy of La Provence and started to read it. After a while, Smith, having checked with Gentry that the coast was clear, entered the café and sat down on the opposite side of the little circular table.

'Good morning, General. Thank you for accepting my invitation.'

Messaille, always somewhat irascible at best, was clearly not happy and showed it. He remained silent, somewhat put out presumably by the fact that Smith hadn't offered a customary handshake for him to ignore.

'And congratulations,' Smith continued blithely, 'On your promotion.'

Messaille just grunted. In an effort to show willing, Smith nodded at the owner behind the bar. Very soon two glasses of a rich amber-coloured cognac were placed with a thump on the table. Smith was not a keen cognac drinker at the best of times, but this particular bottle had been a gift from a particularly grateful French ambassador rescued by Smith and Deveraux some years ago from a particularly hazardous kidnapping. It was an 1886 Moyet of legendary quality and it amused Smith to keep it behind the bar in a café in which it was almost certainly worth more than the rest of the bar stock put together. He hardly ever used it. Indeed, the last time he had sampled it was about a year ago on the occasion of their first meeting. Again, it had the effect of bringing a small thaw to the icy conversation.

'All right Smith. What do you want this time?

The tone of voice was still somewhat truculent, but Smith understood that it was far from easy for the man. He was one of the most senior policemen in France being faced with an unknown Englishman who had the power over him, if not of life and death, then at least of his continuing professional career. So, Smith came straight to the point. He quickly handed a USB stick across the table.

'On that, General Messaille, are full details of a conspiracy being hatched by one Sebastien Moroni of Toulouse to set up a regular import of groups of illegal immigrants from north Africa into France using the beaches of Beauduc as a landing point. It includes details of the local farmers who have agreed to help him. I thought it would be useful information for the Gendarmerie National who, I think, have the resources to put a stop to it very quickly and with the minimum of bloodshed. The people meeting the shipment will undoubtedly be heavily armed with automatic weapons and you have the resources to meet this with an appropriate level of force. I don't want any of the local people to be caught in any sort of cross fire. I would not wish to offer any advice to you, of course, but if I was planning an operation to mop these bloody people up, I would intercept the immigrants out to sea. Whatever you decide to do with them, at least they wouldn't fall into the hands of Moroni's thugs. It would also make a beach operation to catch the bad guys simpler, I would have thought.'

The little memory stick vanished almost as soon as it was placed on the table. Messailles took another small sip of the Moyet and paused to savour it.

'Why?'

'Why what, General?'

'Why are you giving over this information, why to me, and why do you have it at all?'

Smith also followed suit in sampling the brandy. He had forgotten how very good it really was. It was true that the man opposite merited some sort of an explanation.

'Well. I'm telling you about it because I want it stopped and you can do that better than I can. I may have a somewhat strange sense of morality by some other people's standards and I don't particularly care about that. But this is a business I don't like at all. Additionally, I know that many people who live and work of the Camargue think the same. Even some of the farmers who might have agreed to help Moroni are not entirely responsible. If you are very poor and can hardly heat your house or feed your family and someone comes along and offers you a great deal of money essentially for doing nothing, it must be hard to resist.'

Messaille just nodded his understanding as Smith went on.

'I'm telling you as opposed to anyone else for the same reason I got you involved last year. You may have a somewhat unorthodox relationship with Alexei Girondou, unorthodox by the customary standards of a senior public servant, that is, but I take you to be a good policeman; an opinion shared by Alexei, by the way. I have no opinion at all about your little Swiss nest egg – or rather not-so-little might be a better expression. I happen to think that you probably deserve every penny of it. I know Girondou quite well and I am pretty sure he doesn't do anything for nothing. But my guess it that you'll not only polish these disgusting people off because they are major law breakers and you are sworn to uphold that law. You will do so because you share my moral dislike to this type of crime. It is a trade based on people's misery and I suspect that you are the sort of man who abhors that as much as I do.'

Again, Messailles inclined his head slightly in agreement.

'Finally, in answer to your last question. I have this information because I found out about it almost by chance from some people who live here in the Camargue who have become my friends but who are not able to solve a problem like this that will be happening on their doorstep.'

'And you can, Monsieur?'

'Yes, Monsieur.'

'Could you also solve this problem without my help?'

Smith looked directly into the man's eyes with a look that never wavered as he spoke.

'Yes, Monsieur, I could. It would be very messy and cause a public scandal. Many people would die, and you would know nothing until it was all over. The problem would be solved using people who weren't French and I suspect that wouldn't go down too well with your chums in Paris. Questions would be asked and as one of the law officers most responsible for law and order in France your next step on the career ladder that you are climbing so successfully would be a dishonourable discharge rather than promotion to Major - or even Lieutenant General.'

There was a silence while the Frenchman absorbed this.

'Yes, monsieur. I saw last year some evidence of you approach to these things on the Beauduc beach. The place was littered with dead GIGN men.'

Smith just shrugged.

'Only guilty ones and I hardly think that three dead traitors constitutes littering. However if I have to solve this particular problem myself then litter, as you so delicately describe it, won't begin to cover it this time'

He waited while the man made his decision that, in reality, was no decision at all. Whatever the niceties of the meeting over a vintage brandy, Smith had the policeman over a barrel and they both knew it.

'Very well, Monsieur Smith. The Gendarmerie will take over. How much time do we have?'

'I don't know. I am pretty sure of the why and we have to wait for the when. I suspect it will be soon. I would guess three or four days. I will let you know as soon as I know myself.'

'Good. I'll give you my mobile phone number.'

Smith smiled and raised his hand slightly as he said: 'Don't worry. I have it, thank you.'

The gendarme coloured slightly as Smith spoke again.

'One thing is important. It's pretty obvious that Moroni himself won't be within a country mile of events on the beach on the night and I think it would be nice if we could use this business to get him locked away for a good number of years.'

Messailles nodded in agreement.

'Yes, he has been a thorn in our side for years in the south west but, while we have arrested many of his people over the years, we have never got near him.'

'Well,' replied Smith, 'We may be able to do something about that. It looks as if the man whose farm is going to be used is called Franco Cordiez. He is also someone who I would like to shield from his own stupidity. He's just an idiot who has been seduced by money. Essentially, he is just a man down on his luck and although that is a situation entirely of his own making, I don't like the ideas of kicking a man when he's down. If you can arrange to have him spirited away on the day into protective custody, he could well furnish you with some testimony that might incriminate Moroni.'

'OK. I think we can arrange that. It certainly would be good to put Moroni out of circulation for a while.'

'Good.' Said Smith. 'Then as soon as I know the precise date, I will let you know. The rest is up to you. I'll bid you goodbye. It was nice meeting you again.'

He began to get up but was halted as Messailles had something else to say.

'Monsieur Smith, I have a small favour to ask of you this time.'

Smith was intrigued enough to set back down.

'Monsieur General, I would be delighted to be of service if I feel I can. Although I should inform you that I don't really see it as my duty to assist the police.

Messailles smiled glacially.

'Monsieur I thought it was the duty of every citizen to assist the police if they can.'

'Ah, you forget,' replied an equally smiling Smith, 'that I am only a resident here in France not a citizen.'

'Perhaps, Monsieur Smith, that is something that I could do something about.'

Smith stopped smiling. He was bored with the game.

'You could certainly try, General, but I wouldn't recommend it. The result would probably be that I might be deported back to spend the rest of my life in England's green and pleasant lands but you, my friend, will spend yours viewing the French landscape though a set of bars for as long as it takes the other inmates to find out that they have a senior bent cop as a fellow inmate. You will probably find that in some places the death penalty is still enforced.'

Messailles raised his hands defensively.

'Monsieur, it was only a small joke.'

'Very funny, monsieur,' replied a distinctly unamused Smith. 'So, what do you want, Messailles?'

'You have, I believe, a man called Nasir ibn Salman ibn Amin al-Farsi living here in Arles. I gather he is some sort of imam. I was wondering if you had come across him at all.'

Smith paused for thought. Not, of course, to try to remember the name although he hoped possibly that was the impression he was giving. It was clear that the imam was on the official radar and that

255

indicated that he would usually be trying to operate either off or below it. In any case, Smith wasn't interesting in helping and told the man so.

'Ah that's a pity. I had hoped for some sort of exchange of information.'

'So far, Messailles, I have given you details of a major crime about to be enacted here in the Camargue. Now you are asking me to spy for you. Well bugger that. In any case, I'm afraid I don't see much coming in the opposite direction.'

'Monsieur Smith. I would like to know a little more about you. You are the man who seems to know everything about me and feeds me these pieces of information that I will admit are very useful indeed, but you are also a man about whom I know nothing. Even more interesting is that fact that even with my resources I can't find out anything either.'

Smith put on his best insouciant expression.

'Surely Monsieur you know everything about me. I live here in France where your bureaucracy insists in documenting everything. I am sure that a combination of your tax authorities to whom I make a return every year and the sous-prefecture here in Arles will furnish you with everything. There is nothing more I can offer.'

'Yes, I know all this but what is interesting, if not unique, is the fact there is no information anywhere else. Nothing on the dreaded internet and nothing available from your life in England even through police or official channels and, as you might imagine, I have access to many of those. Nothing.'

Smith shrugged.

'I really can't help you there. Perhaps the records have been mislaid? You know what government departments can be like.'

'Mislaid or, perhaps, hidden?'

Smith said nothing as the policeman went on, musing:

'Perhaps I should dig a little deeper, Monsieur Smith.'

Smith finished getting up and fixed his companion with a very steely look indeed.'

'Oh, Brigadier General. I really wouldn't recommend that at all. If one digs too deeply into anything, who knows what might be discovered'.

It was only then that he broke eye contact and the Frenchman addressed his parting remark to the back of the retreating Englishman in a very soft tone.

'Perhaps you're right, Monsieur Smith. Perhaps you are right.'

Chapter 17: An Invasion Thwarted

Chirosi wasn't happy. Not at all. He had spent much of the last few years behind the scenes as befits the man who was in charge of a considerable part of Moroni's eastern territories. His usual policy was to put others in the firing line so if anything happened, he wasn't the one to catch the flak. Now Moroni wanted him on the job personally to make sure things went well. He also hated beaches. Even as a child he disliked them when his parents insisted that it would be "fun" to spend the day in Palavas-les-Flotes or Sète or Adge. The first shipment of immigrants was coming and, being part of a very small group on the beach, he felt very exposed and he didn't like it at all. For the first shipment Moroni had wanted to use the simplest alternative. A straight landing on the beach, into the trucks and away up the main road. The problem was the track between the beach and the main road was full of potholes and any ordinary lorry would have to go very slowly indeed if it made it out at all. It would also be noisy. He had finally persuaded Moroni to spend a bit more money on a more sophisticated approach. They would transfer the immigrants quickly into small boats that were designed to go over the marshes that ran back from the beach out to sea directly from the fishing boats that brought them from North Africa. They would then run inland and only use the beach at Beauduc as an access point. This way they wouldn't lose time with a beach landing. Once through the beach they could go via Cordiez's farm on to any number of points on the edges of the Étang de Vaccares or the Étang de Monro. There were good roads running along the west and northern sides of both marshes. The transfer to trucks could then be done easily and quickly in a wide variety of places. He had found three 18ft Delta Marsh boats and put 30KW Aquawatt electric engines on them. As long as they didn't have to run at high speed for a long time, that was easily enough power to do the whole round trip from a small distance out in the sea.

He had kept a close look out as he had driven slowly down from his home near Montpellier to the Beauduc beach. He had kept to the well-known tourist routes through Aigues Mortes, crossing the Petit Rhône at the Pont de Sylvéréal. He then took the tourist route, the D37, along the north of the Etang de Vaccares before turning south on the D38B that would take him to the Cordiez land and in to the narrow, pothole strewn lane across the dunes and marshes, the so-called Route de Fangassier, to the beach. By the time he got there it was late afternoon and he was pleased to see that insofar as there was any traffic on the road, it was all leaving the beach. He was the only person going in the opposite direction. He had called in to see Cordiez but found the place deserted. Presumably having given his advice of the geography of the place, he was getting as far away as he could. Chirosi grimaced. Our Mr Cordiez is going to have to do more in the future to earn his fee that that, he thought.

He looked up and down the beach and saw no-one. It was 2am. He knew that the local authorities had banned caravans and campers for staying overnight. Satisfied he drove back inland. The landing wasn't scheduled until the early hours of the morning. He had spent the afternoon and evening exploring a corner of the Camargue that he hardly knew at all. He had also wanted to find something to eat.

Now, high above his head a French army MQ-9 Reaper drone was cruising silently well out of sight and range at almost eight thousand metres. It was observing a pair of fishing boats currently some fifty miles off the French coast. It had been following them for more than two days as they left Jijel on the north coast of Algeria. The boats had taken the two days to cross the Mediterranean Sea. The drone also saw now the three picking up boats making their way slowly towards a rendezvous point off the French coast.

Chirosi looked out to sea waiting for the moment when the boats came over the horizon. The beach was flat of course as were the sand dunes around it. There were no vantage points to increase his view out to sea. He was limited to the distance to the horizon. Someone had once told him that a six foot that a man standing on the beach to see to the horizon only 5km away. He knew that the transfer from the fishing boats was happening a lot further out than that. Therefore he just had to wait and see. In any case there was precious little light as the think clouds ran fast across the sky and there were only a few glimpses of the moon. He only had one or two men along the beach as observers. They wouldn't have to do anything. The marsh boats would just sweep inland, skating across the watery dunes to the rendezvous point that was at the corner of the Etang du Galabert near the pumping station. It was on Cordiez's land. There the boats could beach and their human cargo could be transferred directly into the lorries. From there it was less than a mile to the road that led north and out of the Camargue. However he saw nothing and as there was radio silence, he had no way of knowing what was going on.

He telephoned the leader of the men with the trucks. All was quiet apparently. They were all in place on the Route de Fangassier with enough firepower to make sure that the transfer went off smoothly. He was nevertheless more than a little uncomfortable. The road where the trucks stood was very narrow with the road falling quickly into marshy sane on either side. Indeed they had had to turn the trucks around in a very small space at the pumping station to get them facing the right way for a quick departure. They were still on a narrow single track road and could easily be blocked in. Next time they did this operation he would insist of locating somewhere that would give them more options for an emergency escape.

It was now considerably beyond the time where something should have happened and he was getting really concerned. In the absence of anything else to try he called the trucks again. This time there was no response at all. He turned back from his mindless survey of the horizon and got back into his wagon intending to drive very slowly back towards the rendezvous point to see what was happening. Suddenly there was a huge racket of a helicopter equipped with searchlights in the sky and a sudden instant intense glow of land based light. It happened in an instant. He swore to himself and swung his Mercedes around and headed north along the beach without lights towards Stes Maries de la Mer where he could possibly escape from the area while the police were busy with the trucks. The operation had gone wrong again.

Messailles had taken Smith's advice. It would obviously be easier and less messy to intercept the refugees out to sea before they got to the beach and they had intercepted radio traffic that confirmed a ten kilometre rendezvous point that was well within French territorial waters. Messaille wanted to arrest the trawler before the refugees were transhipped. A P400 fast patrol boat would intercept the trawler while four very fast Zodiac Hurricane RIBS would take care of the collection boats. The operation onshore was little more hazardous. Again, the drone had picked up two lorries making their way up the road that bordered the Étang de Vaccares. Once the sea operation was complete armed Gendarmerie squads blocked the roads out and squads of heavily armed CRS police coming in behind the lorries on RIBs from the sea, Chirosi's men were completely and instantly surrounded. It was over in an instant. Chirosi's men had no stomach for a firefight with CRS men armed with sub-machine guns and grenade launchers.

As he drove away having seen what was going on on shore he assumed that the fishing boats had been intercepted as well. Yet again the police had found out about the plan somehow. They had lost the shipment and he was pretty sure that, in spite again of getting the money up front again this time Moroni would be very angry indeed. A second operation going wrong, especially one that had taken so much preparation would mean that the whole idea of importing refugees would be called into question. That would mean a significant loss of future income. He waited until he had reached the Gacholle lighthouse and the narrow road that led towards Stes. Maries before steeling himself to call his boss.

The news was greeted in silence while the boss listened.

'Who the fuck grassed this time. Pierre?'

Chirosi was under no illusion that this was only a delay. However, he knew his boss wanted something specific. Bullshit wouldn't do.

'Well, I don't think it was one of us. In the first place there were precious few of our people who were involved. The people who supplied the boats and the lorries had no idea when they were going to be used. The drivers and boat crews got their orders at lunchtime today and were under our surveillance all the time after the briefing. In any case that wouldn't have been enough time for the police to have arranged their ambushes especially at sea. Actually, the boat crews didn't get the rendezvous coordinates until just before they left. No, I really don't think the leak came from us.'

'Who, then.'

'The only person who knew the date and time outside our people was Cordiez.'

'I can't believe it. He was on to a good earner. Why the hell should he fuck it up?' Doesn't he know what will happen to him? Doesn't he know me at all?'

'To be frank, boss, I don't think he would have done this on purpose. There is no good reason why he should. If I had to guess, I would think it was a mistake. Maybe he flashed some of the money around unwisely and someone got onto him. If he was as poor as he said, he may not have understood how to handle a fistful of cash. He may have just talked casually to friends or family. Maybe someone suspected him and put the arm on. I don't know, obviously. But he is the only one other that you and me and the people in Algeria who knew the date and time in advance. I think we can rule out the Algerian end. They aren't going to piss on a good earner either. No. my money's on Cordiez. I note, incidentally, that he seems to have vanished today.'

Another long silence followed. When he did speak again, it was to head off in what seems a totally random direction.

'Right. Find Cordiez first. He may have conveniently vanished today but he's bound to come back to his farm sooner or later. Don't do anything to him. Just make sure that he's the one who let the information out. Make sure that he knows that he is responsible. Then make contact with that Dutchman who works for Girondou again. I don't care how you do it but set up a meeting as soon as possible. Pay him a lot of money if necessary. You be there as well. Don't contact me until it's done.'

With that the man in Toulouse rang off. Chirosi was under no illusion that there would be consequences for all this but he was relieved that, for the moment at least, he was still in the game and taking instructions. He sent half a dozen men to keep watch on Cordiez's farm with instructions to keep him when he returned.

It was not far into the next morning when he got the call and by lunch time he had driven down from his house in Montpellier and was sitting in what passed for a farm kitchen. Cordiez was tied to one of his own kitchen chairs and looked decidedly apprehensive. Two very large goons stood on either side.

'Well?' said Chirosi.

Cordiez just shrugged and said nothing. At a slight nod from Chirosi, one of the goods stepped forward and slammed an enormous fist into the farmer's face sending him and his chair flying across the room.

'Mr Moroni has instructed me not to kill you yet but he left no instructions as to how badly you should be hurt. I would recommend that you co-operate. It might be less painful.'

He paused while the bleeding man was put back upright.

'It's pretty obvious that someone talked. Now very few people knew the details of last night's operation and we are pretty sure that none of us would have talked to the flics. That sort of leaves you and, er, you. So if you don't admit this, I'll ask one of our friends here to start castrating you with a penknife.'

Cordiez did at least begin to look scared.

'I swear I didn't tell anyone. No one. Why should I? I had every reason to keep it secret. I didn't want anyone else muscling in on my deal with you.'

Chirosi realised that this was obviously true. This stupid man would certainly have kept it to himself. He began to have a sinking feeling that he might have to start an internal investigation within their own organisation to find someone who might have been turned. Even with their firm there was only a very small number of possibilities. It was all going to get a bit bloody. Clearly relieved that he had neither been hit again nor had his manhood been filleted yet, Cordiez continued rather without thinking.

'I told nobody. It only came up briefly in a conversation with my son when he came to visit.'

Chirosi pounced.

'You mean you told your son about this?'

Cordiez seemed surprised at the question.

'Of course I did. He is my son. He's family. He would never had told anyone.'

Chirosi just sighed.

'And did you tell your son what you had agreed to do to help us and did he approve?'

'Well no. To be frank he was pretty bloody angry. But he's my son. He would never have told anyone else.'

There was little more he needed so he got up and left leaving his men to spend some more time with Cordiez. Damaged but not dead was his parting instruction.

'I thought so.' was Moroni's reply. 'It had to have been him. Have you got hold of that Dutchman yet?'

'Yes, I set up a meeting for tomorrow afternoon. Three o'clock at the apartment in La Grande Motte.'

'Good. Let's see if we can dream up some particularly impressive way of teaching these fucking farmers a lesson or two. Something that even they will remember. I want to go through some ideas with you so let's meet in the apartment at midday. Get some food brought in. It'll be a working lunch.'

Chirosi wondered how many Michelin starred chefs did take-away but, as usual, Moroni's name would be enough to find one.

In the end the meeting went well. Moroni had a lot of experience with hired bodyguards and he knew full well that loyalty wasn't usually high on their list of attributes. Money bought most things he had always found and the services of even the best could easily be secured with enough of it. So it proved with the Dutchman. As Moroni was prepared to offer an indecent amount of money and a suggestion that he should run the Marseille end of things after the removal of Girondou, an agreement was swiftly arrived at. Much to Chirosi's relief, for the moment at least, Moroni had even put the disappointment of the fiasco on the Beauduc beach to one side as he had planned his revenge on the wretched farmer. Chirosi also understood now that his boss also had bigger fish to fry.

267

Chapter 18: Corrida and Death

Smith sat on the hard, knobbly stone seat with surprising contentment and it was not just the contentment that came from the knowledge that the stone under his bum had been laid two thousand years before in the reign of Roman emperor Vespasian. He hadn't exactly been looking forward to this. Not that he was uncertain about the bullfight. Quite the contrary. The two Arles Ferias were highlights of his retirement. He had been brought up to love them primarily because he had been brought up to understand them and what they meant. It was a necessary consequence of his belief in Baxendall's historical eye concept that there should also be a cultural eye as well. He had taken the trouble and afforded the courtesy to history of finding out about bullfighting very early in his life. He had made his decision about it and didn't really care to much about the others who thought differently.

A few weeks before, when they had all been discussing arrangements for the Autumn Feria, he had feared, if not actually the worst, then the less-than-ideal. The Aubanet family would certainly have their usual seats in the Tribune C nearest the president, of course. They would be surrounded by the great and the good of Arles and of the Camargue; the greatest and the best, in fact. He would surely have had to endure the constant rubber-necking of many of the twenty-odd thousand people who would fill the amphitheatre to say nothing of the company of people he neither knew nor particularly wanted to if truth be told. Before he had met Martine, his customary seat had been further back in the *secondes,* a good ten or fifteen rows back and above the privileged occupants of the Tribunes. His seat in the *secondes* was still in the shade, the *ombra,* to use the often confused franco-spanish language that is used in bull-fighting circles in the south of France. It was also about half way around the long side of great oval that forms the arena proper – the actual sanded oval on which the fight would take place – and usually gave the best view of the whole corrida which traditionally reached its climax on that side of the ring. It was also high enough above the Tribunes to be at least affordable for someone on his limited budget. Seats on the opposite side were cheaper but he was too old to enjoy sitting three hours at a stretch in the direct sunlight.

There was another reason he preferred his old seat. He had lived off and on for many years in his little house facing the great two thousand-year-old Roman amphitheatre. Over that time, he had seen it wearing many faces; drenched and blackened with winter rain, standing hard and firm, hard against the worst of Mistral winds that could blow at more than a hundred kilometres an hour down the Rhône valley, baking silently in the sun that could reach above forty degrees. He had even seen it shrouded in snow and ice from time to time. But on all these occasions, and a myriad more, what he saw, for all the great building's many faces were just dead stones; stones perhaps redolent of two millennia of history and human use, but dead stones nevertheless. The Roman amphitheatre in Arles had been built two thousand years ago for people, to collect them together, to entertain them, to instruct them, to be an instrument of administration even, of social control as well as a symbol of power and Roman permanence. Now in more modern times it was seldom full. The pop concerts of the past, concerts that used to fill it, were, indeed just that; past. Few of them could guarantee to fill the place these days and concert promoters usually opted for the safer, smaller and heavily restored – one might say re-created - antique theatre next door. No, the great old building lived now mainly only as the passive object of a million camera lenses or the occasional home, less than half full, of the Camargue games where athletic young men tried to snatch coloured ribbons from between the horns of young bulls, that were held each week through the summer mostly for the benefit of the tourists.

It would be one of fewer than ten days of the year when the place would be full, and Vespasian's great building would live again, albeit briefly. It would be full of more than twenty thousand noisy enthusiastic people, an equally enthusiastic, strident and not always completely musical brass band and, of course, the six great fighting bulls and their individually choreographed paths to their deaths in the afternoon sun. Not only was it a good seat to watch the fight, it was the place where all parts of the audience seem to meet. Around him, in the *secondes,* the crowd was as passionate as it was knowledgeable. They were simpler too. No one here had a season ticket but generally it was the same people who, more or less, sat in the same area, year after year.   There were always strangers there too; tourists, holidaymakers, followers of the bullfight from other places and countries. They all came for a variety of reasons and with a variety of opinions. He himself had brought many people to the fights over the years, some with as strong opinion as to the cruelty of the whole thing as it was possible to hold. He had, of course, forced none of them to come but he had always said that, given that more than twenty thousand people were usually there, one person leaving at any stage would hardly be noticed. In fact, given that the seat markings on the stone rows were extremely narrow, anyone leaving would be more likely to be thanked than abused. He remembered, not without slight amusement, that no-one actually had ever left. There were every year, of course, many who protested outside the arena and against a sport they held to be barbaric and uncivilised, cruel and disgusting. Few of them ever found their way into the *secondes*, or even anywhere inside for that matter, unwilling as they were to pay any money actually to see first-hand that which they so passionately condemned.

His bit of the *secondes* was a lively and agreeable place to him and much preferable to the more significant places a few rows below.

Some weeks ago, they had been walking – ambling almost - her arm looped into his, slowly along one of the many tracks that criss-crossed the Mas des Saintes, the great Camargue farm that was home to Martine and her father. It was a brisk early spring morning and they were both rugged up against the cold. A few birds scudded arrow-like

271

on the wind across the wide sky. The sun was out but it offered no heat, only light. It was the sharp winter light that had so entranced van Gogh, not the summer haze and today it picked the farmland out in precise and vivid detail. These were the days he liked most. Arthur was, as usual, running free and chasing everything imaginable. They looked on in contentment. The racing greyhound had been Smith's only real companion for a few years after he himself followed his dog's example and retired. Now the dog had full reign over the thousand-odd hectares of the Aubanet farm. It hadn't taken him long to realise that there was no fun in chasing Emile Aubanet's prize bulls. They were no-where near fast enough to catch him nor to give him any sport. They were much too big to do anything with even if he had decided to try to hunt one down. But here were rabbits and rats, water voles and otters to be hunted and the dog was completely content as he ranged about.

The woman had come into his life only a year or three earlier and they had shared an adventure or two as his past had shown an annoying habit of refusing to remain dead, or when his well-buried and unconventional talents had refused become redundant. He and his previous employers had spent a considerable amount of time and money burying his past and establishing a quiet and unobtrusive retirement for this retired and slightly overweight Welshman who had spent his life teaching art history in a number of American and British universities, then tried his hand at business when he finally tired of his students getting lazier and more stupid in equal measure. Throughout both careers he had worked from time to time as what modern parlance calls an unofficial asset for the British secret service where he found, much to his surprise and slight annoyance, that his considerable talent for deciphering antique sarcophagus iconography was matched by his ability to kill people. It was considerably to his regret that it was this latter talent that survived into his retirement as a more useful one than the former. However, he thought to himself as they strolled along, it was also this latter talent that had brought him close to the beautiful and powerful lady who was now carelessly draped over his arm. Again, to his surprise he had found that over the last year or two he had gradually fallen for this woman to the extent that, had he admitted it to himself, he was in love. He had retired to Arles with every intention of sitting and drinking himself into what he had hoped would be a very long and gradual oblivion, left alone by a modern world with which he felt progressively little kinship. His retirement ambition echoed that of one of his university professors, a man of impeccable scholastic lineage and a fierce and unfriendly, unbending intellect - he had been a German after all - who when asked how he intended to spend his retirement, replied that he intended to spend it learning more and more about less and less. Smith was not sure that Arthur actually shared this ambition but both of them had been shaken out of their respective lethargies by this extraordinary beautiful woman and her life in the Camargue.

Today he found himself, not in the *second* but feeling very uncomfortable in a Tribune, the most expensive seats in the house.

Down here on the first row just behind the *barrestre*, the wooden barrier between the sanded ring and the outside of the arena. It was the narrow passage that allowed the participants of the fight to move around the arena safely. Undeniably it was the best seat in the house and one that he had never occupied. It was way too expensive. Now he sat beside Martine who was attracting more than her fair share of attention with Emile on her other side. Also, in their Tribune was Cordiez's estranged wife who had come for the event and some others that he didn't know. Franco Cordiez was down in the ring in the *callejón*.

The late afternoon heat seemed to rise from the ground now that the first fight was about to begin. The brass band's trumpeter signalled the entry and almost immediately the first bull of the afternoon came out of the *corril* at speed. The first matador stood quietly by the side of the *barril*, as his three helpers waved their yellow and purple capes and got the bull pointed in the right direction to make its first pass by the man who would ultimately bring be its nemesis in about twenty minutes or so.

Like most of the bulls that were bought to fight in Arles, this one was Spanish, expensive and not particularly impressive. It was still half a ton of rage. That was expected. But rather like many of the new generation of bullfighters the matador seemed somewhat too show biz for Smith. He had been coming to the fights since he was a boy and he would be the first to admit that he was rather old fashioned in his tastes. His grandfather who had come to Spain to fight Franco had ultimately buried his disillusionment with the republican cause, perverted, as it had been by the Bolsheviks, in a study and ultimately an educated passion for bullfighting. They shared a preference for the rather quiet and dignified style that had progressively fallen out of favour. Now, Smith felt show business seem to have taken preference over skill, or that is what it seemed to him. His grandfather had told him to look at the feet. The less the feet moved as the great animal rushed past the better the bull fighter. These days it seemed all shouting and stamping, bells and whistles. But if you looked closely through all the noise and excitement you saw young fighters increasingly taking safe ways to earn their living. Close passes were made only on tired bulls when the bull could no longer turn so quickly or so dangerously. Bandilleras were placed with great flourishes but from further away. Picadors and their horses took increasing advantage of the horses protective armoured skirts to stay engaged and close to the bull to cut more of the neck muscles than they should. Matadors themselves increasingly took safe routes into the kill, to the sides or further away. They seemed unwilling to lean in over the head, between the horns and follow the sword, relying on the perfection of the thrust to ensure their own survival. More and more bulls were not killed correctly and the *descabello,* a short dagger, used to finish a bull that was on its knees was more and more prevalent.

As Smith looked around at the cheering crowd, he also realised that two of the three matadors were locals, men who came from Arles or the locality. The senior one, Bautista, had achieved world fame and had been the darling of the Arles crowd for years. As is traditional, he fought the first and the fourth bulls. Then, of course, was the junior Roger Cordiez who would take the third and the last. Whether or not they were any good – and all three performing today was certainly that – the triumphal severed ears or even a tail were regularly demanded by the chauvinistic local crowd irrespective of whether or not their hero of the moment had really performed well. However, given that the matadors were of high standard and the bulls equally were fast and fit the corrida proceeded well and the quality of the fight was very high indeed.

The first three bulls came and went. Cordiez first bull, the third in order was fought and dispatched with skill and much to the approval of the vocal partisan crowd. The next two fights were also played out to their inevitable conclusions with much excitement and skill and crowd satisfaction. To be honest the fights, no matter how good, were some distance from Smith's own taste. These days the style was more flamboyant with much shouting, stamping and gesticulating. He found his attention drifting. He remembered a day many years ago in that same arena when Antonio Ordoñez had fought a bull in that calm dignified style that gave respect to himself and his opponent. No shouting or stamping. He used to remain almost completely static while the bull raged around him; feet firmly planted on the same spot from pass to pass. When the moment for the kill arrived, he had followed the *estoque* over the lowered head of the bull whose horns passed on either side of his slim chest as he lay squarely over the great head. The sword found the aorta cord as it was supposed to and the bull was dead in an instant. But it hadn't fallen but had stayed completely upright. The bull was just dead on its feet. Literally. Those who wonder about the origin of the expression needed to do so no longer. The vital signals from the brain had yet to penetrate to the animal's extremities and the bull just stood immobile. There was no spinal cord connection to pass the message. Ordoñez just drew back from his sword and turned his back and walked away. The crowd, imagining an incomplete kill started to boo and whistle. He quickly bored with this silly crowd. He had done his job correctly as he had been taught by his father Cayetano and that was enough. The crowd continued to boo and hiss as they imagined they had been denied their theatre. After a few steps, he paused and without either fuss or even actually turning around towards the immobile bull behind him just raised his hand in a final salute. At that same instant the bull collapsed in a dusty, inanimate heap and the crowd hushed instantly into silence as they realised the genius of the man who a few seconds before they had been deriding. They started to cheer but the matador just remained grim faced with contempt and walked straight out of the area without a backward glance. In spite of many offers over the years, he had never returned.

The last bull of the corrida came into the ring with a great roar of approval from the crowd. This was the moment that after his kill, Robert Cordiez would be awarded his much-anticipated *alternative*.

The bull was a good one, strong and nimble. It was not as heavy as some but it was a good fast bull for the young man to show his skills. The fight went through its defined phases. the *tercio de varas* where the bull is played with a cape showing the matador's skills followed by the work of the picador. The second phase, the *tercio de Banderillas* where again the bull was plays and the three pairs of be-ribboned *banderillas* placed. The picadors arrived to do their part to the traditional mixture of praise and abuse that always follows the men on horseback. Finally, the *tercio de muerte* and the young Cordiez was on his own. He dedicated the bull to his mother and set about a long and complex series of passes with the *muleta*, a small red cape supported with a short cane, each series of four or five passes greeted with great roars from an approving crowd. Smith could see that the boy was, indeed, rather old fashioned, quiet in his footwork and silent, relying his cape work to make the bull charge or stand. It was a skilled performance and much to the approval of the partisan crowd. Even his father stood to the back of the *callejón* with a broad smile of pride on his face.

Finally all the preliminaries were over. The final *tercia* was drawing to an end. Cordiez had exchanged been handed his *estoque*, the killing sword, by one of his assistants. The final few passes were complete. He was satisfied that the moment, the *suerte suprema*, had come. The bull stood, head lowered, its shoulders glistening darkly with the blood running from the small wounds made by the *banderillas*. The great chest heaved slowly but the eyes were still bright, looking up through the top of his eyes at the slim figure standing a metre or two in front of him, twitching the muleta very slightly from side to side. The great head followed it warily; two great pointed horns pointed directly at the matador moving equally from side to side, drawn by the cape. With the control that only the matador has at that moment the movements were gradually lessened until the muleta and the horns were locked together, completely stationary, facing each other from less than a metre's distance. The crowd fell silent and the matador edged very slightly closer to the bull. He then slowly turned half sideways, pivoting to stand with his weight on one leg only, raised the sword up to his eye line and sighted along it to the spot behind the neck between the bull's shoulder blades where he aimed his final and fatal thrust. The sword momentarily caught the sun and glinted along its length down to the tip which curved slightly downwards. He raised his left leg slightly and dipped the *muleta* down to the ground. The bull's head followed it down thus opening the tiny narrow space between the shoulder blades that would allow the sword to pass through and sever the bull's aorta.

There was a second where nothing moved, and nothing sounded. Then the matador, leaving the cape down, just kissing the ground, stepped forward in a fluid and fast movement and, leaning over the top of the bull's horns, began the lightning-fast thrust that would kill the bull. The point of the blade had just entered the bull's neck. The end was a fraction of a second away. The crowd was just drawing in that collective breath that would be released in a great shout to greet the kill.

Suddenly the young man seems to stumble slightly. He swerved a little and the cape on the ground moved sharply to the left. In a fraction of a second, just as the tip of the sword broke the skin on the back of the bull's neck, his hold over the bull was broken and, feeling the prick of the sword tip between his shoulders, the great beast, sensing that something had changed in an instant jerked his head violently upwards. The left horn entered the young man's chest and came through to his back. The great animal took off and. standing high up momentarily in his back legs, tossed the body free in a single great shake of the head. The man's body spun away into the air and fell violently to the ground. The bull turned in a flash on his axis in a great cloud of dust and sand and bent his head again to gore the body that was now lying prone on the Arena floor. Twice he tossed the rag doll far across the arena before the helpers, rushing in, waved their big *muletas*, distracted the now enraged bull and lured him away from the bleeding matador, by now lying completely motionless. With the bull finally distracted at the far end of the arena, a medical team rushed into the sand and unceremoniously picked up the lifeless corpse and ran with it out of the Arena.

The crowd sat silent, subdued and shocked as the second matador, as is required in such circumstances, approached the bull and commenced the *faena* again. This time the whole event was received in almost complete silence and it was only after the final act of killing and the bull was dragged out of the arena that the crowd stood to applaud. They were applauding the bull not the matador for it is the bull rather than the man who is the true hero in a bull fight. It is usually the bull that pays for his courage with his life in a bullfight, not the man.

The closing ceremonies, the departing parade of the remaining two matadors and their teams, the final salutes from the arena staff all passed almost in silence as the recent events remained fresh in the crowd's mind.

The remainder of the corrida had passed without incident or, from Smith's point of view at least, much interest. He was mulling over what he had seen; or at least thought he had seen. By his side, Martine also was quieter than usual. She turned to him.

'My darling, since Robert was gored you seem to have been somewhere else. What is it? What did you see that all the rest of us didn't?'

Smith had indeed been distracted. Just after the young man was tossed to the ground for the first time, he had been standing like everyone else in the Arena but he was looking around at the crowd not down at the sand. Then he had fixed precisely in his mind the exact place where the man had first fallen. After that he had just really been re-running those few seconds over in his head for something wasn't right. He avoided her question by asking one back.

'Tell me my dear, what exactly happens to the injured man after he is taken from the ring? Where does he go?'

However strange a reply it was, she knew him well enough to know he had his reasons.

'Well, unlike many of the larger arenas, we don't have a proper medical facility here with an operating theatre and emergency facilities. We are too small. Roger would have been left on a stretcher and put immediately into one of the ambulances that are always here. Then he would have been taken to the town hospital.'

Smith remembered with limited pleasure his own visit to that particular institution a year or two before. She went on.

'If he is alive, they'll operate on him of course. If he is dead, then they'll certify that and return him to his family.'

Smith knew that his next question would give him away, but it had to be asked.

'If he dies, would they normally do an autopsy?'

Martine was silent for a moment before replying. Smith's questions were getting stranger.

'No. I don't think so. There is really no reason. We all know what would be the cause of death. After all there were thousands of witnesses.'

There was a pause in their conversation not just because the final bull had entered the Arena but she was trying to work out what he was thinking. At length she continued.

'Unless, of course, there is some reason to think that it was not just the bull that killed him. Is that what you're thinking; drugs or a heart attack or something? I mean, apart from the usual amounts of stimulants that bullfighters often take before a fight. But he didn't look under the influence to me at least.'

Smith nodded but remained silent. After a while he came up with another disturbing question.

'Do you and your father have enough pull around here to get an autopsy done if the man dies?'

Now it was an even deeper frown on her face as she replied.

'But why? What on earth are you thinking, Peter? What possible reason can you give for an autopsy to be carried out? We would have to consult the family. It would be their choice, after all. But I suppose the answer is yes, we probably could if we really pushed for one .'

Smith had a further request.

'Can you get me some time alone in the arena directly at the end of this performance as soon as it is cleared of the arena staff? I need about five minutes undisturbed. Please just get me that time and I can answer your questions.'

She leant over to her father on the other side and talked briefly to him. The old man frowned but in any event, he beckoned one of the arena staff who was stationed behind them. A word in the man's ear and it was done. The last fight came to an end with a certain degree of competence but in front of a still solemn crowd. As the final parade was mounted Smith got up and went into the darkness of the arena passages and started to make his way to the level where all the matadors' staff and supporters were beginning to clear up. As he passed Martine he whispered:

'I'll see you back at the house in half an hour. Just make sure that if Roger is dead, they don't release the body until they hear from us.'

He entered the back of the *callejón*, the alley that surrounds the arena proper running behind the *barrestre*. The message had got through as the few remaining people there made way for him. Some even touched their caps as he passed.

He waited a few moments until the crowd had almost cleared before setting foot onto the sand. It was still bloodied and stained after the last bull, but he remembered the spot where it had happened very clearly. Holding one of the sand rakes that the arena staff use to tidy the surface before each fight he went to the spot where the young man had fallen and started very gently to examine the surface, pulling the sand about very gently as he did. It wasn't long before he felt a slight bump as the flat blade of the rake travelled over the surface. He bent down and sure enough he found what he feared was there.

As far as he could see it was a standard 7.62mm NATO round used in hundreds of thousands of rifles around the world. Possibly more informative was the fact that it had hardly deformed at all on its way through. Nor had it impacted the sand particularly violently. It seemed as the point was largely intact. If the shooter was a professional, he had chosen the more penetrative round so that it wouldn't stay caught in the body. Or at least that is what Smith would have done. If aimed for the heart it would probably have passed through instantly killing the man instantly leaving the bull and its subsequent actions as the immediate and completely credible killer. The bull's horn would have followed almost exactly the same path as the bullet but would have inflicted much more damage. The bullet's part would have been completely obscured. Smith smiled grimly as he squatted in the sand. Score one for the bull, he thought. He saw that the rifling marks on the bullet were still intact, but he very much doubted whether they would get much useful information from them. Perhaps Gentry would be able to do something with it. He slipped the bullet into his jacket pocket and rose to look briefly around the now deserted amphitheatre. For a few hours the venerable building that had been his neighbour for a number of years had lived again, full of people, action, passion and violence. The great building was no stranger to death. Tomorrow there were another two fights but on the Monday, the stones would sleep again and revert to being the passive and uninterested subject for a thousand and one tourists and their cameras, none of whom, of course, thought of asking the building's permission to take it's portrait or, indeed, thanking it after before they rushed off to search for another attraction to add to their digital memories. It took the death of a 700 kg bull and a young matador to bring the building back to life albeit momentarily. He shook his head. There was a lesson there, somewhere.

He left the arena, nodding thanks so some of the men who were standing back, waiting to prepare the surface for the next morning's *corrida*, and made his way back up the little hill to his house. He found Martine and her father sitting in his garden, each with a glass of whisky. One had already been poured for him. Arthur, of course, had rushed to the front door but now had resumed his position under the table. Smith slumped tiredly into a chair and just took the bullet from his jacket and put it on the table between them.

'Roger was killed by this an instant before he was gored by the bull. This shot was so well timed that I doubt that anyone noticed.'

Emil Aubanet looked very old and just sighed.

'Except you, Peter. Except you.'

Smith shrugged.

'Perhaps I have had a little more practice at this sort of thing than others.'

'So, what does this mean? ' Martine asked.

'Well quite simply it means that someone wanted to murder Roger Cordiez and devised a plan to make it seem as if the bull did it. Rather a good plan, actually. No-one would look further if the poor man has a bull horn going in the front of his chest and coming out of his back. I have to admit to a certain professional admiration. It was rather well conceived. The shooter was probably up in the tower on the top of the east side of the amphitheatre. He obviously had a well-silenced gun and the shot was a relatively easy one. No more than forty metres. Couldn't miss I'd say. I'd be very surprised if your friend was still alive. This is a big round to take anywhere in the chest. The only question is why would anyone want to kill a bullfighter especially a local boy in this rather arcane way? Personally, I haven't the faintest idea. But judging from the looks on your two faces, I suspect you both might. So unless you want to tell me a bit more about all this. I can't help you further.'

At that precise moment Martine's telephone rang. She put he hand over the microphone and looked at him.

'He's dead. Do you want me to try to get an autopsy done?'

Smith shook his head and she rang off.

'I can't see the point now. It would raise some very awkward questions for the family. I would think that it's highly unlikely that any real proof would be established by a PM even with the bullet in evidence. The damage caused by the horns would be massive. If this death is part the more general conspiracy, then I suggest that we are more likely to be able to unearth the killers than anyone. Perhaps you don't want the family to know while we do. From that point of view we know what happened and it's probably as well that as few people as possible share the knowledge, for the moment at least. However, that's your decision not mine.'

'This was Moroni's revenge on Cordiez for grassing him upon the illegal immigrant thing. That hit him in the pocket. I'm sure that a lot of people saw me back there in the arena digging around in the sand and they will soon guess that something untoward happened. More importantly Moroni will have wanted it to become public knowledge as a warning to Camargue farmers not to cross him. A pretty effective one too, I should think.'

287

They just sat there in silence. Both Martine and her father looked miserable. Smith was just feeling a bit like being in the presence of King Canute trying to keep the realities of modern life at bay by sheer faith or hope or something. The Camargue and its people may well be regarded by most everyone to be good only as camera fodder, but modern life occasionally intruded and some of that wasn't particularly welcome. Smith though grimly that if you were poor or out of work living in a half-derelict suburb of Marseille or in the Arab ghetto of IIII violence and murder, crime and drugs were everyday facts of life and had to be dealt with. This was the world controlled by men like Girondou and Moroni. Men with power and money and it took an equivalent amount of money to keep men like them away from one's life. It was a lesson, he felt, that the Aubanet family and the community they protected had yet to learn. He knew full well that the only real reason that they had been left alone by the outside world was that there was very little nothing in the Camargue that the outside world really wanted other than to be able to visit, take pictures and go back home.

Chapter 19: Shared Truths

Girondou was sitting at his desk, calmly going through paperwork. He smiled slightly as he thought of how the life of a major league criminal had changed. At the time when his father had run the territory forty years ago, he had been a very rough diamond indeed. Young, arrogant, rich and violent, always sheltered by an adoring father. But the old man knew what he was doing. The young Girondou soon was diverted from a highly successful career on the streets of Marseille to the more prosaic waters of the Collège Adolphe Monticelli in Marseille then to Paris to the Sorbonne and thence to *Institut d'Études Politiques de Paris*, more colloquially known as "Science Po". After that came Harvard business school for a post graduate degree. A few years later the young Dr Alexei Girondou came home to Marseille to manage the family business. Now, after much change, he found that his life was increasingly spent at his desk rather than in the streets, working out how to minimise tax rather than how to avoid paying it.

He sat with the current mountain of paperwork spread out in front of him as the door to his study was flung open and his daughter Solange burst in, face incandescent with anger; as close to complete hysteria as could be imagined. She rushed up to her father's desk, crashed both hands down in it and thrust her face as near to his as she could. The words came out in a torrent of inventive and spittle.

'You bastard! You complete and utter bastard! You disgusting piece of shit. I will kill you for this, mark my words.'

Girondou was completely frozen to the spot. All he could do was to stammer out:

'But, what my dear. What do you mean?'

Her anger continued.

'You fucking bastard. Now after all these years, I find out.'

Still Girondou was utterly at sea.

'But what? What have you found out?'

'I've found out, you miserable cocksucking animal that you murdered my father, stole his wife, our mother, for yourself and us too, bringing us up as if we were your children. No doubt there's a whole lot more but that'll do for starters. The whole of our lives have been a lie. This man Moroni and you are brothers, for Christ's sake. I hope he destroys you.'

She turned abruptly away and fled from the room as quickly as she had arrived, leaving Girondou completely paralysed. He was still sitting completely motionless when sometime later Angèle came in, tears streaming down her face and collapsed into one of the armchairs. She just looked at him. The children finally knew their great secret and now that the moment had come, they were completely unprepared for it.

'How?' cried Girondou in a broken voice. 'How?'

His beautiful wife looked at him through her tears.

'I talked to Amy. It was your brother. He somehow found them when they were shopping in town. I don't know why he told them, but he just did.'

He looked up.

'Amy?'

'She's obviously very upset but seems to be taking it better that her sister.'

'Why? Why now after all these years. Oh my God, I should have told them the whole thing years ago.'

Angèle grimaced through her tears.

'You wanted to tell them many times in the past, but I didn't let you. I was the one who wasn't brave enough. Now your brother has done what we should have done and perhaps he has cost us our family, our children.'

'How did they find out? Have you talked to them?'

Angèle shook her heard.

'They just told me that they were shopping in Marseille and had stopped for a cup of coffee in a café somewhere and this man I assume was Moroni came up to them and just started talking to them.'

'Who was with them?'

'Henk apparently.'

'Why didn't I know about this? Why the hell did he not stop it?'

Again, Angèle looked miserable.

'I don't know.'

He looked at her hopelessly.

'What can we do? Obviously, Moroni is up to something and he is not just shitstirring. If he has done this then there is obviously more in his mind. He has finally decided that the way to me is through my family. He knows if he can destroy that, he destroys me.'

Their father Girolamo, a lifelong supporter of Mussolini and his Fascist Party, had been a refugee from the partisans and had fled to Toulouse where he reckoned that he was safe from the vengeful Italian left. He had prospered mightily during the war servicing both Mussolini and then the Nazis, supplying them with everything from food and weapons to soldiers and intelligence. The man had been a thug and a killer and in the power vacuum that followed the German withdrawal from the South of France in 1944 he had quickly established a large criminal empire while the French themselves were trying to rediscover democracy. In the time of virtually everything being rationed, he was the man who ran the black market throughout the south. Clothes, food and wine, medicines; anything and everything that was in short supply, it came though Moroni and his network. Anyone who opposed him was simply killed with impunity. There were no almost police nor was there any justice system to speak of. The French were just obsessed with executing collaborators. The father had prospered and his three sons all entered the family business and by the time the men were old enough to do their own killing the eldest son, Sebastien, had responsibility for the west between Toulouse and the Spanish border, the middle son Fernand for

Toulouse to the Rhône and the youngest, Alexei, for the region between the Rhône and the Italian border.

Girondou reached for the phone and dialled a number he knew be heart although he had not used it often. Moroni answered in a mocking voice.

'Alexei, my dear fellow. How nice to hear from you. How can I help you on this fine sunny day?'

'Sebastian what have you done? Why?' Girondou could hardly get the words out. 'What have I done that you can hate me and my family so much?'

'You have a short memory, Alexei. You don't remember what happened back then.'

'I remember perfectly well, Sebastien. I also remember exactly what happened rather than just the fantasy version that you seem to have created in you own mind.'

'You killed our brother. I remember that.'

'I killed him as he broke into my bedroom in the middle of the night intending to put a bullet in my head, as I recall. I tried not to, but he gave me no choice.'

'You were screwing his wife, for God's sake.'

'We were having an affair and had been for some time.'

'She was still his wife, your sister-in-law,' Moroni replied in a voice that was getting angrier

'Fernand was a bastard and you know it,' said Girondou. 'He was vicious and nasty. He was a psychopath. He used to beat her up and abuse the children. She wanted to leave him and when she told him, he tried to kill me. It's just tough that I came out on top.'

Moroni spat the words down the phone line at Girondou.

'You killed my brother. Then you stole his wife and his two children and fled to Marseille. The whole thing killed father. So, in essence, you killed him as well.'

'That's bloody nonsense and you know it. He was eighty-eight years old and had had lung cancer for years. If you remember he had been dying for months. He spent the last six months of his life in agony in bed.'

'So, having killed your brother and your father, you left your family, changed your name and set up with the whore Angèle and her children in Marseille and became a king in your own country.'

Girondou said nothing. There was nothing to say. These were old bones that had been picked over many time before.

'So now your beloved daughters know that you're not their father.'

There was no disguising the triumph in Moroni's voice.

'Now they also know that you killed their father and their mother is a whore who was screwing you while she was having them. Perhaps I felt that the time had come for them to know that you aren't their father and that their mother is just a common slag. Good luck dealing with that, brother.'

Girondou was left staring sightlessly at the dead phone in his hand. After a while Angèle gently too it from him and replaced it, keeping hold of his hand as she did. She tried to offer something to the stricken man.

'I think it would be better if I talked with the girls. I am, after all, on their side of this story. Perhaps I could try to straighten things out a little.'

Girondou thought about it but not too long. There were really no options. He just nodded, eyes full of tears.

She got up and drew her distraught husband to his feet.

'Have courage, my darling. Perhaps we should have seen this coming and not allowed Moroni the chance of getting to you like this. But you and I know what the truth was all those years ago and we should trust that our children – children that you have bought up as your own family for all of their lives – they'll understand. I am also pretty sure that they've not been told the whole picture; what a monster Fernand actually was. I can tell them the whole story, not just a partial one created to harm you. At least let me try.'

She put her arms tightly around him and held him for a long moment. She could feel that he was shaking almost uncontrollably. After a while he whispered softly.

'All right. I'll leave it to you. They probably wouldn't listen to me anyway.'

She reluctantly turned away to find her shattered family leaving her husband behind silent and numb.

Smith's mobile phone number was a closely guarded secret. He had never liked telephones at the best of times and calls from unidentified people tended to be ignored. He had an equally tangential relationship with answering machines. So, it was unusual when a completely unknown number appeared on his phone that he answered the call. But these were unusual times. However, an equally unknown female voice awaited him.

'Monsieur Smith?'

'Yes?'

'This is Jeanne Hegeau, monsieur. I am Derek Deveraux's friend.'

Smith thought this was a fast response as he had only just asked Deveraux to see if she could help.

'Madame Hegeau, good morning. How nice to hear from you. How can I help?'

'Monsieur. I am not very sure what is going on, but you may not know that I am usually assigned to protecting Amy Girondou as Henk is more concerned with Solange these days. She seems to trust me and she's asked if I can contact you. She would like to talk to you in confidence.'

This was all rather startling. However, Smith remembered that Deveraux trusted this girl and the news that one of a pair of twins that he had hitherto thought of as inseparable wanted to talk to him in secret should be taken seriously. But he couldn't resist asking the obvious question.

'And why, madame, can Mademoiselle Girondou not ask me herself?'

The woman's voice sounded uncertain and lowered noticeably.

'She thinks that her mobile phone may be monitored, monsieur,'

This was not an explanation that Smith wanted to hear at all.

'Very well madame. What do you suggest?'

'Amy suggested yesterday that we might come into Arles to visit the shop of Christian Lacroix. It is Madame Girondou's birthday soon, so we could shop for a present for her. There is no Lacroix shop in Marseille. I would accompany her and perhaps we could meet somewhere.'

'OK. It's a good idea.'

He glanced at the kitchen clock. It was 9:30am.

'How about you come to my house in two hours? Keep your phones tuned on in case someone is actually monitoring them and wants to see where you are. As you enter the town turn both the GPS locators off at the same time. This will at least stop anyone tracking your movements too precisely. We can always think of an excuse if someone is unwise enough to remark on it. Don't worry if someone actually follows you by car although I doubt they will. The twins have been here many times before and in fact it would be unusual for them to visit Arles and not come to see me.'

'Very well, monsieur. Thank you.'

'Just keep a view behind you as to drive. Look for motorbikes as well as cars. I'm sure Deveraux has offered you advice on this. Until later then. Drive carefully. Something odd is clearly going on as I'm sure Deveraux told you and I think we should be careful.'

The two hours passed quickly and soon there was a knock on the door. Smith opened it to see Amy standing on the top step of the four that led down to street level. Below he was Jeanne at the wheel of one of the Girondou armoured Citroen limousines. Arthur was, as usual, delighted to see a visitor. Having greeted her with the customary kiss on the cheek Smith led her through the little house into the garden terrace where they sat at the table under the thick canopy of vine by now burdened with a heavy crop of grapes.

'Jeanne will do my Lacroix shopping and wait till we have finished.' she said by way of explanation.

She was certainly not the carefree cheerful beauty that he was used to. She looked drawn and very nervous. He poured a glass of cold fresh orange juice for them both and took her hand.

'Take all the time you want, my dear. Say what you want however it comes out. Remember that this visit will remain secret as will everything you tell me. That includes, if necessary, from your sister and parents as well.'

She hesitated for another moment, took a deep breath and started in a bit of rush, all the time holding tightly on to his hand.

'There's a lot you don't know about our family. I'm pretty sure that daddy has never told you. I would also never have told you now, but I think that our family is in great trouble and I can't see anyone else being able to help. There have been plenty of times in the past when daddy has said that he thinks you are the only person he really trusts outside the family. So, I have decided to trust you in spite of the fact as you will see it means betraying my sister and possibly my mother as well. What you don't know is that daddy is not our real father. Mummy was originally married to daddy's brother; Fernand and we are his daughters not Alexei's. Fernand was killed in a family fight when we were two years old. Daddy married Angèle almost immediately. According to mummy Fernand used to abuse her and beat her up.'

She paused a moment as if to gather a little strength. Smith intervened gently to give her time. Alexei rescued her from that. He killed Fernand. I think he and mummy were having an affair as well.

Smith listened quietly without, he hoped, letting her know how little he was actually interested in this family history. He wasn't even interested in his own let alone that of a French gangster.

'I understand but I am not sure where this gets us in explaining the present situation.'

She raised her hand. There was clearly more to come.

'Solange and I have always suspected something but it was never talked about and we basically ignored our feelings. However, what we didn't know until recently is that there were originally three brothers, all members of the same criminal family lead by their father that controlled almost the whole of the southern half of France. It was divided up between the three of them.'

Again, Smith couldn't see where this was leading. There seemed nothing that could cause the present difficulties. So, he just waited as Amy took if possible, an even bigger breath.

'Yesterday Solange and I were going shopping in Marseille and having a coffee and when we were approached by a stranger who identified himself as the third brother. He also told us that the man who killed our real father Fernand was his brother Alexei who was now, of course, our own daddy. It was part of one those family power struggles that happen from time to time. This man's name was Sebastian Moroni. He is the third brother'

Suddenly a number of possible explanations of the current situation sprang into Smith's mind. But while he began to digest them, she indicated that there was more to come.

'This where it becomes rather complicated. Henk and Solange had already started to get rather close some time ago. They regularly went off on long walks together and Henk seemed to be devoting more time to her than to guarding daddy and the rest of the family. I didn't think much about it really. Solange has always been rather headstrong. Then I remember that one day a few weeks ago when we were swimming, by mistake I picked up Solange's mobile instead of my own. We have the same model. I wanted to check on my messages. Her phone was unlocked, and I saw that she had been getting a lot of messages from Sebastian Moroni. I didn't have time to read any in detail, but I saw Henk's name mentioned more than once.'

'You remember that Mummy took us away for a few days to the house in Chamonix. That was when you came and made us all come back without realising that it was the last thing daddy wanted you to do. Apparently, he had just been told by this Moroni man that he was going to tell us about it. Daddy just went to pieces. Since then they have both been a complete mess and nothing is getting done. Daddy's business is in a mess and there are many of his people who are beginning to talk about getting rid of him and talking to this Mr. Moroni about taking over. He seems just to be completely upset all the time. Now Solange has confronted daddy with it and there was a terrible row. Mummy was very upset too, and daddy was completely shattered. I really don't know what to do so I came to you for help.'

Smith leant forward and took her hand.

'Amy have you talked to your mother or father any more about any of this?'

She shook her head.

'No. I thought about it obviously, but I felt I needed to talk to someone outside the family and who could be trusted. So, I came to you. I know that the mummy and daddy need help and I know they trust you. I did think about talking to Solange. We have always been close, and I wondered if I could talk to her about whatever she has been so involved in. But in the end, something stopped me.'

'What was that, Amy.'

301

She sounded very hesitant.

'Well before this happened, she had changed a lot, Peter almost completely. Since getting together with Henk she had kept herself to herself and only really talks to him. They have gone away together sometimes, and I know that Jeanne doesn't always know where they are. She doesn't seem to go anywhere near daddy and even mummy has difficulties talking to her. Henk has given her a new mobile phone. I've seen it. But she hasn't given me or mummy the number. I don't know what she is using it for. Jeanne told me not to use mine either except for non-confidential stuff. But not all this has come to a head with our meeting Mr. Moroni yesterday. Solange has gone crazy.'

She stopped suddenly as if running completely out of breath all of a sudden.

Smith stood up and took her in a big hug. He held her tightly and for a long time before gently sitting her down at the table. Smith took rapid stock of what he had just been told. Certainly, it explained Girondou's situation. It also explained the danger he was facing. Somehow, he felt that there was a connection with the Camargue matter as well although he couldn't figure it out yet. However, there was a few more practical things to arrange.

'Amy. Firstly, thank you telling me all this. I understand how difficult it is. It was definitely the right thing to do. You were right to come to me, and I will do everything I can to help sort things out. Although you should understand that it is really your father who should be doing this. Talk to your mother and keep each other strong.

She knows everything that happened all those years ago and what is happening, and she need to know that you are on her side. Really, Amy, that is really, really important. You must also remember that it is Alexei who has loved you and cared for you all these years. He is your father, not some dead memory.'

He changed his tone of voice to a more business-like one.

'Now listen carefully to me. We better be getting you back home soon now. Given what is in the wind at the moment your parents are probably anxious about your return. Unless the question of visiting me comes up in conversation I wouldn't mention it. It might start some sort of cross examination. If it does, of course, then just talk about brief social call to see me. If anyone mentions your phone being switched off, just say you ran out of battery but remember who asks you about it. Nothing more. Please write down your mobile phone number and your sisters. Do you both have the same type?'

'Yes,' she nodded. 'That's the reason I made the mistake of picking hers up in the first place.'

'Good. In a day or two you'll get a new one. It will be identical to your current one, but it will have a second number that will be completely secure. Jeanne will give it to you and tell you how it works. I want us to be able to talk whenever we wish and in complete security. Apart from that try to act as normally as you can. Please trust Jeanne. She can always get in touch with me via Deveraux and that might be safer for you too. I know that will be difficult, but you must try. It may be that Solange is being misled by Henk or indirectly by

303

Moroni or both. At this stage it's useless to try to intervene, especially as you are supposed not to know too much about it all. Just try to do the usual things and stay near to your mother. Act normally with Henk but make sure you're never alone with him for the time being. Above all don't try to do any amateur sleuthing. Just leave that to me.'

They stood, and he gave her another a long tight hug.

'Keep brave, my dear. We'll sort this mess out, don't worry.'

With that and another kiss on the cheek he let her out of the front into the waiting Citroen. As he watched it speed of down the hill beside the amphitheatre, he hoped that he had sounded a good deal more confident that he felt. His next call was to Gentry.

'You available for half an hour, Gentry?'

'Of course, old chap. However, I should say that I haven't got much for you yet.'

'Don't worry. I got some stuff for you, for once.'

The call ended, and Smith threw out some biscuits for a sleeping Arthur before locking the house and making his way quickly to Gentry's lair in the town below.There was something of a silence after Smith had relayed his news while Gentry assembled their usual brace of whiskeys. Unusually it was Gentry who was first prepared to guess.

'So, having completely destabilised Girondou's family, Moroni is using the dubious charms of Henk to create a vengeful Solange to divert her father while he takes over Girondou's patch. Bit of personal vengeance in this I feel. For the moment I can't see where cuddling up to a bunch of discontented farmers fits in now, especially as we put a very large spoke in the works of his first Camargue venture but I'm sure it does somewhere. In any case I am pretty sure that he won't give up, even if you put yourself in the firing line.'

'Not for the first time, Gentry, I have a feeling that you are spot on. However, proving it might be a bit tricky.'

There was something of a snort from the opposite armchair.

'Can't remember your being unduly worried about such niceties as proof in past times, old friend. However how do you want to progress?'

'As before, I think. You continue to keep tabs on Moroni. Sooner or later this will come to a head and there will be a solution one way or the other. I just want to make sure that there is a little collateral damage as possible. In spite of my apparent refusal to need proof, It would be a pity to start killing people if they didn't really deserve it.'

'OK. I have to admit that I am finding the farmers to be slightly more difficult. Not too many records or electronic devices to look for.'

'I may be able to help here, I think. I've got Deveraux and his new girlfriend digging around a bit there and, of course, Madame Durand's team of boy spies as well as Madame Durand herself. I might talk to Emile Aubanet too. I must admit I am surprised that Moroni hasn't given up after the failure of last week. There must be an awful lot of money in this trafficking.'

Gentry sighed.

'Millions. The average price is between five and eight thousand dollars each. Say a low average of six. If the average shipment is, say, one hundred people, and you do two a month, then simple arithmetic gives an income of about nearly fifteen million dollars a year.'

'Christ,' muttered Smith. 'I had no idea.'

After a silence, Gentry went on.

'As I said I haven't been interested in why Moroni hasn't given the whole thing up. The numbers show why he is persisting. But why he is not adopting his usual method. By reputation his general approach is more muscular but here he seems to be persisting in just trying to persuade people onto his side. Maybe he understands that these farmers aren't his usual soft clients who can be scared with a gun out bought with cash. Apart from the kill at the bullfight, which was a very public demonstration of what he does to people who double cross him, he has been quite gentle by his standards. Perhaps he doesn't want to rock the boat with whatever he had got in play in Marseille.'

'We a lot of background on the people Moroni is still talking to. That might lead us somewhere. I think we might do some electronic snooping on Henk and on the two girls. We should have Henk's telephone details or be able to trace a new one if he has got one. Here are the girls' phone numbers and types. I want an identical one made up for Amy with secret second number and the usual secured access if someone who shouldn't gets their hands on it. If the ungodly are doing their jobs properly she'll be monitored, and I want her to feel she can contact us if she wants to. This may entail a bit of time-consuming surveillance. Do you know anyone we could use for a while?'

Gentry nodded.

'Won't come cheap though.'

Again, Smith smiled grimly.

'Don't worry, Girondou will pay.'

With that the two parted and Smith made his way back up the hill towards home.

Chapter 20: Funeral

The little church of the Nativity of the Virgin at Le Sambuc was full and there was even a large crown left outside. The most important were inside, of course. A broad cross-section of locals from both town and country, bullfighting and farming. As ever in Provence, the two were intertwined. Some also came from the bullfighting fraternity in Spain, other bull fighters and some breeders too. It was a rare tribute to a young man who had not yet even achieved his *alternativa*. Smith had already made his apologies. He didn't want to take he pew next to Martine and her father, surrounded by people he didn't know. Martine understood. He was happy to stand outside, on the outside of the crowd. No matter what happened and no matter how long he would be here, this was a part of Provencale life that he would never completely join. He felt a little like an intruder. Oddly, that didn't concern him very much; or rather at all. He had always made his own way, perhaps too much and too well. An ex-wife might have been evidence of that. He had always felt a bit an observer when he was forced into contact with life outside his own immediate circle, so there was no real reason not to feel one now. His observation was actually not quite as casual as it seemed. Apart from father and daughter Aubanet and, of course, Deveraux who was certainly present but, as usual, not visible, he was the only person present who knew what actually happened at the corrida. While everyone at the church was engrossed in mourning another, fortunately rare, death in the bullring, he was more interested in seeing if anyone else who also actually knew the truth turned up. He thought it unlikely. Whatever else he might be, Moroni was no voyeur. He was also no fool. He had certainly disposed of enough people in his life to make anything special out of this one, no matter novel was his chosen method. To him it had just been making a point. Now these bloody little farmers would take him seriously just as everyone else in his world did.

The church in Le Sambuc was off the main road down a lane that, like so many of the smaller roads in Provence ending up in a dead end at the side of the river Rhône. In fact, most of the village had developed either side of that road. It left the main road at right angles as the Rue de L'École as that is where it went. Having got there it continued as the Chemin de l'Eglise as its next destination. Its final length was as the Rue du Grand Paty that it took it to the Rhône.

Smith had already looked quickly around the graveyard. It was a calm little place that also housed the Aubanet family plot. Slightly unusually, it was across the road from the church, bordered by a freshly painted white wall and, equally unusually, it had room to spare. Something, Smith wondered, to do with the longevity of the local residents. A cursory examination of the tombs and inscriptions revealed that they obviously thought that the biblical three score years and ten was merely a starting point. Arles, after all, had been home to the legendary Jeanne Calmet who died as the longest-lived woman whose life was documented in history. She made it to the age of one hundred and twenty-two. Like many such cemeteries, most of the plots and the graves that occupied them were rather grand, being given over to families rather than individuals. That of the Aubanet family was elegant and well-kept but not significantly grander than many of the those that lined the cemetery walls.

Le Sambuc was the closest church to the Cordiez family farm. It had never been a big place; numbering only five hundred souls at most but, like most of the villages of its size throughout the region, it still had its own bull ring and the young Cordiez would have started his career there as a child. Even now, he had returned regularly to the little circle on the Place des Sureaux just to the west of the main road to practice on his own or to give demonstrations to local children whose hearts were set on following him to the great arenas of Spain and France. He would still visit the cafés in the village to chat with friends all of whom were interested in him and his stories of increasing fame in spite of his curmudgeonly father. The boy's success bought credit to them all. It was something in their hard lives on the land that they could share in and which bought a sense of pride to them all.

Smith just stood quietly on the outskirts of the crowd that was waiting patiently for the service to be completed. It was a good place to look around and try to see if anyone untoward had turned up. Finally, the service was over, and the congregation filed out after the coffin and the six pall bearers. The coffin was plain varnished wood with the sole decoration of a single bullfighter's sword, an *estoque*, un-sheathed; its short hilt and handle dressed in the traditional blood-red linen binding, lying gleaming down the length of the coffin, the sun glinting off its polished blade. They were followed by Franco Cordiez and his wife, united for a short while, at least, in their grief. The rest followed, and Smith waited until Martine and her father had almost passed before falling in beside Martine who immediately threaded her arm tightly through as they crossed the road and entered the cemetery.

As the company surrounded the grave to witness the interment, Smith again looked around at the assembly, but he still couldn't see anything suspicious. Most were in full Provençale costume. The women in muted colours and the men wearing black jackets in spite of the heat. Those that weren't wore suits. It was a show of respect. The coffin was lowered into the grave, sword and all and the crowd waited their turn to pass by the grave, mumble a few words and throw down a handful of earth. Both Cordiez and his wife were tearful, and they weren't the only ones.

A few went up to Cordiez to offer personal condolences; not many. Martine took Smith by the arm and led him across to the grieving father.

'This is a sad day for all of us, Monsieur Cordiez. Please accept our condolences. Please remember that you can always come to us if there is anything we can do to help,'

Cordiez had tears in his eyes and just nodded his thanks. Then quite suddenly he reached forward and took Smith by the elbow and pulled him firmly away to a little distance from the others. He turned and looked Smith directly in the eyes.

311

'More than anyone I knew my son, Monsieur. I followed his life and his training minutely. I knew his abilities and his weaknesses. Above all I knew exactly how he fought his bulls, his timing and his balance. I knew the way he moved better than he did himself. That is why, monsieur, I saw him stumble at a moment when I knew he would never have stumbled. I didn't understand but then the bull got him, and I felt that my life too was ending, and I forgot what I had seen. Then, monsieur, after the corrida had finished, I came back to the Arena to collect the last of Robert's possessions and I saw you out there looking at the ground where Robert had fallen. I saw you rake the sand and stop to pick something up. At that moment I knew that something wasn't right.'

It was clear by the man's unremitting grip on his elbow that Cordiez wanted something more.

'Mr Smith, I know of your reputation and I want you to answer me truthfully on this the day when we bury my beautiful son. How did my son die? Was it the bull or something else?'

Smith had no option. The man deserved the truth. In a low voice that couldn't be heard by the others he replied:

'You son was killed by a rifle bullet, Monsieur Cordiez, not by the bull. He was shot the very instant he began to place the estocada. He was murdered.'

Cordiez just stood without a flicker of emotion. The stare didn't waver.

'Do you know who it was?'

312

'Yes, I rather think I do.'

'Then, Monsieur Smith, when you are certain, would you please bring me this man?'

Smith had no choice.

'Yes, Monsieur Cordiez, I will.'

The man released his grip and nodded curtly before walking back past Smith and returning to the small group that was still waiting.

Smith just felt he wanted to get out of there. Some sort of wake had been organised and was to take place in the little community centre in the village across the main road and Smith was desperately trying to think of a way to get out of going. He just wanted to get back to his little house in Arles for a while. Fortunately he had had the foresight to leave Arthur back in Arles to provide just such an excuse should it be necessary. He was on the point of using the excuse when his phone vibrated in his jacket pocket.

'Monsieur Smith,' came the unmistakable voice of Sheik Nasir. 'I hope I haven't interrupted anything but if you're coming back home later I would be pleased to see you tonight for dinner if you're free.' Perhaps because it provided such a ready-made solution to his problem he was delighted to accept. The Sheik sounded genuinely pleased.

'Good. Then I'll be honoured to see you at my house at about ten. Please bring Arathar. He too is always welcome in my house.'

The conversation was ended. Smith smiled at the fact that the old ways of late eating were alive and well in the Arab quarter of

Arles. He quickly made his excuses, drawing a somewhat arch look from his beloved Martine, and took his battered Peugeot from the equally dusty roadside and made his way towards Arles with a deep sense of relief.

Much later was with a surprised but highly delighted greyhound that he set out from his little house down the hill beside the Arena just as the last of the light seeped out of the day. The Sheik's house was only two of three minutes away and as he turned through the low arch on the Rue August Tardieu into the little courtyard from which the Sheiks house gave, he was astonished to see that tables and chairs had been set out and oil-fired lanterns hung from the surrounding walls. A large desert canopy had been erected over the whole yard. What was more the courtyard was full of people, all standing as Smith and Arthur entered. There was no applause but the Sheik came forward to welcome his guests.

'as-salaam 'alaykum,' was accompanied by a slight bow.

'wa 'alaykum as-salaam,' replied Smith correctly to the obvious pleasure of the assembled crowd.

'We wanted to thank you, Peter.'

Smith was completely baffled. He had absolutely no idea what was going on and said so. The Sheik just patted him on the arm that he had taken.

'Patience, my friend. There will, I'm afraid, be a little speech later.'

The feast was long and extensive. Plates of food came and went and even a freely wandering Arthur finally collapsed at Smith's feet replete and dropped off to sleep. Smith glanced down in wonder. He had never seen such a thing. Everyone was clearly having a very good time. The guests also wandered freely amongst each other's tables and everyone as they passed behind Smith's chair touched him gently on the shoulder. Finally the Sheik stood.

'Friends. I won't make a long speech but you all know why we are here. Over the last few weeks some people who are not our friends have been making money by offering to bring many of our countrymen illegally into France from out homelands in North Africa; from Algeria and Morocco, from Libya and the Sudan. Some came from your own families or at least were our countrymen. Many suffered, many died and few arrived safely. All had paid – money they couldn't afford or had to borrow – but few actually succeeded in achieving this new life that, even if they succeeded in the crossing, would entail their looking over their shoulders for the gendarmes for the rest of their lives.'

'That dreadful trade has been stopped, for the present and in this area at least, by the personal intervention of one man; the man who is our honoured guest here tonight. So, Monsieur Smith,' he said looking down at him, 'we thank you for saving many of our fellow countrymen from getting involved in this terrible business. We have all worked hard to be honest French citizens since we came both here to Arles, to Mas Thibert and other places in the south. Much prejudice still remains but the very least we can do is to abide by the law of Allah and the laws of France. You, my friend, have helped us do this.'

With that the Sheik sat while the assembled company lifted their tea glasses and offered the toast. Smith just remained still in his seat, completely astonished. He looked around and recognised the young man with the greyhound he had met by the side of the canal at Mas Thibert. Realising how well he had been outsmarted he raised his own glass in the direction of the smiling young man.

It was well past two in the morning as he and Arthur walked slowly up the hill to his house of the place de la Major. It had been a memorable evening, of course. He felt both content and proud that this group had seen enough of him to trust him. That meant a lot. But he had also solved the mystery of the Sheik. The General was a long way from being retired. He was still employed to keep the peace amongst his Arab compatriots. As international terrorism grew, men like Sheik Nasir would use their connections and their mosques to keep their little bits of the world calm. Retired or not, the man still worked for the Elysée.

Chapter 21: Martine Takes Lunch

The whole thing started the day before as Martine was sitting at her office desk when the call came.

'Martine? Hi. This is Angèle. How are you?'

Somewhat surprised as it was the first time that she could recall Alexei Girondou's wife making contact, Martine's reply was somewhat guarded especially given what was going on in that particular family.

'Er ... fine, Angèle. Thank you. How are you?'

'Martine. I was wondering if you would like to come here tomorrow for a spot of lunch? It doesn't seem that us girls have much of a chance to chat these days.'

In reality, Martine thought that the opportunity had never really arisen before and, to be frank, she hadn't particularly missed it. However, she knew that her husband was going through some sort of difficulties and that would certainly be impacting Angèle. So, in spite of the fact that she was extremely busy and had much more on her plate than she had time to deal with, she offered an enthusiastic response.

'Well, how kind, Angèle. Of course. I'd be delighted. What time do you want me to come?'

So now she was sitting in the back of the Range Rover being whisked along the familiar road from the Arles river crossing down the road Sausset-les-Pins. However, she had no time to gaze out of the window as she was balancing a lapful of paperwork in the hope of at least getting some of it done before they got there. Jean-Marie, as usual, was her driver.

Soon that they drove through the gates and down the long drive that led from the road down the hill to the house. Jean-Marie was a little surprised that the pneumatic bollards that were usually raised to protect the access were lowered. But he just shrugged mentally at this apparent lack of security. It wasn't particularly good practice, but he presumed the gate man had been warned of their arrival and had done the necessary in advance. He raised his hand in the direction of the gatehouse but couldn't actually see the man who usually staffed it.

Angèle was there to greet them and quickly took Martine into the house while Jean-Marie went in the general direction of the kitchen. He looked around him as he went but couldn't see either Henk van der Togt, Girondou's bodyguard or his deputy, Jeanne Hugeau, who he knew was rapidly becoming an serious item with Deveraux. In fact, the place was rather quiet altogether but as he wasn't really too familiar with the place he wondered if that was normal. He left the ladies to it and just as he turned into what was essentially the staff entrance, he heard a call from behind him. Jeanne can across the courtyard waving in greeting.

'Jean-Marie. How nice to see you.'

The pair exchanged the customary kisses before she continued.

'I hadn't heard that you were coming today.'

Jean-Marie replied: 'Well, it seems a bit of a last-minute thing. Madame Girondou invited Madame Aubanet for lunch, I gather. So here I am.'

'Well, I'm delighted to see you. Let's go in and see if the cook can rustle up something for us as well.'

So, they went into the house together and were soon seated either side of a long scrubbed wooden table each with a glass of wine. A few niceties were exchanged before Jean-Marie got to the point that was worrying him.

'I didn't see Henk when I came in. Is he around?'

Jeanne grimaced.

'He seems to be absent quite a lot of the time these days; either with Solange or just plain missing. Between us, it is a bit of a worry.'

'Have you seen him today?'

'Well, come to think of it. I haven't.'

Jean-Marie was immediately concerned. Something was obviously awry with security surrounding the Girondou household. Normally it wouldn't bother him too much. It was none of his business, really and they could do what they wanted. But on this occasion, his boss could be in firing line and for that he was responsible.

'Well I suggest we take a look around, you and I. I don't know what the usual standing orders are around here but when we arrived, the entrance barrier was lowered, and we weren't stopped or challenged. In fact, the old guy who usually sits in the gate house didn't seem to be there.'

Jeanne frowned.

'No, none of that sounds right. Look, let me quickly go out and have a quick look around. There's probably nothing out of the ordinary going on. It's probably better if I go to start with. You're not very well known here, and I don't want some trigger-happy local making a fool of himself.'

With that she left him seated in the kitchen to read the paper and firstly drove up to the gatehouse. She immediately knew something was wrong. The door was swinging open on its hinges and when she went in she saw the gatekeeper was lying on the floor behind his chair, blood pooling around his head. She bent over to check him and saw a single bullet hole in the centre of his forehead. She quickly operated the controls that raised the barrier, but it had been disabled. The huge electric gates were also stalled fully open. She lifted the telephone and found it dead, as were the telephone lines. Looking out from the hut she saw that neither of the gun positions set back from the drive and concealed in the undergrowth that usually guarded the top of the drive were pointing at the sky. Something clearly was going on. Rather than take her car back she ran down the hillside taking a direct route through the tree and shrubs rather than following the winding drive. A movement seen through the bushes just short of the house caught her attention. She dropped down to observe an SUV drawing up outside the house and group of three, Henk and two others, all carrying guns about to go into the house. A fourth man stayed with the vehicle.

The door they were entering was the same entrance that Jean-Marie had used but there was no way to warn him now. He would just have to take care of himself. Her priority was the family. That was her job. She knew that Angèle and Martine were in the drawing room, and she presumed the two daughters were there as well when she last checked while Alexei was working in the room beyond that in his study. The drawing room had full length windows that gave out on to the terrace as did the study. She circled at speed around the house and approached the study room hoping to get there in time before Henk did. Girondou was her prime responsibility and she knew that he would be the main target of any attack.

The earliest causality of the invasion was Jean-Marie. He was sitting in the kitchen have a cup of coffee while his boss was beginning her lunch. The door was opened and in walked Henk. He still had a smile of greeting as two other men dressed in black jeans and T shirts and wearing a black balaclavas came quickly in behind them. One hit Jean-Marie very hard over the temple with a short leather cosh. He was knocked clean off his chair and to lie unconscious on the floor. Henk pushed the two cooks out of the door telling them not to come back. Another man arrived together with Solange.

Jeanne came in through the portes-fenêtres into Girondou's study with a rush, her gun in hand.

321

'Monsieur Girondou. We are being attacked by a group of men. They seem to be led by Henk. Please get up and go to the safe room immediately.'

Faced with an almost complete paralysis on the part of her audience she took Girondou by the hand and wrenched him to his feet and started to drag the across the room towards to door that led down a corridor to a safe room. He gasped:

'Angèle!'

Jeanne almost shouted at him.

'Get yourself into that room and close the door. I'll go and get Angèle.'

She thrust him into the corridor and waited just long enough for her to be sure the he was doing as he asked. She turned around and headed back through the study and into the sitting room. There she found Angèle and Amy talking to Martine.

'Quick, you must all get up, go through the study and get into the safe room. Monsieur Girondou is already there. We are being attacked. I don't know who they are, but I am pretty sure that our bodyguard, Henk van der Togt, is with them. Please go now!'

Solange and two men burst into the room. Solange went straight up to her mother.

'Where is he, mother? Where is that bastard who killed my father?'

Angèle was shocked.

'What do you mean, Solange? Why? What's going on?'

The man came forward and thrust Solange to one side and pointing his gun directly at Angèle's head.

'Tell me where your old man is, you bitch, or I'll blow your head off.'

There was a shot as Jeanne put a nine-millimetre slug into the man's neck, knocking him off his feet while covering Angèle in a spray of red. The second man immediately aimed at Angèle and was about to fire as Solange cried:

'No no. Not my mother,'

She flung herself across in front of her just as the man fired. The bullet hit her squarely in the back. She too fell to the ground in a bloody heap.

Martine who had been standing slightly to one side then hurled herself at the gunman but was easily caught by him in an arm lock. Taking advantage of the diversion. Jeanne managed to drag Angèle and Amy out of the door and through into the study, shutting the door and bolting it behind her.

Angèle was still struggling, crying out.

'We must see to Solange, Jeanne. I can't leave her there.'

'Madame Girondou, I must get you and Amy to the safe room. If we go back in there, they will kill you. I'll go back to find Solange. Now go to join your husband and lock yourself in that bloody room until I tell you to come out.'

She waited until the door was closed and locked before turning back towards the study. With luck she could get out of the house again. She couldn't see whether Solange was alive or dead but going back into the sitting room would be suicide. She had a much better chance if she was outside.

Back in the sitting room, the second gunman was still trying to deal with the struggling Angèle when Henk burst in.

'What the fuck's happening here, you moron. Who told you to come in here before I was ready. Where's Girondou?'

'Escaped into some safe room or other. Frank is dead, shot by some French bit. God knows where she come from. So's your girlfriend.' he said, gesturing at the bloody little pile of bodies on the carpet.

Henk looked at the firmly closed door at the far side of the room and decided that cutting his losses was about the best he could achieve. He knew that Moroni would be furious. But perhaps Madame Aubanet would sweeten the pill slightly.

'Get Madame Aubanet secure in the car then come back to get the bodyguard from the kitchen. He's still out cold.'

'What about Frank?'

Henk sneered at the corpse.

'Leave the asshole there for someone else to clear up. Serves him fucking well right.'

The man left dragging Martine with him. Henk went across the room and tried the door to the study. It was locked but one kick was enough to open it. The study was empty. He crossed that room too and carefully opened the door into the corridor. There was nobody behind it, but he saw that the door at the far end was closed. He knew that the door was solid steel. He also knew enough about the little safe room to know he wouldn't get in alive if Jeanne was in there too. He felt an idiot. He had forgotten all about the bloody woman. There was nothing he could do. At least, he thought, he could get away easily. The safe room was not a particularly sophisticated one. It was more a large reinforced cupboard. It wasn't equipped like some he had seen, with survival kit, secure ventilation and so on. He also knew that there were no comms and no phone signal. But they wouldn't risk coming out for some time.

One of the assailants had got Martine out to the car and set about bundling her into the back seat and tied her feet and wrists with cable ties. He sent the driver into the house to get Jean-Marie. Jeanne came slowly around the side of the house from the garden. She had a clear shot at the man but there was a strong probability that she would hit Martine. She waited until the man straightened up then she stepped out and shot him through the chest. She was just aiming a second shot when Henk appeared from the house. He hesitated before loosing off a fast shot at her which caught her in the shoulder and spun her to the ground. The driver arrived hauling a still unconscious Jean-Marie by the collar of his shirt.

'Put him in the back of the car and tie his ankles and wrists. Then get us the fuck out of here.'

Before long they were away up the drive and on the road out. There was a chartered helicopter waiting in a secure hangar at the airport at Marignane only ten minutes away. Once there, no one would catch them.

'Christ. What a cluster fuck,' thought van der Togt. Girondou was obviously very much alive thanks to that French bitch. God knows what Moroni was going to think about it all. With any luck their hostage might save his neck.

Chapter 22: A Second Rescue

The call had come in to Smith from Amy. They had waited for ten minutes or so before coming out of the room. They had found Solange dead and Jeanne outside bleeding heavily from a shoulder wound, fading in and out of consciousness.

'Peter. There has been an attack here. Henk and three men came to try to kill daddy. Solange is dead and Jeanne is wounded. Two of them are dead too. Jeanne got them. Solange was with them.'

As usual, Smith felt very calm indeed as he found out what he could from a surprisingly rational young lady.

'Your father and mother?'

'They're safe. Jeanne got us into the safe room. But, Peter, they took Madame Aubanet and Jean-Marie away with them.'

Smith felt his heart lurch.

'Were they harmed?'

'No. I don't think so. They seem to have been taken hostage or something. Jeanne got two of them, I think.'

'Deveraux's training paying off,' he thought grimly.

'OK. Amy. How are your parents?'

'Daddy just seems in shock and mummy is hysterical.'

'You're doing very well but you have to hold it together a little longer. First, I need to call the police and tell them to get medical help to Jeanne. So, I'm going to ring off and do that. Then I'll call you straight back. OK?'

'Yes.' Came the answer.

Smith made the call and then phoned Amy back

'Your house will soon be swarming with police and medical people, Amy. Your father won't like that but that's just tough. It's more important that Jeanne gets treatment. Please let me know when they arrive. Are there any other people around?'

'Well that's the strange thing. The whole house and grounds seem to be deserted.'

'Right. Just sit tight with the family. Call me immediately if you need anything or want to talk. Perhaps the sight of hundreds of policemen will bring your father to his senses. If you can find out what hospital they are taking Jeanne to and perhaps you can give me a call. Deveraux will want to know. I'll check up on you from time to time but now I must see about getting Martine back.'

'OK', came the surprisingly calm young voice and she rang off.

The next call was to Deveraux.

'Where are you, Dev.'

'Doing some shopping the Arles. I was thinking of going down to Marseille unless you have anything for me.'

He listened in silence as Smith told him of events at Sausset. It didn't take long.

'Where do you want me, boss?'

Smith knew exactly what he was getting at. Deveraux would naturally want to find Jeanne, but he also knew that she would be in hospital and there was very little he could do. Steering clear of Sausset would also be a good idea with all the police having fun there as they finally had a pretext to peer into every bit of Girondou's private life.

'I suggest you get yourself to the Mas as soon as possible. Émile will be there on his own and someone needs to tell him what happened and stay with him. I doubt there is any danger to him, but it would to as well to have you there. I'll get to Gentry and get a rescue plan under way then I'll join you. I'll tell you as soon as I have news of Jeanne, obviously.'

The next call was to Gentry with the same story. Gentry just listened in silence. Gentry had also understood what was necessary. That had been his job throughout the years of his friendship with Smith. He had been the organiser, the supplier of equipment, the enabler. He had done the planning with and Smith had carried it out, often at times when success was unlikely. The conversation had been extremely brief.

'Moroni's got Martine, David. She was visiting Angèle. I need a plan.'

There was no hesitation as if the request was the most normal thing in the world. This sort of thing had happened before.

'Leave it to me, Peter. Do nothing until I contact you again. Nothing. OK?

'Yes.' The answer was a hard one.

"Do I have 12 hours?'

'Yes, I think you do. Presumably if Moroni wanted Martine dead, he would have done it then and there. I've no idea why she was there but my guess is that she is collateral damage to a plan that went wrong. But Henk has obviously taken her for a reason. That means he wants to bargain in some way. '

Gentry knew his friend well enough to know that bargaining was actually a long way from Smith's mind.

'All right. I'll be back to you within the hour with a rescue plan. I'll need 12 hours to organise things. If you get any indication that things are more urgent, let me know immediately.'

'I want to have Devereux. It's up to you to add however many you want to make the thing work. Don't include anyone from Girondou's lot. He's as useless as a chocolate teapot at the moment and has got troubles of her own. Once the police have finished there get some people there to lock the place down. God only knows what happened to the people who were there originally. Bought off probably. That's Girondou's problem but we need to keep him safe for now at least and preferably isolated. The last thing we need is Girondou doing something silly and getting in our way. I'm going out to the Mas des Saintes now to talk to Émile. He'll probably be having a heart attack or soon will be.'

With that the connection was cut. His next call was to Émile. The old man also listened in silence as Smith told him the story.

'Émile, I'm on my way to see you and Deveraux should be with you very soon. Please do nothing until I get there. If you get a telephone call from Moroni answer it but just listen. Don't talk to him. Don't bargain with him. Don't even demand to talk to Martine. You must say absolutely nothing. If he issues any threats or instructions try to remember what he says but do not reply. Trust me, Émile, I will get her back. Have absolutely no doubt at all about that. You know I mean what I say. Tell the men on the gates that I will be coming.'

The old man's voice came back sounding very faint and querulous.

'I understand, Peter. Again I seem to need you look after my family for me.'

It was not a conversation Smith had time for.

'All right, Émile. I don't think you're in the immediate danger but get a few of your people with guns into the house and all of you stay put. As I said, I'll be with you in half an hour. '

With that he rang off and closed up the house. He extracted two Glock Pistols from his floor safe; a 21 with a 13 round magazine and a smaller 39 with a 6 round capacity. As a second thought struck him, he pulled out of the safe his father's old Fairbairn-Sykes services knife. Positively ancient by modern standards but it had seen service during the Second World War and he had seldom operated in the field without it. An extremely battered metal leg sheath came with it. Old it may have been, but it still did the job. Smith remembered grimly that a solid gold FS fighting knife formed part of the commandos Memorial at Westminster Abbey. His father's old knife could well be doing service again soon. He also stuffed some well used but serviceable combat gear in a plastic bag, put it and Arthur in the back of his old Peugeot and headed once again out of the city towards the Mas des Saintes buried deep in the Camargue.

When he got there, he found Émile in a state of shock and the rest of the household in a state of confusion. Deveraux was nowhere to be seen but that was nothing unusual. Someone had obviously spent a little time sorting out a rudimentary defence.

'Émile. What do you know about why Martine went to see Girondou?'

To give the old man credit, he thought a bit and then made perfect sense.

'I was just out on the farm so she just left a message. She just said that she had got an invitation to have lunch with Angèle. She took Jean-Marie and left about half past eleven. It was all a bit last minute, I think. She certainly hadn't mentioned it before.'

Smith explained that they were making a plan to get them back. He didn't admit to the possibility that there might be no-one to rescue - alive, that is. He explained about Gentry, a man whom Aubanet had never met and that they would just have to wait for

Gentry to do his job. There was no point in rushing off to a completely unknown place in the hope of doing any good at all. They had to have a plan and it had to be a good one and for that they had to wait for the expert to do his job. There had been no phone call from Martine the meantime. In all probability it had taken Moroni's men considerable time to get themselves and their prisoners home. However, in all likelihood, they would receive a phone call within the next hour or two. So, they just settled to wait in Émile's study: Smith moodily cleaning his two guns and sharpening the knife and Émile simply staring into space.

Waiting for Gentry to do his planning felt like the longest time of his life. There was simply nothing he could do. Once the operation was started and he was in charge then he knew what to do. Having spent a considerable amount of time trying to live down or at least forget his past, he now was profoundly grateful for it. It was precisely those skills he had learned over many years that would now guide him. As usual, he felt quite calm and quite determined. People might well die later in the day. No more than necessary perhaps, but enough. Moroni certainly; others if they got in the way. But to get that far he needed what Gentry was now organising for him and no matter how difficult it was he kept his hand away from the phone. Two Glocks lay in front of him in pieces on table desk as he methodically cleaned them. To be honest there were already completely clean already. They were kept that way. But it was a therapeutic exercise; something to keep his mind occupied while he waited.

The expected call from Toulouse came about an hour later. Having been briefed more fully by Smith, Émile answered with a plain "yes". To do the man credit, Moroni didn't bother with any threats. He just got straight to business.

'Monsieur Aubanet, all I want to do is talk with you. Your daughter and her bodyguard are completely unharmed albeit a little indignant. And for the moment at least, they will stay that way. I want to meet with you for I have some plans which I prefer to carry out with your cooperation rather than against your opposition. Our little plan to eliminate Girondou did not go as intended but that had nothing to do with you. And taking your daughter, whom we didn't expect to see there, as a hostage is simply a method of trying to take business forward. The whole operation was bungled by my people, and I regret the death of the girl. But at least now perhaps Girondou will understand that I'm serious.'

To do him credit the old man came through with the response that he and Smith had prepared. He was terse and composed.

'Mister Moroni. You will understand that if you want to meet, I must consult some of my fellow farmers because I suspect what you want to talk about involves them as well as me. This won't not take long but it will take a few hours. However, I want your word that if we do agree to meet that my daughter and her friend will remain safe and will be treated well. You must understand that the outcome of any discussions you might want to have will depend very much on your keeping that word. '

'Very well, Monsieur Aubanet. I give you 24 hours. This time tomorrow you must give me the answer that I want and that will determine whether your daughter remains alive and unharmed. My man panicked a little and I apologise for his taking Madame Aubanet. I assure you that she will be treated with courtesy and respect.'

With that the man rang off and Émile slumped back in his chair and looked across his desk at Smith who looked grim.

'I'll take some pleasure in butting a bullet in that man's head before the week is out.'

'Is that enough time?'

For the first time Smith began to feel confidence coming back. He knew what Gentry was capable of.

'Oh yes, Émile, more than enough.'

He picked up his phone and called Gentry.

'Moroni has given us twenty-four hours, the idiot.'

'We need sixteen maximum. I'll be with you in less than six. Tell the wild men on the gate to expect me.'

Now that really surprised Smith. Very seldom, if ever, did Gentry venture out into the field. Smith assumed there were maps or plans to be shared and that couldn't easily be done electronically. He also knew that Gentry wouldn't expect Smith to leave Émile Aubanet on his own any longer than he had to. He smiled slightly at the warning to the gate guards. Gentry drove a British Racing Green open Morgan sports car, usually at suicidally high speeds, around the narrow lanes of Provence and they wouldn't find it difficult to recognise him. There were very few Morgans per square kilometre in that part of the world. So, having made sure that Émile knew what was going on, the two men just settled down to wait. Smith noticed that the evening was approaching and this it would be a fully dark 10 o'clock by the time Gentry arrived. Given the speed with which things were having to be organised, nothing was going to happen before the following morning and Smith's mood deepened a little. Daytime operations were always the worst.

In fact, it was slightly less than five hours later that the Morgan made its noisy entry into the Mas courtyard. Smith helped Gentry out of the car and carried a laptop into the house. Introductions were made but the business at hand made the usual ritual somewhat perfunctory on this occasion. Much to Smith's surprise a solemn-faced Deveraux was also in the car. He passed Smith with a nod and a slightly mischievous wink of the eye. This sort of thing was meat and drink to the man. Soon they were sitting at the kitchen table and Gentry started his briefing. Smith was used to Gentry in organizational mode and he was very far indeed from the dusty old bookseller he pretended to be normally.

'Right.' He said briskly, 'Listen up as you need to concentrate, my old friend.' And then with a nod and a charming smile towards Émile. 'and new ones.'

Gentry continued.

'Moroni lives in a large modern house in the countryside just outside St Sulpice la Pointe which is a large village about 10km to the north east of Toulouse. The house has about 30 rooms on two stories. The house has a completely flat roof and is surrounded by various small, single-storey outbuildings. It is also surrounded by a large garden and then slightly further out by a thick wood that encompasses approximately three quarters of whole estate. As I don't want to answer questions at this point you must just take my word for the fact that I know that Mme Aubanet and Jean-Marie are in the house and are moving around . They don't seem to be tied up or anything unpleasant. Their movement, however, seems to be limited to three of the upstairs rooms that I presume are two bedrooms and a bathroom. There are 12 other people in the house at the moment although the surveillance helicopter that we've had on site last two hours can't say whether they are all hostile whether there is a mixture of other civilians. For the purposes of this briefing I am assuming that there are all hostile.'

Smith could see that Émile was struggling with the idea that a foreign civilian could conjure up a surveillance helicopter at a couple of hours' notice but then again, he didn't know Gentry.

'You remember, Peter, that we managed to get hold of rather a special helicopter a little while ago. Well that came from the 4th Special Forces Helicopter Regiment who if you recall we came across in Chad a year of two back. Luckily the regiment is based in Pau which is only 150km away. Their current commandant is an old chum of mine and when I offered him a night's hostage rescue training exercise at very short notice he immediately volunteered as, after all, they are supposed to be France's premier rapid reaction force, and this would certainly require rapid reaction however you might define it. He was also very interested when I told him that Moroni is involved. I gather the government doesn't like Moroni very much.'

He broke off to consult his watch.

'In four hours, time, two of their nice but very silenced Tiger Mk IIIs attack helicopters will land behind the woods and will deposit a total of twenty soldiers who will surround the house. Luckily the house is near one of the usual routes taken on training exercises by these machines, so they shouldn't be thought of as too unusual even they are spotted. This will be done as non-violently as possible. Their job will be to mop up an of the opposition who might be outside the house. They will not enter it. They will do this as silently as possible. They will also take care of anyone who might wander outside for any reason and stop anyone venturing in. Fifteen minutes later a third Tiger will deposit you Peter, two members of B Squadron 22 SAS who happen to be at Pau at the moment to help with training the people there in certain things that they are not meant to know and, of course, Deveraux. We are, just borrowing the SAS people of course. The ground assault group will also cut the power to the house, all telephone lines and intercept any intruder alarms and stop them making a nuisance of themselves. Your helo will jam any cellular or satellite signals for the duration of your visit.'

Again, he broke off to look directly at Smith.

'I emphasize that Deveraux is in charge of this operation, Peter, not you. It is a measure of past reputations that they agreed immediately to Deveraux's command. One of the SAS instructors actually muttered that he was pleased it wasn't you as they hadn't come all this way from Hereford to the sunny South of France to get their asses shot off. In any case Dev has received a full briefing from me and knows the layout of the house.'

So that's where Deveraux vanished to, Smith thought.

'I emphasise again that you are to be the last one off the helo which will land on the house roof just after the guys on the ground have started making a lot of noise to distract the ungodly inside the house. If I could stop you going in the first place I would, but I know that's impossible.'

Smith simply grunted.

'Now this next bit is serious. The guys on the ground will not be using live ammunition. They are French nationals and could get into a lot of trouble if people find bodies. Only you four guys on the third chopper with have live rounds. You're all British or at least not French and we can lose any comeback of a few of dead people if all the occupants prove to be hostile in the general fog that surrounds all SAS anti-terrorist operations. If there are all hostile, then you four have a lot of work to do very quickly. At least the SAS guys have up-to date training in differentiating between friendlies and hostiles in action through night vision goggles. I would emphasise that you should wound not kill if you are in the least uncertain about who is

338

what. By the way, although someone close to the Elysée will obviously not sanctioning any of this, they have indicated that they would not be desolé to hear the Moroni is no long part of the scene here in the South. You and Dev will bring Martine and Jean-Marie back on the helo you came on while the two SAS guys go back to Pau with the others after the op.'

'My general thought is that Moroni thinks that he is safe at home surrounded by his own people. He's assumed that he is just up against a Camargue farmer and a few pitchfork-waving chums and is neither expecting nor remotely prepared for a full night-time military armed assault that kills people.'

Gentry again glanced down at his watch.

'It is now 23h15.Your transport will be arriving here at 12h00. It will contain the two pilots who will, of course, develop instant amnesia the second they return to Pau. They will also deliver your two SAS guys and all the equipment you could possibly need. Deveraux has an assault plan and he will do the briefing. You should spend any spare time getting some food and resting. You will take off at 02h30 with a flight time to target of 50 minutes. Your ETA is therefore 03h20. I estimate that the operation should take no longer that 5 to 8 minutes, possibly less depending on the amount of resistance, so you should be back here by 05h10.'

'So that's it from my point of view. The helo will bring a complete field communication set so Émile and I here can keep an eye on you all. The surveillance helo has departed of course and headed back to watching traffic on the motorway which is actually what the French tax payer pays it to do, but I have borrowed a surveillance drone from another local friend. We'll have a video should Girondou want to look later. I see no reason given the opposition that there will be any great difficulty. If there are any civilians, servants and so on, the ground troops will have a word with them after you leave and inform them of the desirability of keeping quiet. In any case if they are just domestics, they should see that the men are firing blanks and soon cotton to the idea of a training exercise. They are something of a loose end but there is not much we can do about that. Given that everyone will be in full unmarked combat gear and full-face goggles they will look more like creatures from space that recognisable humans.'

The briefing seemed to galvanise Émile into action. He got up and smiled down at Gentry.

'Well, thank you for that. It all seems very clear and well-organised. I gather that food is on the agenda and is something I can certainly contribute. You just carry on and I will make some pasta.'

And with that he turned briskly and made off towards the business end of the kitchen. Deveraux took up the briefing. He flicked a button on the PC monitor.

'We'll do the operational briefing when the others get here but I thought you might like to see the layout. The others on the helo also have this and are monitoring the feed from the drone.'

'The roof is just big enough to land on. There is some satellite gear at the north corner next to the air conditioning units and a small access door leading inside. This is the way in. Fortunately, this comes out into the first-floor corridor very close to the rooms in which we think Madame Aubanet and Jean-Marie are being kept. By the time you get there hopefully the household will have thinned out to just those who would be resident and are staying overnight. With luck the rest should have left. We put the SAS people in first from the roof. It depends on whether there are any hostiles on the move, of course, but their first job will be to secure the rooms where Madame Aubanet and Jean-Marie are. They signal me in and we will clear the rest of the house while you Peter get the hostages back up onto the roof and into the helo.'

Smith sat quietly frowning slightly. It was certainly true that of the four, he was the least qualified by both age and recent training to do operations like this. However, it came hard. But he nodded his understanding at his friend.

'OK Dev. You're the boss.'

Deveraux smiled grimly.

'No. You're the boss, Boss. I'm just trying to save myself the trouble of saving your ass again.'

Smith grunted. He knew that this was something entirely too close to the truth for comfort. The next was an instruction, however.

'I want them dead, Dev; especially Moroni and I want the movie for Girondou. He has just lost a daughter over all this and Moroni is responsible.'

'Understood. I'll just get the people out and you'll do the rest.'

341

Émile Aubanet had been standing at the cooker slowly stirring a pasta sauce.

'If it's all right with you I'll ask Jean Marie's parents to come and be here. They know something of what is going on and they'll be worried.'

Smith nodded.

'Of course. We should all be back about five.'

'All right. Now there is something I can contribute. I have some supper for you all.'

They waited for the two pilots and two SAS soldiers to arrive before eating. It was a surreal gathering. Around the table were grouped 6 large men in full assault outfits, dripping with equipment and arms, David Gentry dressed as usual in a tweedy british Provençale, and Émile Aubanet in a sleeves rolled up basic farmers clothes with baggy canvas supported with braces worn outside his shirt. Arthur had set himself to a regular circuit around the table receiving regular titbits from everyone. All were eating vigorously, and Smith was pleased to see that Émile was very much restored. Surrounded by the men who were going to rescue his beloved daughter, and a television screen that was now showing a live feed from the surveillance drone above Moroni's house. The infrared showed that the two hostages were in separate but adjoining bedrooms with no guards in immediate attendance. It also showed that there were now only five others in the house with two in bedrooms and three on the ground floor. The heat signatures showed that the two in the bedrooms were asleep and the three on the ground floor were moving occasionally but not much.

Before long they were airborne. Émile had bid them good-by and thanked them.

'Gentlemen, I can only thank you from the bottom of my heart. I am in your debt and there is always be a welcome for you and your families here at the Mas de Saintes. I wish you God speed and a safe return. Whatever happens today and whatever you do, I am pretty sure that God will understand - my God at least. Peter come back safely. Both Martine and I need you. I'll take care of Arthur.'

Now they flew on. The Tiger may have been fully equipped with all the latest stealth equipment that made it quiet from the outside but this was still bloody noisy of the inside. Smith was seated next to Deveraux but was fortunately equipped with a comms device that enabled them to talk. He was pretty sure that Gentry, for all his organisational skills, had been less that detailed on the wet end of this operation

'I've changed my mind, Dev. I think we forget the pictures. I want Moroni out alive. I also want Henk if he's there. According to your girlfriend he left with Martine which would indicate that he is one of the house occupants. My guess is that if Moroni is one of the three on the ground floor and Henk will be one of the other ones. I'll get Martine and Jean Marie onto the chopper as instructed. That's fine. You get our two soldier friends to secure the ground floor while you do the bedrooms. If neither of the two in the bedrooms are Moroni or Henk, kill them both whoever they are. Close the doors afterwards and don't let the SAS guys in. I don't want any more witnesses that necessary. Get the SAS to get Moroni and Henk onto the chopper and make sure they're secured then go down yourself and finish the third who is surplus to requirements. With luck all that will be found will be three dead gangsters and I don't think anyone is going to cry much over them. By the way tell them about Jean Marie. I don't want them shooting him. I intend to give him a Glock as soon as I see him. It's more for his ego than anything else.'

Deveraux nodded. He understood all too well that the young body guard would be acutely embarrassed about not being able to resist Moroni's men and being given a role in the rescue, ever if it was a completely symbolic one, would do him a great deal of good. He changed his radio so he could talk to the two SAS men leaving Smith to run through the operation in his head a few more times. On one hand the whole thing seems a bit excessive but that was generally the way Gentry did things. Unless he was planning something extremely secret, he usually went in well over the top. It was an approach that usually succeeded and minimised the risks. In this case if Moroni was sitting there like any common or garden gangster in his nice house expecting at the worst either a few heavies rather like his own rolling up in an armoured Range Rover or even worse a bunch of farmers in theirs, he would be thoroughly disconcerted by fully armed combat troops in full night combat gear, Heckler MP7A1 machine guns and night vision goggles dropping out of the sky in the middle of the night. It would be enough to scare the shit out of most people.

The pilots had been giving them a countdown for the last fifteen minutes so they knew that they had arrived. A metre or two before they touched down the two soldiers vanished from the open side door down onto the roof and had the roof door open within seconds. They vanished inside. Deveraux was next and somewhat more sedately came Smith. As usual Smith was struck how fast these things seemed to happen. By the time he reached the foot of the short staircase from the roof, the doors to the end rooms were open and both Martine and Jean-Marie were standing seemingly unharmed in the corridor, Martine with a broad smile on her face. Smith's appearance was anticipated. Smith pressed his Glock 21 into the young man's hand.

'Please get Martine safely on the chopper and stand by guard there. Two of our soldiers will come upstairs in a moment with Moroni and Henk van der Togt. Can you make sure they are suitably bound and loaded securely onto the chopper?'

He then took Marine's hand. Over her shoulder he saw Deveraux coming out of the bedroom further down the corridor towards the stairs to the ground. He closed the door behind him and nodded at Smith. He raised two fingers before heading for the stairs. Two dead gangsters. Job done, thought Smith.

'Are you OK?' he asked her. In fact, she looked remarkably well considering her ordeal. She reached up and kissed him lightly one the cheek.

'What kept you, dearest?'

With that she followed Jean Marie up to the roof. Smith turned and listened for a moment. He had competent people on both floors who were perfectly capable of carrying out their instructions without any interference from him. So, simply by listening he could gauge what was going on. A glance at his watch told him that precisely 30 seconds had passed since the helicopter touched down. Within a few more seconds the two SAS men brought Moroni and Henk up from below. Each was hooded and wasn't making any noise. A liberal application of duct tape would have seen to that. Both had their wrists fastened tightly behind their backs with plastic ties. They too were escorted onto to the roof where they would be secured. After a few more seconds Deveraux came up, nodded once at Smith and passed him on his own way. Finally, Smith left the scene and climbed onto the helicopter. He looked again at his watch. 90 seconds start to finish. Not bad he thought.

He was pleased to see that Martine and Jean Marie were seated together on one of the benches that ran longitudinally along the two walls of the passenger cabin, both clothed in voluminous padded jackets, scarves and gloves. It may have been a warm Provençale evening, but it was still going to get cold on the way back. Yet again Smith was impressed with Gentry's attention to detail. The two

346

prisoners were tied tightly into their seats but had been afforded no such luxury. Deveraux was seated beside Jean Marie while Smith sat next to Martine. Just as he was getting into the place one of the two SAS men poked his head in through the open door and took off his goggles and light assembly.

'Nice to serve with you again, Sir,' he said with a broad Glaswegian accent and an equally large grin on his face. 'Your quiet retirement doesn't seem to be working out quite as you hoped, I think.'

'No sergeant, it isn't. Thanks.'

The man just nodded, shut the door and vanished back into to join his fellow soldiers. Smith remembered of course. The man had been a member of the Special Forces detail who had accompanied him to Chad a good few years ago. Not a good place, Chad. The second pilot looked back into the cabin and saw Deveraux's curt nod. Seconds later, they lifted off, rose a few hundred feet in the air at a speed that left everyone's stomachs on the floor and turned violently east towards Arles. Smith consulted his watch for the last time. They hadn't even reached the two-minute mark. The trip home was fast, rough and noisy. Conversation was impossible, but Martine had her arm tightly threaded through Smiths and her head lay heavily on his shoulder. There it stayed for the duration of the flight. It didn't seem very long before they landed again in the field behind the Mas des Saintes. There was no reception committee. Smith handed a couple of well-stuffed envelopes to Deveraux before helping Martine to the ground and towards the house. Deveraux went quickly into the cockpit and addressed the pilots.

'Messeurs, this is a token from Monsieur Aubanet. He has asked me to thank you and to say that if you or your families are in this region again, you would be honoured guests at his table. He also asked me to tell you that he is in your debt. Thank you also from me and from Mr Smith.'

He stepped out the helicopter and slammed the door shut. It took off like a rocket and was soon invisible as it headed at thirty feet above the ground at very high speed southwards out to sea on a circular route that would disguise their trip home.

Smith addressed Jean Marie.

'Please escort Madame into the house, Jean Marie. Her father is waiting and I'm pretty sure that your parents are there as well and will want to see you.'

He placed his hand roughly on the man's shoulder and held him tightly.

'Jean Marie. Both Deveraux and I have been in many of these things over the years. They are never easy, and one always tends to blame oneself. Remember this was not your fault. Your prime responsibility was Madam's safety and you have protected her. It was not your job to stop her being kidnapped. Your job was to keep her alive. You did that, and I am profoundly grateful. You were taken by surprise in a place where you had a right to expect to be protected yourself. You were also outnumbered and outgunned. Sometime soon we will talk about this and we will see we can both learn about it, because learning it all part of the game. But for now remember that you stayed with her and she is alive. That was your only job and you did it well.'

He clapped his young friend on the shoulder.

'Now on with you. Get Monsieur Aubanet to pour you a very large drink.'

He kissed Martine.

'I'll be in in a moment. I just need to accommodate these two for the night.'

He watched for a moment as they left before turning to the next job in hand. He and Deveraux walked the two men towards a range of small stables and found a couple of empty horse boxes. Having checked the cable ties and renewed those around their ankles, they secured them to the heavy steel rail railings that surrounded the enclosures. Smith bent close to Moroni's ear so only he could hear.

'Who shot the matador? The Dutchman?'

The hooded figure just nodded. Smith got up and left the building. Deveraux was waiting just outside the door.

Smith thanked his friend and then said:

'I'll decide what I want to do with these two when I've had a good drink. If you want to get yourself to the hospital in Marseille and find Jeanne, please do. I gather she is not too badly hurt. Let me know how things are. Don't contact the family. I'll do that.

'Well, I just pop over there to check things over. As long as you don't need me for a while, that is.'

'No,' said Smith. 'You go ahead. Jean Marie will be back in harness before long. Take one of Aubanet's Range Rovers.'

They both remembered the small arsenal that the cars carried. It might be useful. They walked on a little further.

'Thanks for your help, Dev. God job, as usual.'

Deveraux just nodded.

'So, what was the tip?' he asked.

Smith grunted.

'Probably a good deal more than they earn in a year.'

It wasn't the first time he remembered his father's words. One day soon after the first of his two unsuccessful marriages, he had been talking with his father in a pub in the north Derbyshire hills where he lived. The two didn't often talk together but neither thought it particularly unusual when they did.

'Perhaps I should give you a bit of advice about this marriage thing.' His father had said, well down his fourth or fifth pint and thus suitably emboldened.

'If you want to keep a marriage together,' he opined, 'you should never go to sleep angry.'

Now Smith knew that his father was the last person, almost on earth, who should give advice about marriage. His own was a disaster. He and his mother were constantly bickering. He was always away on mysterious business trips or the golf, or the masonic, or the rugby club or whatever. He spent little enough time in the marital bed to offer any advice at all on how to occupy it. But the comment had stuck and now it came back to him as he and Martine lay in her big bed in the *cabane* they increasingly lived in. The night was hot, of course, and they lay naked, covered only by a thin cotton sheet. Holding hands was all it took for them to feel in contact. It was the time that they had to talk and to go over whatever had happened during the day. Most days had not been this exciting, but the same principal applied. She gently squeezed his hand.

'What are you going to do with them?'

'Not sure. I thought I'd sleep on it.'

He knew that he would have told her, so she left the subject alone.

'In any case, thank you, my love. Yet again you had to save me. I'm sorry.'

He was somewhat startled.

'What do you mean, sorry?'

'Well, I shouldn't have gone. It was so unexpected. Angèle called and that was that. If I hadn't gone then all this bother might not have happened.'

It was true, of course, but Smith had never been one to dwell in the past.

'The point is that you are OK. Here and now, OK. That's what matters'

She squeezed his hand.

'Don't be too hard on Girondou.'

It was an odd thing to say for he had never thought that anyone would guess what was in his mind.

'We'll see my love. We'll see.'

She paused.

'Just remember, my dearest. He's not the man you are.'

She moved across the bed and laid her head against his shoulder. Her breathing deepened as she fell into sleep. The last thing he thought as he followed her was:

'Too fucking right, he isn't.

Chapter 23: Death of a Traitor

It was after a late family breakfast that Jean-Marie got a sorry looking Henk out of his horse box and loaded into the boot of Smith's old Peugeot. The man had peed in his pants overnight and Smith felt that he was too unsavoury a specimen to grace an Aubanet Range Rover.

'Where are we going with this piece of shit, Boss?'

Smith was amused that he had picked up Deveraux's way of addressing him.

'Well, I thought that given that it was this piece of shit as you so accurately describe him who shot Roger Cordiez, I thought we should ask the boy's father what we should do with him.'

Jean-Marie nodded in approval.

'Not too much doubt there then, I should imagine. Old man Cordiez is never a particularly forgiving type at the best of times.'

They drove down the Route de Fielouse that ran down the eastern side of the Étang be Vaccarès. Being so close to the heavy salt concentration of the étang this was difficult, unforgiving country. Smith wondered if the rather dour farmer was a result of that. If anything, the land seemed in worse condition than on their previous visit. But as before Cordiez was out ready to see who was coming, his customary shotgun crooked in his elbow. He was glowering at them.

'What do you want now?'

Smith remembered recent events and resolved to be as patient as he could. He also wasn't going to beat around the bush. He nodded to Jean-Marie who went around to the boot of the car and hauled out their prisoner to stand in front of the farmer. Jean Marie yanked off the hood.

'You probably don't know this man, Monsieur Cordiez. But at the funeral you asked me to bring him to you. He's the man who shot your son.'

There was a silence that you could cut with the proverbial knife. Very slowly Cordiez walked up to van der Togt and stood very close, their faces a few centimetres apart. The moment lasted some time. Smith was relieved to see that the arms holding the shotgun remain relaxed with the gun pointing at the ground. After a long time, Cordiez turned away and came to Smith and held out his hand.

'Thank you, Monsieur. I owe you a debt.'

Smith just wanted to get the whole thing over with.

'Do you have a nice quiet barn where we could take this meeting further, Monsieur?'

His host just nodded, and the group trooped off together and before long they were established in a very run down, low shed that hardly merited the description of a barn. Smith asked Jean Marie to stay outside and to ensure they weren't disturbed. Various rusty bits of farm machinery lined the walls and there seemed to be more holes in the tiled roof than tiles. Some chairs were found from somewhere. Henk van der Togt was seated on one of them against one wall; Smith

354

and Cordiez side by side facing him some five yards away. The prisoner was now free of gag and cable ties. All three were completely still. Smith's arms lay relaxed along his legs, his right hand laying quietly over his Glock 30. It seemed almost to hover. Cordiez had his shotgun across his knees. Henk van der Togt was much less relaxed as his eyes flicked between Smith's eyes and his right hand. He knew that in spite of being completely un-restricted, he had no chance to gather his feet under him to try a lunge across the small space between him and his adversary. There was no time. He would be dead before he got halfway to his feet. So, he just sat nervously wondering what was going to happen. The man opposite knew.

'In a way this could be seen as my fault,' Smith mused out loud. 'Or at least partly. I realised when we first met that there was something wrong. Perhaps I am getting old and perhaps I felt that the standards I had lived by and which had always seemed to keep me safe were no longer the right ones and that maybe you should be given a chance to learn or at least to do the job differently to me. I remember that you were reluctant to see killing as a part of your work for us. Perhaps you felt that you could protect someone without being prepared to kill someone. I don't know. Probably I should have got rid of you immediately. However, you remained and now we have come to this.'

'To be honest, the matter of you changing your mind about killing people and your accepting a contract on Roger Cordiez is a matter between you and Monsieur Cordiez. He'll decide what he wants to do to you. But before I hand you into his tender hands, I wanted to say something to you.

He sighed without lifting an unwavering gaze from his companion's eyes.

'Above all, Henk, life, my life at least, is about trust. Truth and falsehood, honesty and dishonesty are all relative; subject, more often than not, to a sort of moral flexibility that serves only to make them fallible. Trust and loyalty are what makes human relationships work for they are absolute things. You seem to have forgotten that your responsibility was to protect this family and you betrayed them. You have reneged on the trust that Mr Girondou, his family and I placed in you and that has led to the death of one of his daughters. At a time and in a profession that depends completely on trust and loyalty you have completely abused precise those qualities. You have abused the trust that your colleagues placed in you and that has put those people in danger; people who have a right to rely on you and who entrusted the safety of their lives to you. For that, Hendrik van der Togt, in my view you should die. Here and now.'

The young man finally stirred as a last note of contempt entered his voice and he snarled sarcastically:

'So, if I am going to be dead soon, why bother telling me all this garbage? Why not just get on with it?'

Smith's look became sad for it was a good question.

'None of us knows what happens to them after they die, Henk. Some people hold beliefs about it, but no-one knows for certain. But in case some bit of you survives in some form that is capable of understanding then learning a lesson from the past might be of use for whatever lies ahead. If there is nothing in the life beyond then you have won a few extra seconds of life and I have wasted a few.'

The man snarled a final question, his face a mask of hate.

'And what makes you God, judge and executioner, all of a sudden?'

With the slightest of movements of his right hand, Smith picked up the small automatic from the arm of the chair, aimed it at the precise centre of the Dutchman's forehead.

'Amongst other things, this gun, young man,' he replied as he looked unemotionally across at the man. 'This gun.'

'This man killed your son, Monsieur Cordiez. He did it for money. Only you really know what that loss means to you. But if you believe that this man should die then I would ask you to do it now. If you don't want to do it yourself, then I will do it for you.'

For the first time Henk van der Togt seemed terrified as he looked pleadingly across the room. The Frenchman hardly hesitated. He rose, sighted and loosened both barrels of the 12 bore in quick succession. The headless body of his son's murderer was catapulted backwards over the chair.

They both stood for a moment in silence before Smith raised a somewhat practical issue.

'I hope you can dispose of the body quickly. It doesn't do to keep this sort of thing around for too long.'

357

The man nodded.

'Pigs.' was his only reply.

They left the barn, collected Jean-Marie and made to leave. Cordiez came to Smith. The man had tears in his eyes, so it was no surprise that he was incapable of saying anything. He just took Smith's hand and shook it with a fierce strength.

As Jean Marie drove them out of the farm and headed back north towards home, Smith gave a convulsive shudder.

'Boss?' asked the driver.

'Pigs,' replied Smith with another shudder. 'Never liked them,'

Chapter 24: Brothers' Business

Deveraux knew better than to make conversation. He just concentrated on driving. Smith was seated motionless, slightly slumped in the passenger seat, just gazing out of the window as the countryside flashed by; seemingly deep in thought. Their passenger was fixed in the back seat of the Range Rover. Not only handcuffed by feet and wrists but also shackled by Deveraux firmly into the seat itself by its seatbelt mountings. He was also blindfolded and gagged.

In fact, Smith was dreaming slightly. After they left the Autoroute east from Arles just before St Martin de Crau and turned south towards the Mediterranean, the flat Provençale landscape gradually changed from one of fields and pine trees and hedges so by the time they were nearing the coast the industry and commerce of Fos sur Mer began to replace them. It was a gradual process. First a few scattered warehouses appeared; storage and distribution centres but soon real industry appeared. Many of the huge oils refineries that used to cover much of the north shores of the Étang de Berre had long since been dismantled. But there was still enough left to remind Smith that this was the moment where Girondou's homeland really started. It was an invisible border to be sure but it nevertheless it was what much the drama of the last few days and weeks had been all about. Smith felt a grim satisfaction that the man who so wanted to cross that border in triumph was now doing so but under very different circumstances;

locked ignominiously into a captive bundle being hastened on his way, in all probability, to the violent end of his life.

'Why is he still alive, Peter? I admit that I'm surprised.' Martine had asked.

They had been sitting together on the veranda of her *cabane* in a pair of old cane recliners angled together so that she could rest her bare feet in his lap. He was absent-mindedly stroking them with one hand while holding his dilute whisky and soda in the other. They both looked out of the marsh as the warm evening got slowly darker. The sun had just dipped below the horizon painting the cloud-flecked sky above in a violent crimson and the flocks of pink flamingos that wandered moodily about the shallow water in search of food quickly changed from pink birds to black silhouettes. The evening was still alive with the sounds of other water birds, water voles and rats plopping about in the little canals and waterways that fed off the marsh. A few Herons still stood about peering down into the water as lugubrious now as they had been for most of the day. There were less attractive features about this evening world too. A whole host of insects whose thirst for human and animal blood seemed to Smith to reflect very well that shown by some of their human neighbours on the Camargue marshes. Fortunately, Martine's *cabane* was equipped with some very high-tech anti-mosquito devices that enabled them to enjoy this evening sight without losing similar amounts of blood to those spilt a few hours ago in St Sulpice la Pointe. Smith realised that an explanation of sorts was in order. All he had to do was think of one. A large mouthful of whisky helped.

'To be frank, so am I. Despite Gentry's orders, I went in fully intending to put a bullet or two in the man's brain. In fact, I was a few grams of finger pressure away from doing precisely that. But a number of things occurred to me all at once and I stopped.'

Martine looked across at him across the top of her glass. This was a surprise and, perhaps, a side to Smith that she didn't see too often. He didn't often change is mind about things; things like killing someone, at least. She waited.

'Two things struck me. Firstly, and most importantly, was that he didn't actually want you. You were there when they attacked and that so-called guard, van der Togt, panicked and took you as some sort of hostage. You were never a target per se and I suspect that Moroni was just as surprised as anyone to see you turning up on his doorstep. Whether or not you and Jean-Marie were actually in real danger I don't know but somehow, I doubt it. It therefore struck me as too flimsy a pretext to kill the man no matter how dislikeable we might find him.'

Martine waited for the second reason. It was a longer wait as she suspected that Smith had not really formulated it yet. When it came it was deceptively simple.

'Girondou is a friend. But he's not family.'

It was the first time she had ever heard Smith mention his family. As far as she was concerned, he hadn't got one. But he knew

361

what she was thinking. He looked across at the face he had come to love as he now admitted it, as much to himself as to her.

'You are my family.'

She put her glass down beside the chair and rose slowly. She took him by the hand and led him silently inside.

It was later in the middle of the night as she was lying quietly in his arms that he continued.

'This is Girondou's family problem not ours.'

She gently squeezed his hand at the use of the word "ours" as he went on.

'This really is a family matter. His family. This story starts years ago with three brothers then was down to two. Very soon I will present one brother with a gift of the other. It's up to him how he enjoys his present.'

She realised that it was costing Smith a good deal. She knew what friendship meant to him. Somehow Alexei Girondou had let him down and he was sad about that. Perhaps it was that he was never really a proper friend and, ironically, that had probably saved the gangster's life. Smith did not usually forgive such lapses. She moved up the bed until their faces touched and then planted a long, gentle kiss on his lips.

Smith's gaze out of the Range Rover window was thus not as vacant as Deveraux might have imagined. As the car passed Martigues and headed on the road to Sausset-les-Pins and Girondou's home, he

362

was thinking about what to do. It was unusual, and he knew it. Usually things came quickly to him. But this took a bit more sorting out. They had telephoned ahead. So the barriers were down as they swept through the gates and down the steep drive to the house. The gatehouse was manned and he saw the LMGs tracking them automatically as they passed. His instructions had got through. No-one met them when they arrived at the house.

Deveraux stayed in the car as Smith walked around the car to the driver's window.

'Take off his leg ties but keep everything else in place. Bring him.'

Deveraux just nodded and took their prisoner out of the car. The three went into the house. Girondou, Angèle and Amy sat together on a sofa in the sitting room, holding hands, each in their own way looking anxious. Deveraux threw Moroni to the floor and retied his ankles before walking back to the door. He stood there guarding Smith's back. It was his chosen role. Smith took a seat facing the group on the sofa. He was saddened a little at how different this was to his usual welcome in this house. He had decided on keeping it simple and brief.

'This is your problem not mine. This whole bloody business is yours not mine. This, Alexei, is your family's business. It dates from before I came here and will, I would guess, continue after I am gone. I am therefore leaving it to you for you to sort out. I am here only because you and your fucking family have betrayed my friendship.'

363

He walked slowly up to the seated Alexei Girondou and stood over him. His voice was very low and very calm.

'Alexei. I know who you are, and I know what you do. I know your strengths and weaknesses; more than you might imagine. You should also know enough about me to stop you doing something ill-advised. There are people out there; people who owe me favours. People who live in a world that you can only imagine; people who are my friends. People who can get to you no matter what surrounds you. Your only defence against them is friendship and loyalty and those are attributes that you are rather short of at the minute.'

'Make no mistake, if you, or,' and he gestured behind him, 'this piece of shit, or anyone connected with either of you ever touches Martine again, I, or one of my friends, will kill you all.'

He let his eye move over the three seated on the sofa.

'All of you.'

He just turned away. By the time he reached the door, Deveraux was holding it open for him.

They were well on their way home, driving towards Arles, before Smith spoke again.

'How are things with Jeanne, Dev? I gather the bullet went through and didn't damage much.'

'No. Everything's fine. Thanks for asking. There'll be a lot of physio and rehab, but she'll be fine.'

'Take good care of her, Dev. She did some courageous things back there. On her own, too.'

Deveraux smiled.

'That she did. I'm very proud of her.'

'I hope this domestic squabble hasn't messed things up between you two. I would have thought that there might be a vacancy soon with Girondou. The top job probably.'

Deveraux laughed.

'I think she'd prefer a transfer into the country. I've been meaning to have a word with you before all this got in the way.'

Smith nodded.

'You?'

'I think I would rather like that, Boss.'

'Well I'm not sure if that's entirely my decision. I'll have to ask Martine.'

'Well, Madame Aubanet has recently offered me one of her *cabanes* at the Mas as I seem to be spending rather a lot of time there these days. Actually, it's just big enough for two.'

Smith nodded with a genuine smile breaking out across his face for the first time in what seemed ages.

'Sounds good to me, old friend. Just make sure you don't lose her to Jean-Marie. He's got a bit of a roving eye.'

'Forewarned is indeed forearmed. Thanks.'

Smith reached across and rested his hand briefly on Deveraux's shoulder. Theirs had been a long friendship. Family.

Chapter 25: Endgame

'So that's that, I presume? All the pieces back more or less in their right positions?

Smith smiled slightly as his friend's enquiry could equally well have referred to their impending chess game as it might their recent adventure. The pieces were set out and Smith had just opened with the traditional "e4". As usual they were seated at Gentry's beautiful Sheraton 1790s chess table, each in a comfortable upright Sheraton Shield Back armchair from the same date. Each player had his particular form of whisky near his right hand.

They played with an equally traditional Staunton chess set. There are, of course, many thousands of designs for chess pieces from all over the world, dating from as far back almost as history itself century. But for Gentry the standard for a working every-day chess had been set by a journalist Nathanial Cook who designed a chess set in 1849 and which was produced and sold in London by his brother-in-law and owner of the firm, John Jaques of London; a firm still famous for its production of games. Cook had been editor of magazine, The Illustrated London News, and the set was named after the famous English master Howard Staunton who occasionally wrote chess pieces for the magazine. The Staunton set has been made in millions since its launch and is still the official design for international competitions. It was typical of Gentry to eschew the many more exotic designs and materials for this most traditional of English sets. It was also typical in that his set was one of the early in the first 500 sets were hand signed and numbered by Staunton himself. It was one of the very early sets too whose King's side Rooks and Knights were stamped with a crown to distinguish them from the Queen's side pieces; a nicety not usually followed in modern times.

It was perhaps also typical that the first game after one of their adventures, the one in which they tended to do as much talking as they did thinking about the game, that Smith elected to play Ruy Lopez again. The 16th century Spanish clergyman's opening was still one of the most used in the modern era and many of its developments had been the basis of some of their best battles. But on this occasion their opening moves were just mirrors indicating that their minds were as much on recent events as winning the match.

After a while it was Smith who broke the silence.

'Thanks David. Good job.'

'Think nothing of it, dear boy. I enjoyed a whiff of cordite from the old days. I assume that the bill will go to Girondou. It'll be rather a lot. I hope he's is a good payer.'

Thinking of their last conversation, Smith was confident.

'I don't think there will be a problem, old friend.'

The game progressed in an unusually gentlemanly manner. They fell into rather an elegant style of play and one got the sense that neither was particularly interested in winning for the moment. Or at least the journey was becoming as important as the arrival.

After a while Gentry was the first to find his attention wandering. When it did his tone of voice was incredulous.

'What? Deveraux is in love?'

He had been in mid-move. His Bishop to King's Knight three was suspended in mid-air.

'Love? Good Lord. Now there's a thing.'

Gentry was so distracted by the thought that the bishop went down onto entirely the wrong square.

'Ah ha!' exclaimed Smith scooping an entirely gratuitous bishop with his pawn. 'You really need to learn to concentrate, old chum.'

Gentry looked down at the beautiful chess table between them with horror. He hadn't made a mistake like that since he was at school – prep school.

'Bugger,' was his only comment.

The game didn't last too much longer. Gentry seemed to have lost his usual enthusiasm. Embarrassment probably, Smith thought. So, they retired to their usual, post-game chairs either side of the fireplace, replenished glasses of whisky in hand.

'So, I gather that this was all a bit of a domestic tiff rather than anything of great significance.'

Smith paused for a moment before replying. Given that Girondou's daughter had died and that his own appointment for the gangster's head of security had turned traitor and had perished as a consequence, he thought that Gentry's tone was a touch flippant.

'Any information as to how this family contretemps has resolved itself?'

In fact. Smith had found out that morning.

'I gather that an amalgamation is proposed.'

'And which of the remaining brothers has the top job?'

'There's only one now. Girondou.'

Gentry nodded slowly.

'Well?'

'Well what?'

'What next?'

Smith shrugged.

'Nothing. I think.'

'Nothing?'

'Well if you want the truth, old chum, I am more than a little vexed with this whole thing. Much as I liked Girondou, and I can't deny that he has been useful from time to time, I am a little fed up that we got involved at all.'

Gentry kept silent. He knew that Smith was talking as much to himself as to him.

'Had Martine and her family not been in the middle of all this. I'm not sure if I would have bothered. Girondou certainly wasn't going to invite us in.'

'Moroni taking over may not have been an ideal outcome, Peter. Better the devil you know and all that.'

Smith just harrumphed before replying.

'To be frank the main thing is that I am very pissed off with having to call in all those favours to go in and get Martine when the whole thing could have been avoided. This was after all just a pissing match between two men who should know better. Much as I liked Girondou, it cost a number of people their lives completely unnecessarily including the man's own daughter for God's sake. Have these bloody savages not heard of families?'

Gentry knew that Smith would calm down in time but now was not the time for that to happen. So, he just offered a gentle reminder.

'Liked?'

Smith was slightly waspish.

'What do you mean: liked?'

'You said "Much as I liked Girondou".'

'So?'

'Past tense, old fruit. Past ...'

An exasperated Smith interrupted.

'So, what if I did?'

'Well, given your idiosyncratic approach to retirement, Peter, old friend, you may have a need of Mr. Girondou and his chums again before too long. Probably not wise to cut all links, I would suggest.'

There was a brief pause while Gentry replenished their glasses. He continued.

'There is one thing that concerns me though.'

'Oh, what's that, my dear chap.'

'Well, I'm wondering if you're not losing your touch a little.'

'What in earth do you mean.?

'Well. We seem to have come through another of your little adventures and..'

'And what?' snapped Smith.

'Er, well, I repeat. We have come through from your latest escapade and, unless I miss my guess, you haven't actually killed anyone. I mean, personally, that is.'

Smith harrumphed and glared at his old friend over the rim of his glass.

'Not yet, Gentry, not yet.'

This observation was the prelude to a long period of silence between the two men as they both stared into the fireplace. This being late summer, it was filled by a large arrangement of sunflowers that had long-since died, drooped, dried and desiccated. The silence was broken only by the occasional clink of ice from Smith's glass has he took another sip. At length it was Gentry, shaking his head gently in disbelief.

'Deveraux. Love. Would you credit it?'

The question, like their mood, was entirely rhetorical.

Printed in Great Britain
by Amazon